MAGICAL WONDERLAND

MAGICAL WONDERLAND

CHRONICLES OF BLOOD

BOOK II

CREA REITAN

Contents

Magical Wonderland

Chronicles of Blood, book 2

www.facebook.com/LadyCreaAuthor

Editing by Alicia Burnett

aburnetteditor@gmail.com

Dragon Fire Fantasy, Inc.

dragonfirefantasy@gmail.com

Version 2021.01.31 - E.NA

Created with Vellum

This is a fictional fantasy fairy tale romance, meaning I made it up and it's not set in this reality. This is a Wonderland retelling. As with everything I write, I go my own way. I'm the god of this world and I make the rules.

One of the things I've always disliked about Wonderland retellings was that they were very basic in making it a retelling and not just a story set within Wonderland. I strived not to do that. I wanted to literally retell Alice's story using the themes, language, tropes, and characters - all reimagined. One of the primary things that had to go, however, was that Alice wanted to get home.

Why would you ever want to leave Wonderland?!

This story is a mystery from the beginning to the end. Something broke Wonderland and it's the job of the Fixer to figure it out and set it right. Along the way she encounters some very nasty people. There's blood, gore, past abuse, death, violence. While this isn't the society we live in, there are many themes that you might recognize. Like the mistreatment of one group of people because of their gender, their sexuality, their race... In a fantasy world, it's handled very differently but it's the same under the surface.

There's also magic, demons, shifters, madness and nonsense, lots of travel, and some tea. There are also some bloodthirsty queens, monsters, and plenty of murder. Mal also has her hands full with a whole lot of men that want to claim her heart!

Oh, and there's sex of all sorts!

This is a polyamorous romance that isn't revolving around a single female who gets all the males' attention. There are other relationships that are just as important as those between the men and the single female.

If anything that you just read bothers you, it isn't what you're interested in, or you find might be triggering, please do not read this book. Otherwise, enjoy Mal's broken Wonderland.

Death

MAL

1

Mal spent a long time sure she was dead. Even when she might have been conscious, a part of her was sure she was no longer in a living realm. The Sheep had killed her. Everything that happened after was simply Mal being tormented in Purgatory.

She didn't know how long she'd been dead. Hours? Days? Years? Longer? There was no way to tell. She'd never been good about telling time in Laddenworn to start with.

When she first opened her eyes, she knew she was in trouble. Also the first sign she was likely dead.

The room she was in was made of stone. Old stone. The kind where the grout sticks out a little because the stone is so worn away. It was rough against her back. Two walls were stone. The other two were thick iron bars. Rough against her torn pants was a hard-packed dirt floor.

A torch flickered a short distance down the hall. There were cells like hers across from her, next to her, and another diagonal. But none of the cells were touching. If she stretched, she could look through the doorless entry to see rooms upon rooms of the same set up.

She could only stretch so far since she was shackled to the

wall, her hands above her head. Her whole body hurt. She was covered in blood, her clothes ripped and frayed. Most of all, her head was pounding and there was an intense pain in her left side. Sight was difficult. As dim as it was, she could barely keep her eyes open. The pain was so intense.

Closing her eyes, she let unconsciousness take her again.

She was awakened to screaming. Screams of pain. Of torment. Based on the begging, she had to assume someone was being tortured. Another sign she was surely dead and in Hell.

Did they know who she was? Was that why she was taken? Safest to assume yes. But where was she?

As if someone saw fit that she needed to know, a man started down the hall, walking as if the screams were not happening. He walked as if in a park. The sun was out. The birds were chirping. He was taking an afternoon stroll.

Mal wanted to close her eyes, pretend she was still passed out. But she couldn't convince herself. She would not hide. She would face whoever had her head on.

Even if it meant she'd die.

He had hair to his shoulders, filled with messy waves and tossed more to one side than the other. It was mud brown, the kind of mud with dark, almost black streaks of mud. His lean face, ruggedly handsome, had a few days' growth, shaped as if it were intentional. Only when he stopped at the bars to her cell could she see that his eyes were a cool brown.

Based on his livery, he was part of the palace guard. Not a soldier. Or at least not an "enlisted" soldier. Perhaps an officer.

One thing was clear. The red and white uniform with a bleeding heart over his chest told her right where she was. In the dungeons of the Queen of Hart. And whoever the man was, he worked for the Queen.

It was too late to rethink her plan to appear passed out. Instead, she sat there and stared at him, attempting to keep her expression blank. She was so sore; she wasn't sure if she managed. Perhaps it just looked pained.

He stopped at the bars and peered down at her. When the next scream ricocheted against the walls, he looked down the hall. After several careful minutes of examining the way he'd come, he stooped down to be on her level.

"Nice to see you're still alive," he murmured.

Mal glanced at the cells around her. There was a heap in the one across from her, but she'd never seen it move. She met his eyes again but said nothing.

"I'm Kav," he offered. "I can't get you out right yet, but I'm working on it. Hang tight, One."

She frowned and rolled her eyes. Yeah, like she was going to trust a soldier of the Bloody Queen. Besides, like she had a choice but to 'hang tight.'

After another quick glance down the hall, Kav pushed a small wrapped package towards her. She rolled her eyes at him again (though, did she or was she imagining she had?) and pulled on the shackles lightly. Just to remind him that she was his prisoner.

The gesture had the desired effect. He looked at the shackles and frowned. "Can you reach that with your leg?"

Mal didn't try. She simply stared at him.

"Look, Princess," he said, his voice getting a little scratchy as his whisper picked up in annoyance. A scream echoed, quieter this time. Weaker. "I'm your best hope for getting out of here. That's food. You've been in there for days with nothing to eat. I can't loosen or release your chains until later so you can actually eat it, but I'll be back to do so. *If* you hide it from view. The Queen will be down to check on you. And I suggest you appear dead."

Mal frowned at him again. He was right about one thing. If she was going to get out, she needed help. Being trapped as she was, there was nothing she could do.

After a minute's struggle to shift at all, she found that she was incredibly weak. The little bit of effort it took to move for the box almost wasn't worth it. By the time she had it safely under her leg, she didn't need to appear dead. She simply passed out again.

Voices flitted in and out for a long time. Pain seared through parts of her body as if someone was playing whack-a-mole. Sometimes there were voices and laughter. Others there was a slight scratching.

Yes, she was dead. Eternally being punished for not fixing Laddenworn. Perhaps she'd find the other twenty-seven failed Fixers. Maybe the heap across from her was twenty-seven.

When the unmistakable sound of her cell door opening broke through her conscious, Mal would have a thought to escape. That was her chance. Then, she'd laugh madly at her own errant thought. She was far too weak to do anything but laugh internally.

Even then, she wasn't sure if it was laughter so much as sobbing.

Most of the time, she wasn't convinced she was alive. She was sure she was in Hell. Life couldn't hurt this much.

The pain continued. Regularly, someone would shift her head back and pour something down her throat. Once, she was sure she drowned while it went down the wrong pipe. She didn't remember coughing. She was too weak to even cough. She just remembered her inability to breathe. And what a relief it would be to die to escape the hellish torment.

Did that mean she was only in the bowels of Hell? Not quite to the true punishment?

That's when the nightmares started. There were giant birds with teeth chasing her, screaming an unbearable sound. She'd be running, stumble and fall. The beak would come at her, its scream splitting her ears.

She'd wake up screaming. Thrashing. Blood dripping down her face.

When the dreams continued, she was sure she was dead and reliving some horrific punishment for failing to fix Wonderland.

Why else would a bird that didn't exist in the Outside torment her own personal Hell?

There were tubes coming out of her arms. She ripped at them, shrieking for help. Or maybe just shrieking in general.

Then, she was being restrained. Tied down. A voice, soothing, tried to calm her.

Yes, she'd died. There was no kindness in the dungeon. Among the torturous screams. At the dark, dank end of the line.

It all stopped, and she floated around in nowhere. There were no sounds. No light. No voices. Was she floating? Sitting? Was she still chained?

The absence of everything made her sure she was trapped in the in-between. That place before she could cross into Heaven or Hell.

But who would choose her destination?

A SOFT TRICKLE REGISTERED FIRST. As if something was dipped in water and raised, letting the excess fall. A gentle pressure on her side was next. It caused a blinding pain to render her near unconscious again.

It must have succeeded. When she was aware of her surroundings once more, the pressure and pain was gone. She spent a long time listening. An immeasurable amount of time passed in which there was no sound.

She was alone. Probably.

She cracked her eyes open very slightly. A light on the far side of the room caused shadows to dance above her. The light caught on something within a frame. Something that looked like a shriveled piece of fruit. There was a knife through it. No, not a knife. A blade.

A plaque glittered in the dancing light. She narrowed her eyes to try and make it out. Her eyes widened when she finally registered enough of the words.

It was a heart.

She screamed and jerked. It was only then that she realized she was not only tied down flat on her back, but she was gagged as well. Panic tore through her as a man came hurrying around a corner. He stopped at her side where he shushed her.

His voice was soothing, lulling.

The panic was still ripe, her eyes wide and terrified. But he looked at her with large brown eyes, cooing at her that everything was alright.

Her heart was still pounding rapidly as she tried to focus on him.

The mess of his hair was pulled into an elastic at the back of his head. The stubble was a little longer. Almost to the point where you could call it a beard.

Kav.

"What do you want?" she tried to ask around the gag.

He washed a hand over his face and looked at her warily. "If I take the gag out, you can't scream. If the Queen hears you, we're both dead."

Mal swallowed.

"Understand, Princess?" he added.

She nodded.

He sat at the edge of her bed to lean over her. It brought his face into hers where their eyes met and locked. Her heart thundered loudly.

The gag released and he gently pulled it from her. Kav sat back slowly, not leaving the edge of the bed.

Mal pulled on her arms, held firmly to the sides of the bed.

"One thing at a time. I can't get you stronger if you continue to pull the tubes out."

She looked at her arms for the first time. There were indeed tubes sticking out of her arm, the one furthest from the wall. A thin tube. Like an IV. Did they have IVs in Wonderland?

"What do you want with me?" she asked. Her voice sounded like she hadn't used it in a month.

"To kill the queens, of course. But first, I needed to get you strong enough to get you out of the palace."

"And you are?"

"The Knave of Hart," he said, giving her a wry smile. "Also, a traitor to the queens. We've been waiting a long time for The One. And since you survived several days in the dungeons before I found you, I think you're it."

"That's nice," Mal said as she turned away. Her eyes caught on the heart again.

"That's a present from the Queen. You see, the knave before me stole some tarts. As punishment, the Queen tore his heart out and staked it to his wall. Now, my wall. She fashioned it with a nice little plaque, so I'll always remember my place."

Mal yawned as if the conversation bored her. It scared her, yes. She was so tired already that the mere idea of more to fear made her want to pass out. Her eyes drooped.

"Sleep a while longer, Princess. You have lost a lot of muscle."

"How long have I been here?" she asked.

She was almost asleep when his answer floated to her like a dream.

"Ten weeks tomorrow."

Oh no, she thought. *My men will be so scared for me*. Of course, they probably thought she was dead.

Then again, perhaps they were still too mad at her to care.

THE DAYS WERE LONG. She'd spent what she thought were hours awake, but it seemed that only minutes had passed. Kav had released her arms but when she'd accidentally pulled the IV out again while angry, she awoke next to her arms tied once more.

She glared at him and refused to speak to him for... well, she thought it had been days, but since there was nothing there to gauge time, she didn't know for sure. It almost didn't matter. With no one else to talk to, she soon forgot that she had been mad at him. He was the jailor to her purgatory after all. If she wanted to escape, she needed him.

Kav spent a lot of time sitting next to her on her bed. Based on what she could see of his room, she assumed it was his bed.

He'd brush her hair back and clean her face and the wounds she still had. He didn't say, nor did she ask, but she was sure she had been injured several times while in the dungeon. There was one particularly painful injury on her side. Every time he touched it, she'd see stars. Pain would course through her so severely she'd have to bite her tongue not to scream.

He spent time on her hair. Washing it. Brushing it. Braiding it. It was a little awkward since she was still tied down. She didn't complain about the restraints anymore. With the nightmares that haunted her, she was thrashing around in her sleep. Not only was she liable to hurt herself further, but she was sure she'd be tearing that IV out. Her muscles constantly ached from fighting the dreamed-up horrors.

Kav finished braiding her hair down the side of her head. He frowned at it after trying to smooth out some bumps. "I used to be pretty good at this," he mumbled.

Mal laughed. "How many women have you had tied to your bed while you braided their hair?"

He grinned. "Just you, actually."

"Uh huh. I believe you."

His smile was beautiful. He surprised her when his lips landed on hers roughly.

She was tired enough, still half convinced she was dead, that she thought he'd simply slipped and landed on her. The thought made her snort and he pulled back to look at her, confusion making his brows pucker.

"Sorry," she said, laughing. "I had a thought of when those

stupid girls say, 'It was an accident,' like they just tripped, and his dick landed in her mouth."

Kav looked at her incredulously before laughing. "I hadn't planned on putting my dick in your mouth."

Mal grinned. "I know."

He didn't kiss her again for a couple of days. Days in which the pain in her side flared up dramatically. It was so intense she barely saw anything around her. She heard Kav's voice sometimes but didn't see him.

The next time he kissed her, she was only slightly sure she was alive. It felt so good to feel something aside from pain. He kissed her hungrily, devoured her completely. His hands on her dulled the pain, even as he pulled at her clothes. His body against hers brought some life back into her dead, limp limbs. His cock inside her made her cry out for a reason other than agony.

She slept for the first time in weeks without restraints. Kav kept her less like a prisoner and more like a lover. He bathed her, fed her, clothed her with beautiful garments. Her muscles didn't work. There was no muscle tone at all. Her whole body looked hollow and sunken.

Still, the IV was stuck in her arm. She couldn't keep down more than a few bites at a time, so she knew she needed whatever medicine he was feeding her.

Mal never questioned what it was he was putting into her body. Since he genuinely seemed to care and tried to help her, make her stronger, she didn't ask. Besides, if it were drugs or poison, would he actually admit it?

"Soon," Kav said one morning, bringing a green berry to her lips. It took her ages to chew. Even chewing was exhausting. "I hope to have you strong enough to at least get out of the palace."

Several minutes later, once she'd finished her berry and regained her breath, she asked, "And how do you plan to do that?" The words were a little slurred, but he seemed used to her jumbled speech.

"I have a soldier's uniform I think will fit you reasonably well. Then, we'll take a tove out of here."

She didn't have the energy to ask what a tove was. It didn't matter. She'd see it eventually.

"What do I need to do?" she asked.

"Just gain your strength, Princess. Carrying a soldier out of here dead to the world will certainly draw suspicion."

Mal spent the remainder of that awake time resting and mentally preparing to exert herself over the next day. Not using her muscles sure as hell wasn't going to help her increase muscle mass.

Following the next sleep, Mal insisted on trying to stand. Kav refused until she could at least sit on her own. It took several cycles of awakes for her to accomplish it for more than a few minutes.

Then, she finally graduated to standing. And walking. By walking, she really meant shuffling a few inches alongside the bed.

Kav came into the room highly anxious one awake. "We need to leave tonight. Queen Redd will be arriving in the morning to see you in the dungeon. In the event my ruse doesn't work, we need to be well on our way."

Mal nodded. She spent hours pushing herself beyond her limits. He made sure she slept for the next several hours with her IV in. It would be important that she keep as much nutrients flowing into her as possible until the last minute.

She watched him pack, resting in preparation for her journey to where they'd get to the tove. Kav prepared a single pack. He left the room long enough to drop the pack somewhere they could pick it up later.

When he came back, he helped her dress in the armor she'd be wearing. The metal was surprisingly thin. It was no wonder Eagy and Ryph could take out so many at once. It wouldn't defend against a steak knife, never mind a well-sharpened blade.

The leggings were stiff. Thick, but in a rubbery way. The

boots were too big. She hadn't tried to walk yet, but she imagined she'd be tripping over herself and dragging her feet. The top was tight with a dent in the side, opposite her injury. And the helmet.... How did one actually see out of it? It made her head feel like it weighed thirty pounds.

The whole getup was heavy and suffocating. When Mal tried to walk, she simply fell to the ground in a crunch, gasping for breath.

"This isn't going to work," she said. "I hope you have a plan B."

The Tove

MAL

2

Kav grinned at her when he finally got her on her feet again. “Guess I should have had you working in this sooner,” he mused.

Mal smiled weakly. Already, she wanted to sleep, her body completely wrung out from that little bit of exertion. It made her feel like she’d been in that dungeon a lot longer than ten weeks. Ten months, maybe.

But then, she supposed that was the point. It seemed like the only way out of the dungeon was death. Unless a treasonous knave took an interest in you. And she hadn’t quite figured out why yet.

Ah, yes. To bring her to her rightful spot in Hell. The part where she was the one releasing those tortured cries.

“We’re going to have to wait until the dead of night. It’s a little later than I had planned, but it looks like we’re going to have to avoid as many people as we can.”

Why hadn’t that been the plan to begin with? There was no way she’d be able to pretend to be a Bloody Soldier convincingly. What if someone had asked her a question? How could he possibly have thought he could just prance out of the palace, dragging her dead weight at his side?

He was as delusional as she was. At least she admitted hers.

While they waited for the night to come on, Kav had Mal standing and walking for short periods of time around his room. Then she'd rest, breathlessly, for many longer minutes than she'd used walking around.

By the time deep night came on, she was ready for short bursts of walking. Unfortunately, Kav's room was deep within the palace. It wasn't a surprise, but still not at all helpful.

Kav left the room, keeping her seated until the last possible moment. After he'd checked the hallway, he returned and helped her to her feet.

"I know the boots are big, but try to walk lightly," he said as he brought her to the door.

Mal rolled her eyes. Sure... no problem.

The corridors were dark and quiet. Kav wanted to walk quickly, but there was no way Mal could keep up. She had one speed and it was a mosey.

"Would be easier to carry you," he mumbled

"So, do it," Mal loudly whispered back.

He gave her a little smirk, raising a brow in a suggestive way. "Soldiers are only carried when they are dead."

She believed that. From the little she had gathered from him, there wasn't an infirmary within the palace. If you were injured or sick enough to need one, the queens let you die or dismissed you from service.

The queens must live in protective bubbles to never need a healer of any kind. Did they not have midwives here, at least? She supposed with the lack of children being conceived, that career choice had died out.

They stopped down the second corridor where Kav shoved her into an empty, and completely dark, room while he scouted the stairs. Once he was convinced they were clear, he pulled her onto his back and hurried down them. Which was good since it likely would have taken her all night to do so.

What felt like hours later, they were out of the main palace.

He pulled her into the shadows where he picked her up again and hurried along to the stables.

Mal couldn't even begin to guess what kind of beast he set her down in front of. It resembled a horse...mostly. Both front and back legs were more reptilian in shape and structure. It stood like a T-Rex, on thick back legs and had shorter "arms". The tail was long hair, as was the mane. Its face was horse-like, too, except for the long, pointed teeth that filled a mouth that extended almost to its ears.

Like Chesh's wide, toothy grin.

It was white with mottled gray fur from its hips down its hind legs. Both the tail and mane were gray. The chest and neck were covered in what appeared to be blood. But perhaps it was just rusty red fur...

On its back was a saddle with the pack Kav had brought out earlier.

"We're not going to ride that, are we?" Mal asked.

The animal looked at her, its large eye narrowing. It might have understood her... great.

"This is Rival," Kav said, running his hand affectionately down Rival's neck. "And yes, we're riding him."

"And what is he?"

"A tove, of course."

"Of course," Mal said

Kav helped her up before he climbed on behind her. "We're going to ride through Silence for the most part. I've taken leave already, but I'd rather stay under the radar as much as possible."

Mal nodded. She'd been traveling in Silence before she was abducted. And possibly tortured. Injured, at the very least.

It wasn't long before she fell asleep. The tove moved surprisingly smoothly and she slept well into the next day. When she woke, they stopped long enough to eat and for Mal to change into something more comfortable. Before they took off again, he had her walking around, over roots and around trees. Practicing picking up her feet higher than a centimeter. In all honesty, she shuffled more than walked.

All the exertion of the ten-minute exercise made her pretty lethargic for the following hour.

Two days later, as Kav continued to feed her and clean her wounds, Mal realized she wasn't actually dead after all. *The pain should have made that obvious*, she thought in hindsight. But the truth was, between nightmares of the Sheep, the bird with teeth, and the constant pain skittering through her body, she wasn't sure she could withstand all that torment if she were alive.

Besides, it was hard to fathom that she had been stuck somewhere her men couldn't actually get to. Couldn't rescue her. She had come to think there wasn't any place they couldn't get. Nothing they couldn't do.

Then again, maybe they were still mad enough that they didn't try.

No, Chesh had forgiven her. Forgiven her cruel words when she was upset and a little frightened. And Wyat had, too. He had been quiet the last couple of days they were together, but she was sure everything had been okay between them. Fairly certain. And although Ryph and Eagy were still very upset with her, she'd gotten Eagy talking a little. That had to count for something. Right?

"Where are we going?" Mal asked after four days of travel.

"Wabe. I know a trainer who can help you regain your strength and muscle mass. Maybe teach you some specialized skills," he said.

"Wabe," she mused. "We'd been heading there before the Sheep."

"Yeah?"

Mal nodded. "There were too many of them. Even for Wyat."

He didn't answer for a minute. "Wyat?" he asked, eventually. There was wariness in his voice. She turned her head slightly to try and get a look at his expression. He was too close over her shoulder to do so, though.

She nodded. "Wyat is my..." she trailed off. The ache of knowing that she'd accidentally canceled their... er... courting?... was still upsetting. "I don't know what he is. I accidentally broke up with them. *After* I had learned that they were my... what's the word? Courtiers? Something."

"Coters. Them?"

"Wyat is my gargoyle. Chesh my demon cat. Then there's Eagy, my sweet eaglet. And Ryph, my mighty golden gryphon," she said, smiling.

Her heart hurt.

"You broke up with them?"

"Not intentionally," she said, sadly. "No one explained things to me. They weren't trying to keep it from me, but they didn't understand that I didn't understand. Everything is different here. My words have power. And I don't mean metaphorically."

Kav sighed. "I see."

"It happened just a couple of days before the Sheep. Ryph and Eagy were still really upset with me. They were barely talking to me. Wyat had forgiven me, I thought, but then he had hardly said anything to anyone. Chesh and I were good, though."

"Forgiven you? Mal, if they kept information from you, you should be the one upset," Kav said.

She shook her head. "They didn't do so on purpose. How were they to know relationships worked differently on the Outside? How was I to know what they were asking me? It was just a miscommunication."

He made an unimpressed, unconvinced sound.

"But then, they haven't come looking for me," she whispered.

"How would they know where to find you?"

"Don't the Sheep work for the queens?"

Kav shook his head. "No, they're free agents. I'm assuming they participated in The Hunt and turned you over to Hart since you were closest to her kingdom when they caught you."

"That's why it was an abduction," she said. "I was sure they were going to kill me. Do you think they killed my guys?"

He nodded. "I'm certainly not advocating for these men who didn't tell you what things meant, but in this particular instance, not finding you wasn't their fault. They'd have no idea where to look. And I don't know if they were killed. The Sheep tend to only terminate someone they've been paid to take out. If your men weren't on that list-" He shrugged.

It made Mal feel a little better. Perhaps they *were* looking for her. But would they have given up by now? It had been almost three entire months! And, the Sheep were known to kill. Not kidnap.

They stopped at an inn a few days later. It wasn't one she'd been in before. She didn't recognize anything about it. Kav gave her her own room, which surprised her. Eagy and Ryph had always said women did not stay alone in Silence.

She was glad for a soak and took a long one. The water was hot, and the bubbles were plenty. She took a note from Ryph's book and piled the side of the tub with several bottles of various scrubs. Mal took her time and enjoyed every single one of them. There was no telling how many times she actually washed when she was done.

By the time she got out, she felt like a new person. She couldn't remember the last time she'd been clean. Being sponge bathed was not her idea of getting clean, though it was pretty close to being pampered. You know, under different circumstances.

The nightmares welcomed her with open arms. The Sheep came bleating at her, large teeth gnashing. Hooves were now claws. Their eyes were bloodshot. They chased her over cliffs where she fell into a mess of broken bones, into rivers where she drowned, and through the woods where she was torn apart and eaten by things she couldn't see.

Somehow, she'd managed not to scream when she awoke. It was almost a pointless victory since she screamed when her door was thrown open moments later. Kav came flying in, securing the door behind him.

"Get up, get dressed," he said, voice low and urgent.

"What happened?" she asked as she climbed out of bed.

It was amazing what a clean body and comfortable bed could do to regenerate one's strength. She hadn't felt this good in ages. Her clothes were neatly folded, clean, on a bench in the washroom. She left the door open to hear Kav's reply as she dressed.

"There are Sheep in the area, and they don't look too good. There are also Soldiers a half a day's walk away that we need to avoid," he answered.

Mal came out as she wrapped her hair in a ribbon at the base of her head. Kav stepped close and pulled her hood over her head. It reminded her of Eagy, always trying to hide her in plain sight. As if a hood could really sell her as someone else.

Her heart ached.

"Ready?" he asked.

She nodded and he led her out. They walked quickly once in the main tavern. Outside, Rival was waiting at the back of the inn, saddled and ready to go. His dark, bloodshot eyes unnerved her, but she offered him a smile anyway.

His lips lifted, revealing a long row of ultra-sharp teeth that stretched all the way to his jaw joint, just under his ears. It wasn't just his eyes that unnerved her. Hopefully, that was a smile and not a show of warning.

They made quick time moving through the forest. Mal wasn't sure Kav was actually steering Rival. It seemed, every now and again, Rival would change their direction on a whim. Kav never corrected him.

"How long will it take to get to Wabe?" Mal asked.

"Few more days as long as we can stay clear of everyone until we get there."

"Surely not everyone needs to be avoided. Eagy and Ryph frequent Silence," Mal said.

"What are they, again?" he asked.

She tilted her head in confusion. "What do you mean? They're men."

"Normal men?"

"Oh. Eagy is an eaglet. Ryph is a gryphon. Why?"

"Ah, they're the duo that kill the Soldiers. The Poachers," he noted, the hint of a smile in his voice. "I'm sure if we're anywhere near them, Rival will let us know."

"How?" Mal asked, eyeing Rival.

Kav chuckled. "He'd tell us, of course."

"He speaks?" Mal asked, incredulous.

"Well, yes. All toves speak."

"Alright," Mal said, glancing back at him. "Remember when I said that there was a miscommunication between my men and me because they assumed I knew something?"

Kav bowed his head, his lips lingering on her shoulder. "Fair enough. Sorry. Rival, this is Mal. Mal, Rival."

Rival turned his head, his one bloodshot eye staring at her. His voice was a low humming growl. To Mal, it didn't look like he was built to be able to speak.

"Mal," he hummed.

"Hello," she said, gripping his mane tightly before she realized what she was doing and released it. "Thanks for transporting us."

His lip lifted a little. Yes, she really hoped that was a smile. He turned back to the non-trail.

He wasn't the talkative sort, apparently. Had he been, she'd probably have figured out he actually spoke far before this point. She'd reserve all her questions on him for later. It was rude to talk about him like he wasn't there.

It was four days before they reached Wabe. She recalled her men saying that Silence had overgrown part of Wabe. It was certainly true. There were trees growing through buildings, roots pushing through stone paths. A fountain in what was probably a town square at one point had a large branch going through the middle of it. The fountain was filled with leaves, growing mushrooms, strange – malformed? - flowers.

As they passed through the tree line right into the heart of Wabe and into the new town-square, she spotted the man from the train who dressed all in newspaper. He was wandering out into the street in a peculiar zagging pattern. He reminded her of one of those people who over exaggerate when they're running away from someone. As if abruptly changing directions would throw them off his path.

Mal shook her head, about to turn away, when a headline on his back caught her attention. TWENTY-EIGHT STILL IN HART'S DUNGEON AWAITING TRIAL. She hadn't realized she'd been scheduled for a trial.

Wait... what was she on trial for?

She pointed it out to Kav. He only nodded, seemingly uninterested.

"I didn't know there was going to be a trial," she whispered.

He shook his head. "There wouldn't have been. Doesn't mean they wouldn't say there was, and you'd been found guilty, sentenced to death."

"On what crimes?"

"Disrupting the utopia that is Laddenworn," he deadpanned.

Mal looked at him skeptically. "You can't tell me people would believe that."

"Not at all. But this is a dictatorship, not a democracy."

They pushed further into town. Mal looked around at the men, the buildings, the layout. It was a beautiful place, really. Very Neapolitan. Neat, but not new. There were preserved buildings in an older style and buildings that were clearly new. The citizens looked well-kept and put together.

No one stared at her like they did in every other city she'd been to.

The inn was a large tea kettle stacked on top of three teacups. Kav left her out back with Rival while he went in to acquire them rooms.

She tried not to stare at Rival. But now that she knew he could talk, she had so many more questions.

He stared right back. It was unsettling. She was ridiculously relieved when Kav returned to her.

"There are no soldiers and no Sheep anywhere around. Nor are the Storeys near, from what I hear. We should be safe in Wabe for a while. Which is good. You need to get back in shape," he said.

Mal nodded as she followed him up four flights of stairs. He opened the door for her.

It was a decent room. A bed big enough for two, a small table with a chest behind it. A fireplace dominated one wall and then a door that presumably led to a washroom. She nodded.

"I'll bring you some food. Stay inside. I'm going to talk with a friend and see if he'll have time to work with you," Kav said.

She nodded. It was almost impossibly fast that he returned with a tray of food. She'd barely eaten much of it when he joined her. He ate with her, informing her that a man named TL would meet them at his Marden first thing in the morning to begin conditioning.

Mal was surprised when he said he had his own room two floors below hers.

"Don't let anyone in unless you're sure you know them, Princess. It's a dangerous time for you right now."

She nodded. He kissed her cheek and left her. It was still daylight but after a soak, she was sure she'd be more than ready to sleep.

Hopefully, she'd think of a way to find her men. They were hers and she wasn't willing to give them up until she was able to set things straight. If they wanted to part ways after that, she wouldn't stop them. It would crush her, but she'd let them go.

The Trainer

MAL

3

The morning was bright. She'd slept marvelously well. The bed was one of the softest she'd been in in weeks. Months. Maybe ever. She didn't remember the beds at DeadEnd being this good.

Then again, maybe it was just because she'd been stuck in chains and tied to a bed for months. Either seemed plausible.

Kav brought her a small tray of food for breakfast. It was edible, at least. She almost didn't care what she was eating as long as she was getting food at this point. Now that she knew she was alive, she needed food.

Still, it had been long enough since she'd eaten a proper meal that she had only been able to keep a bit down at a time. Small amounts of food were better than none.

She finished in relatively quick time before she started on tea. The breakfast tea was good and served with honey. It soothed her throat in a way that she hadn't realized her throat was sore until she'd felt it soothed. She was growing used to tea several times a day.

"Ready?" Kav asked, offering her his hand.

Mal accepted it and allowed him to pull her to her feet. She was surprised with just how weak she still was. Sure, she'd been basically comatose for quite some time, but for the past two weeks (had it been two weeks? Time certainly was different and hard to keep track of in Laddenworn), she'd been working on regaining her strength. Sitting. Standing. Walking. Riding a monstrous tove. She even climbed the stairs to her room.

And still, it was like she was just learning how to walk. How to lift one foot completely off the ground to take a step instead of dragging her feet along. Somehow, it seemed dragging her feet gave her more balance. She was steadier when she didn't have to lift her foot.

She was also noisy and a bit clumsy.

"I guess," Mal said. "Who is it you're taking me to see again?"

"His name is TL. I've known him for years. Great at conditioning and training and he owns the best Marden around."

Mal followed him out the door. He was kind enough that he walked at her pace instead of trying to get her to walk faster. She couldn't walk faster. Not yet. Someday, she'd be able to. Hopefully with TL's training.

"What's a Marden?" Mal asked as they headed out into the street. It was busy. There were men everywhere. Everyone seemed happy, pleasant. They didn't appear to be in a hurry or have any real destination as they wandered around.

Mal was pleased to see a few women here and there, also. Not so pleased to see that they were acting like tyrannical bitches as every other female she'd come across in the cities. Apparently, Wabe was no different. That was a disappointment.

"It's like a gym or dojo. Maybe a little of each," Kav said as he led her down a different street.

The Marden was a large, spherical building, bright green in color with orange trim around the windows and doors. Looking at it hurt her eyes.

Kav led her inside, where it looked like any other gym she might see. There was a track several feet up at the widest part of the structure where a couple of men were running laps. There was a corner covered in mats, floors and walls. There was a weight area and doors all along one stretch of the round wall. One set of doors were huge, like someone might drive a Mack truck through it. She couldn't even guess what they might be used for.

There was no workout equipment, though. No treadmills or elliptical. No rowing machines or bikes. It wasn't that surprising since Laddenworn didn't seem to have technology of any kind to speak of.

They headed toward the back, where a couple of men were following directions from another in the proper stance needed to use a couple of large tridents accurately. Why one would need to use one for anything, Mal couldn't guess.

"TL," Kav called, announcing their arrival before reaching him.

The man turned and Mal felt her eyes widen in surprise.

Taller than Kav. Probably taller than Ryph, though not nearly as tall as Wyat. He was hard and lean, built like a linebacker. His shirt was sleeveless, putting his ridiculously taut arms on display. His short hair was strands of dark maroon and orange. Not quite striped, but there were patchy strands of the two colors intermixed. And, as if that wasn't enough, there were dark, almost black freckles in his hair. Yes, in his hair!

When she stopped in front of him, the finer details of his face made him even more unique. Dark maroon eyes that matched the freckles in his hair. There was stubble along his chin and along his jawline. Lean and rugged and oh-so-stunning!

"Kav," TL greeted, nodding at him without a smile.

"This is Mal," Kav introduced.

Those dark maroon eyes turned to Mal and she froze. She hadn't been moving before, but her entire body stilled further. Even her breathing paused for a few heartbeats. It felt like he was looking *through* her eyes, into her soul.

Mal tried to smile. She wasn't sure she pulled it off.

"Be easy on her for a couple days," Kav said. "She's still barely eating solid food. Walking is a chore, too."

"So you said." TL frowned, his eyes remaining locked on Mal.

"I told you what I took her from," Kav said, lowering his voice.

Was it a warning? Or a reminder? Mal wasn't sure, but she got the distinct impression it was one of the two by the way his tone changed.

TL glanced at him. "You want her up and running, she goes by my rules, Kav. I don't make exceptions."

"You can't beat a dead Bandersnatch," Kav snapped.

Mal would have said something, stuck up for herself, but she wasn't truly sure what they were saying. Perhaps TL knew the right way. He was the successful Marden guy, after all. What did she know?

"I'll be gentler for two days," TL conceded. "I don't spoil my clients."

"We've been over this," Kav insisted. "She was basically dead two months ago! I didn't bring her to you to tear apart more."

"No, you brought her to me because I'm the best and if anyone can get her back in shape, it's me. But you've gone so soft for her that you're trying to make me coddle her."

Kav rolled his eyes. "I'm trying to make you understand that she's a little fragile right now."

That did it. She was not fragile!

"Okay," Mal interrupted. "I'm a little weak, sure, but I need my strength back by whatever means necessary. That means challenging my body however my trainer sees fit. I don't need to be treated any different than anyone else."

It was the first time she'd seen TL even hint at a smile. Her heart fluttered. Perhaps he'd be one of her seven.

Then, she thought that she might have to start over gathering her seven.

She ached thinking about the loss of her men.

Kav frowned at her. "And if you overdo it?"

"I haven't killed a client yet," TL said, the same small smile dancing.

Shaking his head, Kav turned and headed for the door. "I'll be back for lunch. Hopefully, she'll still be standing."

Mal watched him leave and a bit of hesitation trickled through her. He'd left her alone with a stranger.

Then again, she'd entered the world with everyone being strangers. Little by little, she'd found friends. And then, she'd lost them all in one fell swoop.

Fantastic!

"Alright," TL said. Mal turned to face him and he made a show of roving his eyes over her entire body. He frowned, sighed, and put a hand on his hip. "We have some work to do."

"I was in a dungeon for three months," she said. "Chained to a wall. Then chained to a bed. I've only been allowed on my feet within the last couple weeks."

His lids hooded. "So, you are frail is what you're telling me."

"No," she gritted between her teeth. "I'm saying that this isn't my true strength. I've had some setbacks."

"But it is your true strength. *Now.*"

Mal sighed, irritated. "Fine. So, almighty trainer, what shall I do first?"

"Change," he said, gesturing to the doors behind him. "You're going to want to wear something more flexible."

Wariness settled over her. Great. She could only imagine what he had in mind.

Mal found the door to a changing room amongst the many that took up almost the entire back of the Marden. Apparently, a square with a diamond meant locker room. There, she found an entire rack of clothing. Leggings and shirts. A shelf had what closely resembled sneakers lined up.

It didn't take her long to change and find her way back out to TL. He was waiting for her at a ladder that led up to the track spanning the perimeter. She stopped in front of him and looked up the length of the ladder. At least a dozen feet over her head.

"Since walking is such a chore, little weed, let's start with the basics."

His voice wasn't exactly condescending, but it surely wasn't friendly and encouraging. Hopefully, he wouldn't be like one of those unlikable tools she used to watch on TV.

Mal didn't argue. She turned to the ladder and started climbing. As it turned out, climbing was far worse than walking. Her arms could barely hold her weight. Four rungs up, the strength in her hand gave out and she tumbled from the ladder.

TL caught her before she had time to let out a scream. He frowned down at her as she clung to him, panting, fear bright in her wide eyes.

"You were stationary for three months?" he asked, voice low.

Mal nodded. "Mostly, yes. Kav said I had been in the dungeon for nine weeks before he found an opportunity to get me out. What little I can remember of the dungeon, I was shackled to the wall in a heap on the floor."

"Probably a good thing you don't remember anything outside of that."

She nodded in return. "Then, he had me tied to a bed as he attempted to restore my nutrients. I don't recall how long that was."

TL sighed and finally sat her on her feet. "Let's try this again," he said, nudging her to the ladder.

Warily, Mal placed a hand on the rung. Testing her grip, she was sure she didn't have strength to climb the twelve feet to the track, never mind still have the energy to walk it.

But she refused to be that pathetic. Regardless of knowing she'd fall again, she placed a foot on the rung and pulled herself up.

She made it a whole rung beyond the one she'd fallen from last time before she felt her hand loosen. As much as she concentrated on keeping her grip tight, her body rejected the command and she started to fall back.

This time, TL was on the ladder with her. His body suddenly pressed firmly to her back as he pinned her against the ladder.

"Try again," he said, placing her hand back on the rung.

Mal swallowed and nodded.

It was awkward with him so close. She couldn't find a good way to move her legs without rubbing against him. But she was thankful he was there. Every other rung, her grip simply released, and she fell.

TL didn't let her get more than a few inches before he placed her hands on the rungs again.

After the seventh time of her heart jumping from the would-be fall, Mal rested a minute, setting her sweat-slick forehead against a cool rung. "I admit," she whispered, "I didn't think I was this weak. Walking had been coming easier."

He didn't answer. Nor did he insist she keep going. He allowed her to rest a minute. When she finally decided to try again, he answered, "Sometimes true strength comes from within, Sunshine. Your inner strength and determination will have a big impact on your performance and success."

Mal chewed her lip as she slipped again. Three slips later, she sighed in frustration. "It's like I don't have control," she whined. "I keep trying to hold it tight-" her hand strangled the rung "-but my muscles do what they want." As if on cue, her hand released and her back hit TL's chest.

"One thing at a time," TL said. "Up to the track. We'll work on dexterity later."

Mal nodded.

It took her far longer to get to the track than she'd have liked. The prospect of having to climb back down was horrifying.

She spent the majority of the day walking. At first, all she did was simply walk. Sometimes she'd rest, but she was determined to get through walking. After lunch, TL made her take bigger steps, emphasizing picking her knees up. By the end of the day, she could jog three minutes before she collapsed onto her back and gasped for breath.

She slept like a rock that night.

Chesh

HE WAS WHITTLING WOOD. Wasting his days, not getting any closer to finding her, whittling fucking wood.

They were a day outside of Wabe. They'd have been closer, but the two were so obnoxious in their frantic searching that they constantly had to stop and fuck against a tree to commiserate.

Supposedly, they'd only stopped here for food. There was a shop several hundred paces from where Chesh waited for them. Since he'd been waiting a while, he figured they'd stopped at a nice tree along the way.

He much preferred traveling alone. This was ridiculous. He'd have been to Wabe days ago if it weren't for them. They could fly and somehow, they were still all stuck walking, taking time.

Ryph dropped to the ground next to him. Chesh glanced his way before peeling back more of the crude wood. "Where is he?"

"Some people were talking about the Sheep," he said, waving his hand. "I didn't think it sounded like anyone knew anything, but Eagy wanted to make sure."

Chesh nodded.

They sat in silence for some time. They could really use a prophecy-telling looking-glass right about then. They didn't know if she was alive or...

He couldn't bring himself to even think the word. She had to be alive.

"We will find her, right?" Ryph asked.

At his broken tone, Chesh turned his head to face Ryph. The gryphon was a young beast in a man's body. At this moment, he looked like a shattered child. There was such desperation in his voice, in his eyes, that Chesh almost reached for him.

"I don't know," Chesh admitted. "We should have found *something* by now. Anything."

The breath that left Ryph's chest sounded like a sob. There were no tears on his face.

"I don't know what to do," Ryph said helplessly.

Again, Chesh almost reached for him. What comfort could he possibly offer when he felt just as useless? They should have at least had word that the queens had...

Ryph's hand was suddenly on the back of Chesh's neck, pulling him in. Chesh didn't think to do anything but drop the knife he'd been using so as not to stab the brute accidentally. Of course, he wasn't expecting Ryph's mouth on his.

Chesh's eyes widened in shock. His arms pinwheeled as he jerked away and they both went tumbling backwards. Ryph's mouth was momentarily parted from Chesh's, but as they came down on the ground, Ryph landing almost on top of Chesh, his mouth was swallowed by the beast's once more.

For some time, Chesh didn't even fight him. He allowed the kiss, allowed Ryph to drive his tongue deep into Chesh's mouth in a disparaging way.

It had been so long since he'd been kissed. Since he'd been touched at all. Yes, Mal, but those kisses were so few. Chaste, almost. He hadn't even gotten to the point where he could hold her yet before she was taken from them. Before Mal... fuck, he couldn't even remember.

Ryph's tongue was like sandpaper, much like his own. The way he dragged it around Chesh's mouth made him shake. The way he danced it across his own tongue made him tremble. When he pressed it to his sharp teeth, Chesh had to force himself not to growl.

Then, Ryph pulled Chesh fully underneath him, pushing his legs apart roughly. The beast bore down on him, pressing his hips hard against Chesh. Chesh's head spun and for a moment, he forgot that they couldn't do this. He didn't remember until Ryph pushed Chesh's legs further apart and pressed his erection hard against Chesh.

Chesh pulled his mouth from Ryph's and pushed at his shoulders. "Ryph, we-"

A shudder ran through him when Ryph bit into his clavicle. Not hard, not to draw blood, but to excite and make his blood burn. His hand pushed up Chesh's shirt, greedily grabbing at his flesh with sharp nails.

"Fuck, Ryph. Stop," Chesh choked.

"No," Ryph growled.

Chesh didn't really want to fight him. They'd both regret it later. Especially if Eagy came upon them.

"Eagy," Chesh said. "Would he-"

Ryph sprang off him in an instant. He tumbled back several feet and landed on his back. With ragged breaths, his chest rose and fell. It wouldn't take much more for him to burst out of his pants.

Chesh sat up and leaned back against the log he'd been on earlier.

"Ass," Ryph whispered.

Chesh threw a stick at him with a severe frown. "Seriously? You jump-"

"Not you," Ryph said, forcing himself up to his hands and knees. Eventually, he dragged his eyes up to meet Chesh's. "Sorry. I'm feeling a little stressed and I don't know what to do with myself."

"May I suggest that was not the solution?"

Ryph grinned. "I don't know. You taste pretty good, pussy cat."

Chesh rolled his eyes and turned his head. *You too,* he thought, frowning. It had clearly been far too long since he'd had attention. He was craving it. But like the cat, he only wanted it on his terms. This was not his choosing.

Almost too soon, Eagy returned. He was frowning. Fortunately, he seemed to be preoccupied, so he didn't pay much attention to Ryph's awkward change in position as he tried to hide his still hard dick pressing against his pants.

Chesh tried not to grin. Well, he tried to try. It didn't work. Served the damned beast right. Stick to your eaglet and leave Chesh alone.

"So?" Ryph asked. The silence left him uncomfortable.

Eagy shook his head. "The Sheep were last seen in Dymund, except that their numbers are shrinking. They're looking a little haggard."

"What does that mean?" Chesh asked.

Eagy shook his head again. "They didn't know anything else. No one's seen a paper in days so..." he shrugged.

"Should we still head for Wabe?" Ryph asked.

Eagy didn't answer right away. He sat on the log next to Chesh and absently fiddled with some of the shavings Chesh had thrown to the ground.

"I don't know," Eagy said, eventually. "I don't know what to do. Lepa hasn't heard anything. Ache says he hasn't seen her. That literally covers everyone we know who knows about her."

They were quiet for several very long minutes. Chesh was uncomfortable with Eagy not having a plan. Not being sure of their next move. It was one thing when he'd been on his own and only had to think of himself. A plan wasn't necessary. But he'd been with Eagy and Ryph for too long now. They needed to do something. They needed a purpose.

Their purpose was Mal.

Eagy dropped something in Chesh's lap before he tossed another package to Ryph. Food. A bundle of different items wrapped individually.

Chesh smiled. "Thanks, Eagy."

Eagy nodded absently.

Chesh munched on his meal. Each bite was wonderful. He was so sick of dried meat, bread, and cheese. The meat pie, tarts, fruits, and biscuit were almost orgasmic.

When he'd finished, Eagy was still staring off into the trees at nothing. One of the shavings twirled between his fingers.

Chesh reached out and placed a hand on Eagy's arm. Eagy

looked at him. "I don't mean this to sound like I'm putting pressure on you, but we're with you. You haven't led us astray, yet."

Eagy huffed a note of quiet laughter. "I don't know what to do, Chesh. Where to go. Who to ask."

"What does your gut say?"

Ice blue eyes turned vague as he turned his head away slightly. For a moment, he did nothing else. When he met Chesh's eyes again, he lifted one side of his mouth in a half smirk. "We go to Wabe, I suppose. And stay put. If she's... able... she'll find us. She won't find us if we're moving around so much. And Wabe was the last place we were all headed."

Chesh grinned. "Good, Eagy." He removed his hand from his companion and turned back to his misshapen piece of wood that looked like nothing.

Eagy smiled and looked at Ryph. Ryph grinned in return.

Wabe

EAGY

4

They stopped at every inn along the way to Wabe to see if Mal had checked in at any point. After thoroughly questioning the staff, it was determined that no, she hadn't been anywhere near these inns.

They weren't surprised. Even if she had survived the Sheep, she'd lost her bag. She had no currency on her. How would she eat, never mind rent a room, at an inn?

Still, it was worth checking.

The innkeepers were a little annoyed that they weren't renting a room when they'd come in to be harassed with their questioning. Eagy made up for it by purchasing food and whatever equipment they needed replaced. It wasn't the same as a room, but it was good enough.

They needed to keep moving, heading north to Wabe. There, they'd book a room and stay put for a while in hopes that Mal would find them.

Eagy refused to believe that the Sheep had killed her. They had been determined to abduct her. They hadn't even been trying to kill Eagy, Ryph, Chesh, or Wyat in the process. Only to get them out of the way.

The four of them hadn't been able to protect her.

What was worse, Eagy had been pretty cold to her for days. If the last things she remembered of him were how he treated her, he would be devastated.

She had to be alive. He had to make it right. They couldn't lose her like this.

"One more inn on the way," Ryph said quietly.

"There's a Cart just west of the inn, a few hours' walk," Chesh said.

Yes, they'd stop at each. Even if Mal hadn't been to either, they could get clean clothes and warm food. The Cart always had little treats they'd not find anywhere other than the cities, too. The least he could do was spoil Ryph and Chesh a little. Maybe take their mind off their horrible situation.

The inn they came to was no longer in service. How could it be when the whole left side was burnt to a crisp? It was the first place they'd come to that had had any damage at all.

The three of them stopped and stared at it.

"Sheep?" Ryph wondered out loud.

"Torture and slaughter were always their interest," Chesh said, shaking his head. "This doesn't look like them."

"Kidnapping isn't a normal thing for Sheep, either," Ryph pointed out.

Chesh didn't answer.

"More likely, it was Soldiers," Eagy said. "We already know they tried to destroy an entire Patch with fire. Why not an inn deep within Silence?"

"We're not so deep, though," Chesh said. "Wabe is only a day's walk."

Eagy nodded.

"Frankly, I don't care who did it," Ryph said. "I just want to find her. Nothing else matters."

Chesh bowed his head.

Deep down, Eagy wondered if they were giving up hope like he was. Three months. It had been three months since she was taken from their grasp. It seemed so unlikely that she was...

"Let's go," Chesh said. "We can still make the Cart by nightfall."

Ryph nodded and turned toward the Cart.

West would take them further into Silence and away from Wabe but at this point, they were running out of ideas.

They reached the Cart well after it had closed, so they set up camp there. First thing in the morning, they'd question the Runner and see if he had seen their Mal.

Eagy was willing to bet the answer would be no. In which case, they'd change their trajectory again and head straight to Wabe, where they'd wait.

Maybe send word to as many people they trusted as they could. Lepa. Maybe Ache. Lorem? Was he worth the hassle? They'd only been there for a few minutes.

Perhaps the Songbird and Raptor Villages.

A rustle in the trees made the three of them turn. Eagy relaxed when Pat materialized from his camouflage of trees.

Ryph turned away, uninterested. Chesh had vanished. Eagy had no doubt that he was still with them, though.

"Hey, birds," Pat said, joining them at their fire without invite.

Ryph frowned at his intrusion but said nothing.

"Pat," Eagy said.

Pat grinned. The moonlight glittered off the scales on his face and neck. They were pearly and smooth instead of, well, scaly.

"Why so glum?" Pat asked.

Eagy studied him for a moment. It wasn't like Serpents to be solitary creatures. They usually traveled in communities. These days, it was too dangerous to be out on your own. The depravity of the world was catching up to all the small nooks and homages.

"We lost someone to the Sheep," Eagy said, taking scrutiny of his expression. Serpents were very expressive. If he'd heard anything about the Sheep's movements, it would show on his face.

Surprise flickered briefly, followed by interest. "Well, they're getting their wool handed to them these days."

"What do you mean?" Ryph asked, his head jerking up.

"Haven't you heard?" Pat asked. "Someone is hunting the Sheep and tearing them apart, limb from limb."

"Oh?" Eagy asked skeptically. The Sheep had been the best assassin group within Laddenworn. Their acts were notorious. It was said that when they set their eyes on you, you best just lay down and present your stomach because they *never* stopped until you were dead.

Pat nodded. "For the last two months. Their numbers have been cut in half, last I heard."

Eagy met Ryph's eyes. Perhaps he was thinking the same thing.

"Have you heard about their last known whereabouts? Or any captives they might have?" Eagy asked, looking at Pat again.

He shook his head. "The Sheep don't take captives, Eag. You know that."

Eagy nodded, frustrated. He didn't need this information. Just answers to what the reptile might have heard.

"What else?" Ryph asked.

"Six newly dismembered bodies of Sheep were found just outside of Curiouser last week. I hear that someone witnessed them being interrogated before their deaths. Though that might have been fabricated since the questions were never disclosed."

"Have any idea where the Sheep's Field is?" Ryph asked.

Eagy glanced at him. That wasn't a Ryph question. He bet Chesh was hovering by Ryph.

Pat shook his head. "It's been hunted for a long time now. I doubt it will ever be found."

It would be found. Eagy was sure of it.

Pat stayed a while longer. The three remained quiet long after his departure, making sure that he was actually gone.

Eagy was pretty sure Chesh had tracked him.

When they met eyes, it was clear that they all thought the same thing.

"Wyat," the three said in unison.

Chesh grinned and leaned against the stalk of a mushroom.

"It explains why he decided not to stay with us," Ryph said. "Why he didn't like our plan."

"If you want to find something someone takes, you go to the source," Chesh agreed. "So, he hunts the Sheep, looking for their Field."

"You think he's found her?" Ryph asked.

Eagy shook his head. "If he'd found her, I'm pretty sure he'd look for us next."

"What if he's found her, but he's determined to kill all the Sheep as retribution?" Ryph suggested.

They quietly considered this.

As the fire died out and they curled up to sleep, Chesh whispered, "I think he'd still find us first to let us help kill them for taking her from us."

"Maybe not," Ryph said. "It's not like we were exactly pleasant when we were together last. Maybe she doesn't want to see us."

Eagy couldn't let his mind go there. Mal wasn't like that. She would want to see them again. She would!

His dreams weren't pleasant. They were filled with Mal's voice scolding him. Telling him he was a horrible youngling who acted childish for being mad at her when it was she who had the right to be mad. Her beautiful voice turning venomous saying how much they'd hurt her with their silence.

By the way Ryph and Chesh were downcast the next morning, he thought they were likely plagued with dreams, too. Chesh was abnormally quiet as they sat around waiting for the Cart to open.

Eagy pulled out the extra cream he'd kept locked away and handed it to Chesh. He looked at Eagy with surprise. Eagy gave him a light smile.

The smile that lingered on Chesh's face was not nearly as wide and mad as usual, but it was there again. He left Chesh to enjoy his cream while he dragged Ryph further into the trees and fucked him against a tree until they were both wrung out.

Looking for Mal and finding nothing had put them all in a bad place. It made Eagy need to feel Ryph constantly. Have him. Make the beast roar and his wings spring out. It made him desperate to hold on to what he had for fear that it might be taken away.

When they eventually returned to Chesh, the Cart had been open for a while. Chesh was leaning on the mushroom they'd slept under with his arms folded over his chest, his tail flicking irritably.

"Sorry," Eagy murmured.

Chesh rolled his eyes. "I need a whole lot more cream for how long you were gone."

Eagy's cheeks burned. He nodded. "Let's go talk to the Runner."

"I already did. They haven't seen a female in ages. Not in this part of Silence. The only thing of interest they had was that two of Hart's top court have been through here recently," Chesh said.

"Oh?" Ryph asked, stilling as he fastened a bag to his back.

Chesh nodded. "And guess where they were headed?"

"Wabe," Eagy and Ryph said.

Mal

THE DAYS FOLLOWING the ladder failure, Mal found she was making better progress. She spent much of the breaks TL allowed her climbing the ladder and getting back down.

Truth be told, it had freaked her out to see how her body had basically been ignoring her commands to hold on to the rungs.

TL was annoyed with her progress. Actually, he was annoyed

with her lack of progress. She insisted that she was trying. And she was getting better. She could climb the ladder like no one's business. But still, she was ridiculously weak.

"You'd think," Mal said as TL barely blocked her and she stumbled, "I'd be building more muscle by now."

"You're not trying hard enough," he said.

"I'm trying plenty hard," Mal snapped.

"Are you? Then come at me with more strength than a bud," he taunted.

Mal rolled her eyes. "You can be such a jerk, you know."

"If you were making progress at all, I wouldn't have to be. But you're stalling on the 'barely functional' leaf."

"No, being a jerk is a choice. No one's forcing it on you. You're as bad as everyone else in Laddenworn. Let's be an ass just because I can."

Her words must have stung. TL flinched and looked away. When he turned back, anger flared in his eyes. He reached out and pulled her to him roughly.

"Look, I'm doing this as a favor, Sunshine. If you don't like my method, you're free to go," he hissed.

Mal wrenched her arm free. Or, she tried to, but she wasn't strong enough to successfully pull from his grip. He let her go when she stopped trying to jerk away.

"Don't do me any favors," she snapped. "I'm tired of help being offered only when I need to jump through hoops to get it. You want to help me, or you don't, but I'm done sitting around allowing you to be an ass to me because you simply feel like it."

She noted the exact moments that he didn't understand what she was saying. 'Jump through hoops' was one of those times. The confusion on his face would have been amusing, had she not been so furious at him.

Seriously, why was everyone such a tool in this gods-forsaken place?! Yeah, your life was hard. Mal's hadn't exactly been a walk on the beach. Her parents were killed in an accident when she was eight. Her twin brother had only barely managed to rescue her from being molested by their uncle when they were thirteen. Even so, it wasn't like she made it out of that situation fully untouched. Then, she spent the rest of her life training to enter a new world where she'd be leaving everyone and everything she knew behind. Most likely, she'd lose her life in the process since twenty-seven people had failed before her.

Yet was she a bitch because her life had been anything but fun and rosy? No. And here she was, trying to fix *their* world.

Mal turned and headed to the door. The appropriate thing would have been for TL to stop her and apologize. Did he? Not a chance.

She returned to her room at the inn in no time, slamming her door shut behind her. Stripping from her clothes on the way to her washroom, she ran a hot soak and lowered herself in.

Perhaps it was lunch time or maybe TL sought out Kav immediately after Mal left the Marden. Whatever the case was, Kav showed up in no time flat, sitting at the edge of the tub and looking down at her with concern.

"If you're here to tell me I overreacted, I don't want to hear it. I'm tired of being told I'm weak and not trying. I'm really tired of people being asshats just because they can."

Kav nodded.

"I don't care. I'll work on it on my own. It's not like I haven't worked on my own before."

He didn't say anything. She ignored that he was there for a long time until it became clear that he wasn't leaving.

Mal sighed and looked at him, waiting for him to say what he came to say.

Eventually, he did. "He's doing me a favor, Princess. While I try to figure out a plan for us to take down the queens, I need someone else to help you along. Teach you things Laddenworn specific. TL might be a jerk, but he's damn good at what he does."

"No," Mal said simply. "I have more respect for myself than

to be in anyone's company who treats people like shit like an entitled dirtbag."

Kav's lips twitched in amusement. "If I promise he'll be better now?"

"And how do you think you're going to enforce that?"

"I just spoke to him. He's frustrated with your lack of skill, is all."

"Yeah, that makes it alright. Everything's forgotten."

He chuckled. "The next best trainer is in Garden, which is in Redd Kingdom. Obviously, we don't want to go there. Give it one more try. Please."

She glared at him for several minutes. "Fine. When I'm done relaxing my sore muscles, I'll take my time getting back."

His smile was amused. She thought he left when he walked out of the washroom with a nod, but he returned with some tea before actually leaving.

Mal spent several long minutes in her tub, sipping her tea. But she wanted to get the bullshit with TL over with, so she got out. Didn't matter that the stupid man was beautiful to look at. He was a jackass. For no reason other than funsies.

TL didn't greet her when she returned to the Marden. They trained in near silence for the rest of the day. He corrected her when need be but otherwise, he simply repeated 'again' until she was dead on her feet.

Over the next several days, something shifted in their hostile relationship. Maybe TL realized that she was pushing her limits, trying to keep up with his demands. Perhaps it was because he watched as she tried to imitate one of his other client's moves over and over until she was on her knees, breathless. Then again, she could have passed some unknown test in his eyes where he decided she wasn't totally worthless.

Whatever it was, TL's instruction became more constructive. He was no longer barking at her or being a twatwaffle.

Instead, he became a lot more attractive and attentive. It

seemed he got a lot more handsy when giving her direction and correcting her posture or executing moves correctly.

At the end of a week, she had finally gotten to the point where he didn't knock her down immediately when they began sparring. He did, however, enjoy pining her to the wall or ground.

Then, he also liked completely confusing her when he'd make some comment that he was not at all interested in her. He wasn't touching her because he enjoyed it. It was a necessary evil of training properly.

Sometimes, she'd watch him with his other clients. Touching was not as common with them. But she didn't push it.

At some point, she must have mentioned her men because every once in a while, he'd ask questions about them. He seemed to pay close attention to what she said, for he remembered exactly who each was and what they'd discussed about them before.

It both warmed her heart that someone was conversing with her conversationally and made her ache more for their absence.

As the day wrapped up, marking a week in Wabe, Mal helped him straighten the weapons they'd been working with. She didn't necessarily do this as a courtesy. Or because she was kind and generous with her time. There was a blade in his back room that reminded her of the one Eagy and Ryph had had made for her. She often stared at it, running her fingers down its sharp edge.

That was exactly what she was doing when TL spoke behind her, making her jump. She had likely been back there for several minutes.

"You're not quite ready for a blade yet, Sunshine," he said, voice light.

Mal glanced at him. "They commissioned a blade like this for me," she said quietly. "I lost it when the Sheep took me. I lost everything." Her blade. Her bag. Her men. It was all gone.

"Why not write to them?" TL suggested.

She turned to look at him, brows puckered. "And send it where?"

TL shook his head. "No, I mean send a messenger. They'll track down whoever you're looking for and relay your message. It doesn't go to a place, but a person."

Mal didn't quite understand the concept. How would a person get a message if they didn't have an address? If they didn't stay in one place for more than a few nights at a time?

But then, she didn't have any other options. Any other ideas. If she wanted to track her men down, a message was likely the only way she could.

He told her where to find one. That evening, before she returned to the inn, she found a messenger and promised the man that the recipients would pay him when he found them. Mal didn't have any blades or currency, after all.

The messenger seemed okay with it when she told him who she was looking for. They were known for their blades.

Mal returned to her room that night, not daring to hope. She'd do anything to be with them again. Anything at all. Just to talk to them.

It wasn't until her nightmare that night that the thought that perhaps they had been killed by the Sheep tormented her. She'd seen firsthand what the Sheep were capable of. She still remembered Let's torn wing and the way they bled Ves to near death.

Tears stung her eyes as she sat in front of her window and stared into the street. They couldn't be dead. If the last thing they remembered of her was how she broke up with them, she'd be crushed.

A Reunion of Sorts

MAL

5

Her morning was riddled with barely concealed fear of what her dreams had reminded her. Her movement was jerky and more uncoordinated than usual. She tripped over her own feet more than once.

At the third time in as many minutes, TL stopped her and studied her face. "What happened?"

She took a deep breath. Tears stung her eyes, but she blinked them away. She wouldn't cry in front of this man. "The Sheep."

TL raised a brow. "There are no Sheep here, Mal."

Mal shook her head. "No, no. But when they took me, maybe they killed my men. And our last days together hadn't been..." A tear escaped before she could stop it. As it trailed down her cheek, she was sure her heart mirrored the tear.

In a moment of compassion, TL wiped her cheek. "Don't go there," he said gently. "Letting despair take you can ruin you. Use your hurt and fear as motivation."

Mal nodded. TL released her and gave her a few minutes to collect herself. When she felt the moment had sufficiently passed, she went to where he was standing, looking at some strange obstacle course suspended in the air.

"Ready?" he asked.

"Depends? What is it I am supposed to be doing?"

TL grinned. "We're working on your dexterity today, Sunshine." He nodded his head toward a rope ladder. "Head on up."

She looked at him reluctantly before doing as he instructed. She spent the remainder of the early morning jumping from one rung to another. More times than not, she missed and fell. Luckily, TL always caught her. And set her down by sliding her body down the hard length of his.

By lunch, she'd gotten marginally better. She refused to allow the enticement of TL catching her as inspiration for failing. It was slow progress, but she managed to succeed two out of every five attempts. Then, it was three out of every five. TL was encouraging her now. Positive reinforcement did wonders to her stamina and endurance.

No wonder dogs responded so well to a scratch behind the ear when they were being trained.

The door opening distracted Mal right before she jumped. She missed the bar by a foot and fell the many feet to the floor. TL caught her and she slid down the length of his body, laughing. He frowned at her, his dark maroon eyes tepid.

"I'm sorry," Mal said, pulling away. She glanced back up to the bars many feet above their heads. "I heard-" As if mentioning why she'd fallen had reminded her, she turned to the door.

Tears sprang instantly to her eyes and she ran, throwing herself in Ryph's arms. She wrapped her whole self around him and buried her face in his neck. Ryph's grip was tight around her, squeezing her enough that she couldn't breathe. It didn't matter. She wanted that more than anything.

No one spoke. For many long minutes, they remained in this position, silent. When Ryph set her down, Chesh pulled her against him immediately.

"I'm sorry, Mal. I didn't know I couldn't evaporate with you," he said with distress.

"It's okay," she answered, holding him tighter.

She pulled away from him after several minutes and turned to look at Eagy. The expression on his face stayed her approach to him. His face was set, closed. His hands in the pocket of his hoodie. He wasn't looking directly at her.

He was still mad at her. After all this time, he was still upset for the things she'd said.

TL cleared his throat behind her. She glanced back.

"I have a few more hours," she said. "Will you stay?" She couldn't bear them being out of her sight.

No one agreed or disagreed, but the three backed against the side wall and sat to watch.

She didn't go back to the bars but changed to hand-to-hand. Sparring was still strenuous, but with her men back, she felt a renewed motivation. It made the blows and stumbles a whole lot more fun. Mal found herself laughing at her mess-ups and eager to try again.

TL seemed fueled with her enthusiasm and dedication to it, as well. The change in her was something almost extraordinary.

Her muscles were stiff, and she felt sticky by the time TL told her she was done for the day. Her three men were standing at the door when she approached them with a wide smile.

"So, you want to come to my room? I have to take a soak; my body hurts after all that. But we can have dinner after."

Their silence unsettled her. None of them met her eyes.

"We're going to go back to our room," Eagy said, voice low.

The way he said it, it was a clear dismissal. She was not invited. "Oh," she answered. Maybe he was madder at her than she thought.

Kav had told her there weren't many inns in Wabe, so she wasn't at all surprised that they had a room in the same. They parted ways at the stairs. She was a floor above them.

Mal waited on the landing as their door shut behind them. Not one of them had looked at her the entire walk from the Marden. She wanted to cry.

It took a lot for her to trudge up to her room through her

harsh breathing. How had they not forgiven her yet? She was so sure Chesh had three months ago before the Sheep attack. Before they had even left Tulgey.

She hadn't even realized that she'd run the water and climbed into the tub until she was neck deep in hot water. The ache in her chest was worse than anything her body had been through in the last weeks. By the time she got out, she felt numb.

But she'd also determined that she would go clear it up with them. She would apologize for the words she'd said in anger. She'd asked them to be her coterie, her harem. She'd make the move this time.

Mal took an involuntary step back when she opened her door and Ryph was there, hand raised to knock. She wasn't sure which of them had moved, but next thing she knew, she was wrapped in his arms and they were kissing madly.

The taste of him, the feel of him. Gods, she'd missed him so much. She pulled away long enough to say, "I never thought I'd see you again," before kissing him more.

He'd never kissed her like this before. There was a tremor in his grip. His mouth was hard and desperate against hers.

Then, he broke off abruptly and pulled from her arms. He shook his head. "Mal, we're leaving."

"Where to?" she asked and turned to her bag. "I only need-"

"No."

The ache in her chest grew and she sucked in a hard, shaking breath before turning back to face him.

"Eagy, Chesh, and I are leaving."

Mal shook her head. "Why?"

"Three months we've searched for you only to find you here. Laughing. Having a good time."

"That's not-"

"Three months," he said over her, his voice strained. His golden eyes looked dull. If his wings had been out, they'd have been dragging on the ground.

"But Ryph-"

"After all this time, you've been *here* while we looked for you," he demanded. "How can we not be upset?"

"I haven't-"

"And right before, you- with Wyat..." He shook his head and looked at the door. "And said you didn't want us-"

"I do-"

"Chesh assured us that it was all a misunderstanding."

"Ryph, listen-"

"But even he is not so sure anymore."

"Stop talking and listen to me, damnit," she said, stamping her foot.

She watched a flicker of amusement pass in his eyes, but it was gone before it even bloomed.

"I'm sorry. For those horrible things I said when I was upset. I didn't mean any of them and I really didn't mean to cancel this harem thing. Please forgive me."

Ryph shook his head. He opened his mouth to say something, but she spoke again before he could.

"I really do want you. All of you. I didn't understand this whole thing, but once Chesh told me, I didn't mean to undo it. I want to be with you. I swear it-"

"Mal." His voice sounded broken.

"Ryph, please!" she pleaded. "I want your courtship and I want to carry your babies and I want you to be my husband one day an-"

She broke off when a searing pain went through her body, culminating on her left forearm. She shrieked.

Ryph was staring at her wide-eyed. Rattled.

"What-"

"Stay there," he said as he turned to the door. "Don't move. Stay right there."

His voice was tense when he left the room. Mal stood perfectly still, holding her arm and staring at the door. She was shaking.

The Binding

CHESH

6

He didn't exactly say he told him so. But the look in his expression said it all. Eagy was used to being hurt. Mal had done just that.

When the door shut behind him, Eagy went straight to their bag and began packing it.

"What are you doing?" Chesh asked.

"We're leaving."

"But-"

"You can come with us," Ryph said. "If you want to."

Eagy stiffened slightly but didn't argue.

"How did you even decide this? You haven't spoken out of my presence since-"

"There are some things we don't need to discuss," Eagy said. "You're going or you're not. Choose."

Chesh didn't answer. He looked at the ceiling. Somewhere above them was their Mal. Their Mal who had been here for who knew how long with a fucking flower, laughing it up. With a shaky breath, he nodded. "Yes, I'll go."

Eagy nodded.

"I'm going to tell her we're leaving," Ryph said. "It would be rude not to."

Eagy nodded again.

Ryph left. Eagy busied himself packing their bags. Chesh glanced at Mal's. The one she'd always had. The one she carried with her clothes and her blade and... They'd have to at least leave it by her door before they left. Eagy had mended the strap after they found it on the forest floor after the Sheep had successfully taken her.

Taken her. From right from their damned hands!

"Where are we going?" Chesh asked, turning away from her bag.

Eagy shook his head. "Anywhere but here," he whispered.

Less than twenty minutes later, Ryph was in the door looking a little dizzy. He looked like he might be sick. Something had-

"What's wrong? What happened?" Eagy demanded as he walked to him.

Ryph lifted his sleeve. Weaving among his feathers and around his forearm was a purple ribbon embedded into his skin. On it said, 'Promised to Mal on this day and that day forevermore.'

Chesh's eyes widened. Eagy sucked in a breath.

"She didn't know-" Chesh began, but Eagy had pulled Ryph out of the way and stormed out. Chesh followed closely behind him. He felt Ryph on his heels.

Eagy burst in Mal's door and stood staring at her, his ice blue eyes narrowed and angry. "What did you do?" he growled. "He's mine. You can't have him. I won't let you take him from me!"

As Chesh had suspected, she had no idea what he was talking about. Eagy must have seen this, too, although his patience for it was gone. He was pissed. When faced with losing Ryph, nothing else seemed to matter. Not even hurting Mal. Again.

Eagy stomped across the room and pulled her hand up by the wrist. His other hand yanked the sleeve up to her elbow. Chesh almost yelled at him for his behavior. For treating her so rough. But he bit his tongue. Even he needed to know.

There was a purple ribbon wrapped around her forearm as well, matching Ryph's in pattern. There was a circle in the middle with the black silhouette of a gryphon.

Mal stared at it, perplexed. "I don't-"

"It's a betrothal promise," Chesh said quietly.

Her eyes got wide and she looked up to Eagy. "But I didn't-"

"You did," Ryph said. "Unintentionally, but words have a lot of power in Laddenworn."

"The power to save a life, to welcome death, to lose a head, to avow a love..." Chesh said.

"Undo it," Eagy demanded, dropping her arm. "I won't let you have him. Not even *you*."

Mal shook her head. "I didn't mean-"

"But you did and now you undo it!" he insisted. "Undo it, Mal."

"But-"

"MAL!" he hollered.

Mal had finally had enough. She shoved him away from her angrily, her tiny hands on his chest. To Chesh's amusement, Eagy did take several steps back. He was surprised enough by her actions to allow it. Angry tears filled her eyes.

"Not one of you has allowed me to speak and for fuck's sake, you're going to listen to me," she snapped. Her chest heaved. She waited to see if they would let her. Since no one objected, Mal continued. "I am sorry for the nasty things I said. I didn't mean any of them. That includes that I didn't mean to break our harem up. I don't want that.

"You treat me as if I know what the hell I'm doing at all times when in reality, this stuff isn't in the books I've studied. I had no idea what you were asking me when you asked it. I didn't know all it took was my simple words, said unintentionally, to do and undo commitments. I didn't know that I should talk to you before adding someone to our... group. Whatever words you used. Coterie. I don't even know what a coterie is!

"And I sure as fuck haven't been here having a grand time for the last three months. I've been here less than a week. I didn't know how to find you. TL told me to send a messenger out to look for you and I did. I-"

"Where were you?" Eagy asked.

"In the dungeon of Queen Hart." She lifted her shirt to show them a blood red mark deep within her skin, about the size of her hand. "See?!"

"What the fuck?" Eagy demanded, coming at her again. "Why didn't you say this earlier?"

Mal rolled her eyes as Eagy dropped to his knees in front of her. He pushed her shirt up and dragged her pants lower to reveal the whole of it. A heart, but the bottom was pushed in. Like an... apple? "As if you've given me a chan-" Her words cut off with a gasp and a yelp as she tried to push him away.

Eagy had bitten into her skin, the soft spot where the mark was on the side of her stomach, between her hip and her naval. He pulled away and spit out the contents onto the floor. It was almost black with only a tinge of red. Thick like honey. Mal's intake of breath matched the horror in her eyes. Eagy repeated his process, sucking the contents out of her body and spitting them onto the floor. All the while, the mark got marginally smaller.

Ryph left them to go to the washroom. Chesh thought that perhaps he'd run her a tub, but he returned with a pile of cloths instead. His hands were shaking.

When Eagy had gotten all of it and his last mouthful was strictly blood, he stood. Ryph dropped a towel over the large puddle of goo.

"What is it?" Mal asked in a trembling voice.

"A curse," Eagy said, pulling her shirt over her head.

Mal was still staring at the towel with goo oozing through it. Eagy stripped her of the remnants of her clothing as blood freely dripped down her leg from the wound he'd inflicted and not bothered to close. He examined every inch of her.

"What are you-"

"Looking to see if there are any more," Eagy answered before she could finish.

Chesh took a towel from Ryph and pressed it against the still streaming teeth marks Eagy had left on her.

When Eagy was satisfied, he returned to the front of her and stared in her eyes. "How long?"

"I was in that wretched place for something like ten weeks. It took us a week to travel here and I've been here ever since. I was really weak. They don't give prisoners much food or water and I needed to get my strength up. I hadn't so much as moved... shackled to the wall. Kav knew TL ran a hardcore Marden and this was far enough out of the way that he didn't think anyone would come looking for me until we were long gone."

"Kav?" Ryph asked. By the look on his face, he already knew who she was referring to. They all did.

"The knave," she said.

The room stilled for several minutes. Eagy wrapped his arms around her, dragging her feet from the floor and burying his face in her hair.

Chesh felt his muscles relax. He wasn't sure when he'd decided that he'd allowed Eagy to take lead, but the relief he felt that Eagy was going to forgive her was almost intoxicating. A few feet from him, Ryph did the same, letting out a loud breath.

"I thought you were dead," Eagy whispered. "I was terrified. And then I see you..."

"I promise you, I was not having a good time for the majority of the last many weeks, Eagy. And I never stopped wishing that you'd find me and rescue me."

Eagy squeezed her tighter. As if there hadn't been any other response to this whole situation, Eagy kissed her. It was a kiss even Chesh felt from several feet away. They had barely begun when both of their hands were pulling at Eagy's clothes, discarding them as they tumbled to the bed, their lips never once parting.

Chesh had seen both men take Mal many times. The two had no idea what foreplay was. It was simply clothes were off and they were in. This was no different. Except that Mal was still bleeding all over the place. He knew that when he returned to the room, it would be a gory sight.

He turned away and headed for the washroom. Ryph stopped him, his big hand on Chesh's arm. Chesh wasn't small. In both height and bulk, he stood somewhere between Eagy and Ryph. And none of them were as big as Wyat. But with Ryph's hand on Chesh's arm, Chesh felt small.

He met Ryph's eyes.

"Will you join us?" he asked.

Chesh was fairly certain he wasn't asking for the sole purpose that Chesh be with Mal. With the pretense of group sex, Ryph thought he might get a bit on with Chesh, too. At least, based on their last kiss, that was how Chesh read the question.

He shook his head. "Not this time."

"Another time?"

Chesh again was sure he wasn't certain what he was agreeing to as he nodded. But he did all the same.

Ryph held his eyes for a long moment before nodding. He let go of Chesh and headed for the bed, pulling his clothes off along the way. Chesh escaped behind the washroom door.

They were loud that night. It was a very long night for Chesh.

Mal

MORE THAN ANYTHING, Mal was ecstatic to wake up with her men again. She was sandwiched between the two with Ryph below her and Eagy on top. Ryph's tail wound around both her and Eagy and his wings encompassed them all.

There was a long time that she was sure she'd never see them again. It was the worst feeling in the world to know that the last things she had said to them were awful. She squeezed Ryph tightly, never wanting to let him go.

His arms around them both flexed and she felt a little more squished. It didn't matter. Nothing would ever feel so good as waking up in their arms.

The great golden wings unwound and lay flat on the bed on either side. Well, not quite flat. They were giant. One went up the wall when the bed ran out and the other flopped onto the floor.

"Mal," Ryph breathed.

Mal turned her head and kissed his chest. Over and over. What felt like a purr rumbled through him and she smiled. Meeting his eyes, she could see his arousal bright and needy.

Eagy's arms came down around hers then and his fingers laced with hers. He nuzzled into her hair. "Can we always wake like this?" he asked.

"No," Chesh said from somewhere on the other side of the room. "I will not always be so accommodating as to allow the two of you to monopolize her."

Mal was surprised when Eagy only sighed. His body didn't tense, and he didn't scowl. And when he said, "Fine," she grinned. It likely didn't reach Chesh proportions, but she was sure it came close.

Surprised further, Eagy pulled off her. Mal shifted to look. Beyond his glorious ashen body with the weird, wonderful etchings smeared in blood, she could see Chesh sprawled out in a chair. He did not look the least bit comfortable. "Do you want us to give you some time?" Eagy asked.

Mal's eyes widened. Really? Ryph's arms around her squeezed her a moment before he pushed them both to a sitting position. She could study the cat's face clearer now.

Chesh stared at Eagy as if it were the first time they met.

Then he sat up, his eyes dropping to Mal's. He took a breath and held it. "My 'no' now doesn't mean I'm not interested and won't take you up on that later. But no. I think we need to clear the air a little and get Mal back to the Marden. *After* you all wash the blood off of you."

Mal looked at herself. The teeth marks on her skin had closed, but they were still scabbed. The three of them, and the bed, were streaked in blood.

Eagy nodded and turned back to the bed. He offered Mal a hand and pulled her to her feet. "Soak?"

She nodded, smiling.

"Hold up," Chesh said, getting to his feet as well. "I meant what I said. We need to clear the air here. You all hopped over the important parts and went straight to sex."

Eagy bowed his head, a small smile dancing. "Sorry," he murmured.

Mal grinned. Behind her, Ryph stood and wrapped his whole body around Mal's. Over her head, he watched Chesh.

"Okay, pussy cat. Let us talk plainly," Ryph said in a purr.

Eagy looked at him with a frown, rolling his eyes. Ryph flashed him a grin.

"We all screwed up and even though it was unintentional, I propose apologies all around. That way, it can never be said that they were not offered and accepted," Chesh said, hands behind his back. He rocked on his feet, ball to heel.

Eagy nodded and looked at Mal. "I'm sorry that you didn't understand what we were asking of you - that we didn't explain. I'm sorry that... our reaction was..." He trailed off, searching for the right word. "I'm sorry for our reaction. I'm sorry for how we left it and I'm sorry for jumping to conclusions yesterday without asking."

Mal nodded her acceptance. Once more, she was surprised when he turned to Chesh.

"I'm sorry that I'm a little averse to you. Your presence in our harem... or whatever we are or will be, is a good thing." Eagy shrugged. His eyes glanced to Ryph before returning to Chesh. "I get jealous easily."

Chesh bowed his head and thanked him.

Ryph apologized for the same things in almost the same words. He didn't apologize to Chesh, though he did add, "I don't mean anything by my words, Eagy. You know you're my heart."

Eagy blushed and looked away, a bright smile on his face.

"I already apologized for not being able to evaporate with you, but I am sorry for other actions, too," Chesh said. "I didn't know that you were involved in things you didn't understand. I'm sorry for almost ignoring my instincts and leaving yesterday. I'm sorry I didn't *ask*."

Mal nodded. "I'm sor-"

"You've apologized already," Chesh said. "Once is enough."

"But I didn't..." Her eyes crinkled. "I didn't apologize to you."

"You did, actually. In the woods before we made camp that day," he said with a wide grin.

She sighed and frowned. "Fine."

"Okay, next, a little explanation. There isn't any right or better way to ask for a courting. A courting is when someone asks to... what is it in the Outside? You mentioned boyfriend. It's been many..." Chesh sighed. "Too long since I've been there. Suitors. Lovers. When you court with the intent to wed, if you're compatible."

"Date?" Mal asked.

"What is 'date'?" Ryph asked.

"It means you spend time together, just the two of you, to see if you get on well. If you're compatible. Many times, people do this with the intent of exploring a life together. A future together. You go places, do things, talk, connect. Hopefully, your emotions are involved. When you make it official that you're together, and that you're not going to be with another, that is when you're considered a boyfriend or girlfriend."

"Only one at a time?" Eagy asked.

"Well, yes, usually. A typical household is two people, traditionally a man and a woman."

"What about more men and a woman?"

"I've heard of it, but it's not common and many people look down on it," Mal answered. Bigots. That's what she and Reth always referred to those small-minded people as.

"I suppose it means more or less the same thing here. We use different words and we don't limit remcules to one and one or two," Chesh said. "It can be asked in any way, but you'll usually hear one of the words 'court,' 'harem,' or 'coterie' in the question, and it will likely end in asking your acceptance. There's also the Song of Commits that doesn't require your acceptance, however, if you do need to refuse, you do so within three days or it's an automatic acceptance."

Mal looked back at Ryph. "I really did love that little song."

He grinned at her, nipping her jaw.

"And... there is no expiration on a courtship. It can last indefinitely. I think that covers it."

"Understand it all?" Ryph asked.

Mal laughed under her breath. "I understand what he's said, but I don't know if I understand it all. I'm sure there's going to be more that I don't. How can I understand what I don't know?"

He nodded dejectedly.

She twisted in his arms and kissed his cheek. "Can we go in the same order again? Will you ask me first?"

His bright golden eyes found hers. "You... Really?"

Mal nodded. "I didn't mean to break up with you."

His brows knit together. "What?"

She giggled. "Never mind. Just ask me again."

"Mal," he whispered, his hot breath caressing her skin. "I want to court you with the intent that you might take me for husband some day."

She nodded. "Yes."

His grin was magnificent. "Although, I think I should point out that I'm already beyond that stage."

"What do you mean?"

He moved his arm to align with hers, their matching ribbons side by side. "I'm a betrothed now. Even if you didn't mean to do it, your words made it happen."

Mal's mouth worked, but nothing came out.

"You can cancel it out if you want to," Chesh said, voice low. "There's no expiration on a betrothal either, unless you named a specific date."

She stared at the two ribbons. With her other hand, she ran her fingers over it. Since Ryph's wings were still out, his tattoos were dead things. Sitting there on his skin, lifeless. Mal chewed the inside of her lip before looking up to meet Eagy's eyes. "Do you want me to?"

Her voice was small. Vulnerable.

Eagy looked at their arms. At the ribbons. The thing that had had him so upset last night. "Do you want to?"

Again, she chewed her lip. "I'm not ready for betrothals, but I don't want to cancel it either. Can't we just... pretend it's not there for a while? And we can court?"

Eagy shrugged.

"No, I need an answer from you, Eagy," she pressed.

He stared at their arms again. His eyes puckered. A breath escaped him in a harsh puff. For a moment, he turned his eyes away.

"The truth," she whispered.

His ice blue eyes met hers. He closed the space between them in two strides and took her mouth in his, kissing her in a demanding sort of way. She wasn't at all sure what he was demanding, but she claimed him with her own assertion.

When he pulled away, he said, "Don't break it up."

Mal smiled at his attempt to use her words.

"I just... you can't have him without me. And you can't pretend to want me to have him. Ryph is mine, Mal."

She kissed him lightly. "I thought we had been through this already."

Eagy rested his forehead on hers. "We did, but still. I need to say it. I need you to understand. I-"

"I'm yours, Eagy. As much as I want this, and I desperately want it so fucking bad, I'll never leave you," Ryph said.

Eagy looked up. After a moment, he nodded and returned his gaze to Mal. "Will you allow me to court you, Mal? Can I be your *boyfriend?*"

Mal giggled and wrapped an arm around his neck. "You're so cute when you're trying to understand my language."

His smile was timid. "Did I at least use it correctly?"

"Yes. And also, yes."

His grin was brilliant. It was the first time she noticed that his teeth were unnaturally sharp. Of course, they were. He was a bird of prey. Even if birds didn't have teeth, their beaks were incredibly dangerous. Why wouldn't that transfer to his teeth?

Once again, Eagy pulled away from her and turned to Chesh. "Well, cat. It's your turn."

Chesh grinned and made his way to them from where he had remained on the far side of the room for their entire exchange. Ryph released her and Mal met Chesh a few feet away from the other two. Per usual it seemed, he didn't touch her.

His fire eyes looked to crackle as his cat-like pupils dilated. "Can I join your coterie, Mal? Can I court you? Before you answer, I will help you take down the Bloody Queens, even if you don't want me. It's not conditional."

Mal parted her lips to respond when he thought of something else.

"And, so you know how much I mean that I want you, we don't even have to have sex until, *if*, you make me your husband."

"No?" she asked, a brow arched in amusement.

His smile was demure as his lids covered most of his fiery eyes. "It will be quite torturous, but I truly want to be with you. *You.*"

Mal cupped the side of his face. "I don't know that that's necessary, but I accept your proposal anyhow."

His grin spread up the sides of his face as he bent to kiss her. It was brief, a peck, and he stood tall again.

"Now," Mal said and turned, narrowing her eyes. "Where is Wyat?"

"He took off shortly after you were taken," Eagy said. "I don't think he liked the plan we came up with to look for you."

The Magic Within

MAL

7

For the next several days, Mal spent the vast majority of her day at the Marden. Sometimes, one or more of her men would join her. Occasionally, one of them would train with her. It was fun to see the true scope of what they could do. She knew they were skilled, that they were strong, but seeing them unchallenged with the soldiers was one thing. Seeing them challenge each other was something else entirely.

Chesh moved smoothly, lithely, like a cat. His balance was impeccable, and he moved through the air like an acrobat. Some of the ways he twisted and contorted looked borderline painful.

Eagy was elegant in his moves. Even as a person, he could soar through the air as if he were defying gravity. His strikes were sharp, powerful, deadly.

Ryph was a damn powerhouse. A beast. He was stronger than all of them, including TL, when it came to brute strength. He was ferocious. And when he let his beast really flex his muscles, it was damn near frightening. Mal wondered what he'd really look like if he let loose.

And TL? TL was a flower. Yes, you read that right. A flower. All those people they had saved in the burning of the Patch were flowers, too.

Sure, why not? If people could turn into birds and beasts, why not vegetation? TL was also not interested in talking about what he was. "Suffice it to say that I'm stronger than I look. Flowers have their own unique advantage. As long as there are no MutMut Trees around."

"MutMut?" Mal asked, trying not to laugh.

"The trees the soldiers were tying the flowers to back in the Patch," Eagy prompted. "Those are Mut trees. A Flower's weakness. It prevents them from shifting, from fighting back."

"Their kryptonite," Mal said.

Even Chesh looked at her like she had lost her mind. So, that meant Chesh had been stuck in Laddenworn longer than Superman had been around. And he was, what, 1930s? Although, she already knew that. Carroll made Wonderland in 1865. Close to seventy years before Superman. And she wasn't convinced time moved the same in Laddenworn as it did the Outside.

She shook her head. "Never mind. So, a Mut tree renders a Flower powerless?"

They all nodded.

"Actually," TL said, frowning at her, "it binds our ability to shift. We're not exactly powerless, but since the other things we're known for aren't exactly helpful in battle, we might as well be powerless."

There was enough in this conversation where she was filled with questions. Would it be wrong to ask TL what he shifted into? *I mean*, Mal thought, *he's a flower. A flower!*

"So, a MutMut tree is different than a Tum Tum tree?" Mal asked, skipping the whole flower shifting topic.

The four of them nodded. "There are very few Tum Tum trees left," Eagy said.

"Why?"

"Different theories," TL said. "The theory that the Queens believe is that they are the source of all magic in Laddenworn. If they destroy the Tum Tum trees, it leaves very little for residents of Laddenworn to fight back with."

"Every story has a source that generates magic," Mal noted. They looked at her curiously as they usually did when she spoke out loud to herself. "Who can wield magic?"

"Anyone," Eagy said at the same time Ryph said, "Everyone."

"Can I?"

They nodded.

"How?"

They spent the next several minutes looking between each other, as if studying someone else might give them an answer.

Mal sighed. Why did every question have to be so difficult to get answers for?

"Okay, let's start with this. Show me some magic," Mal said.

"Like what?" TL asked.

She shrugged. "Surprise me."

Chesh evaporated. His disembodied voice said, "Does this count?"

Grinning, Mal said, "I have no idea; I guess it does. But if shifting shape, or something that is uniquely yours, is your only trick, I have to say that I'm not all that convinced that everyone can use the magic here."

"But take into account," Chesh said, his wide smile the only thing materializing, "I was not able to do this before I was summoned here."

"What about the fire you created when you took on the Duchess's monsters?" Mal asked.

"That is because I'm a demon. It's Hellfire."

Mal nodded. "It would be nice to talk to someone who came to Laddenworn and Wonderland to see if they acquired the ability to use the magic here."

Eagy and Ryph exchanged a look. It was quick, but Mal didn't miss it. "What?" she asked.

Eagy shook his head. "Maybe you need something to teach you how to call the magic to you."

Mal was not at all convinced that was what their look had meant. Still, if she could wield magic, that was a game changer.

Right?

It was at least leveling the playing field a little.

"We've talked about magical objects before and how hard they are to find," Mal pointed out.

"We were looking for items with specific properties then," Eagy said. "Now, we're talking about an object that simply connects you with the magic."

She nodded. "Okay. Does this object exist?"

"There are a few," TL said. "The most common are kid gloves."

"Always check the gloves before you trade for them," Chesh said. "There are cons everywhere."

"Kid gloves," Mal mused. "Like the ones the Duchess wore?"

Chesh grinned. "Exactly like those."

Mal nodded.

"Alright, we've had enough of a break," TL said, getting to his feet. "Back to work."

Her men left the Marden instead of training with her that day. Now they were looking for kid gloves, she hoped. She kissed them each, loving that they were with her again.

"Sprint," TL said, gesturing to the track above. "Twenty laps. Then, we spar with grown up swords." His words might have sounded like a jab, but the quirk of his lips said he was only teasing her.

Mal grinned and headed for the ladder. She could feel TL's eyes on her, watching her as she climbed.

Since her men had returned, her strength and stamina had greatly come back. She'd been making a lot of progress. It no longer felt hopeless, like her body was rebelling against her. Now, it was just weakness of the muscle mass she'd loss and trying to regain it.

At first, she thought it had been them back in her life. As if their absence had rendered her dead inside. But now that her red mark had been removed, courtesy of the someone within the palace, the curse was broken. That had been what was preventing her from properly training.

She didn't know what it really did. What its intent had been. Most likely to kill her eventually. When she asked Kav about it, he said he'd never seen one before. Not on any other prisoner. He didn't question it because he had assumed she'd had it before she came to Laddenworn. Or, in the very least, before he had found her. How was he to know otherwise.

He wasn't wrong.

With it gone, she'd made leaps and bounds. But she was still tired. Still weak. Regaining what she lost was taxing, exhausting. Now that she explained what had happened to TL, he was pushing her far harder than he had been. She was so tired when she returned to her room each night, she was dozing off in the tub during her soaks.

By the time she made it through her twenty laps and back down to the floor, TL was talking with a Serpent. She knew that was what the man was by the scales covering his chest and left bicep.

Mal didn't approach since they seemed to be in conversation. She went to the weights and began going through some reps he'd shown her yesterday to focus on her back and shoulders. All the while, she kept them in her sights.

She tried to read their lips. TL's expression was grim. Since his back was slightly towards her, she didn't have a good view of his face. He was in profile, at best. What he was saying wasn't clear.

The Serpent smiled. Mal was surprised to see his teeth looked similar to Chesh's, pointed and sharp. She was also surprised to see that he had fangs like a snake. Absently, she wondered if they were venomous. Did the Serpents come in different species like snakes did? Their scales were all similar in color. She couldn't recall the Savage clear enough to remember if the few Serpents she saw as snakes had looked the same or different.

When the Serpent glanced her way, she saw that it wasn't only their teeth and scales that marked them as Serpents. They had serpentine eyes, as well. How had she missed that when she last saw them? She had to have missed it. Or could they change just their eyes?

Mal looked away when the Serpent left, and TL made his way to her. He had apparently seen her come down.

He didn't say anything as he stopped at her side and immediately corrected her form with a hand on the small of her back and another on her stomach opposite.

"Straighten your spine," he said.

She allowed him to adjust her. When he removed his hands, she raised her arm with the weight in it. She paused long enough for him to bring her arm higher, showing her where she should be. Yeah, she could certainly feel it now.

"I didn't realize there were Serpents in the city," Mal said when the weight was at her side. She brought it up again as he answered.

"A few. Most remain in the woods."

"Where they blend in," Mal said.

TL nodded. "Have you spoken to a Serpent?" he asked.

Mal waited to answer until the weight was down. "Not spoken to one. We stumbled upon a Savage not long ago." She paused to do another rep. "I guess it was a while ago, now, actually. We stopped the things from killing all the Serpents."

"That's not how a Savage works," TL said.

She shook her head as she finished the rep. "That's what Chesh said, too. But-" she paused again to do another rep. "- the Duchess screamed that they were supposed to die and was irate when Chesh single handedly destroyed all the beasts instead."

"Odd," TL said. "Why kill the Serpents? They only strike when threatened."

Mal didn't answer for a few more reps. She paused long enough to say, "A while before we ran into the Serpents, we came upon a group of Soldiers systematically burning an entire Patch, all residents were being burned alive, as well."

He stiffened. That must have hit home. Hopefully it wasn't his Patch, the one he grew up in.

"There's a rumor," he said, once more adjusting her so that her back was straight. "That the Queens despise anything other than people."

"I don't understand."

"Those that aren't purely person. Not bird or beast or flower."

Mal looked at him. "She's killing everyone not..." she paused, trying to think of the word. One that wouldn't be offensive, even though she certainly didn't mean it to be offensive.

She didn't need to finish as he nodded. "A second culling, maybe. To get rid of everyone unlike them. Everyone not pure people. Change arms."

It took her a minute to realize the last two words were an instruction for her. She did as he directed. Before she could start her reps, his hands on her back and stomach adjusted her posture again. Her muscles fluttered under his touch. When he pulled his hands back, she began.

They were quiet as she went through the rounds on this arm. Both lost in thought, perhaps. After the third time correcting her back, he kept his hands on her while she continued her reps.

Her whole body ached, and she wasn't entirely sure it was from the weight. She tried very hard not to look at him.

"I thought we were sparring after your warmup," TL said, his voice low.

She tried to stifle a shiver but wasn't sure she managed. "You were busy," Mal answered. Another rep. "I thought it rude to interrupt."

A smirk graced his lips. "Why did you choose to focus on your back?"

"I think my legs are coming along," she answered, her face

heating for some reason she chose not to explore mentally. "My core muscles and back are lacking. As are my arms, probably."

He nodded, a slow bob of his head.

She could feel his eyes on her. Trying her damnedest not to pay attention to him, she focused solely on her weight. When he spoke again, she jumped and felt immediately embarrassed for it. It wasn't like he had moved away from her at all.

"Why do you keep curling your back?" he asked.

Mal glanced at him, just a flicker of her eyes. When he took the weight from her, she backed away and slid down the wall to sit.

"Practicing my inner cat flexibility?" she offered.

TL shook his head, bringing the weight back to the others to put it away.

"I don't know. My posture is shot. Too much time slumped in chains, I think. I'm trying. I swear."

"I know," he said, voice low.

"Can I ask you a question? About Flowers?"

He frowned. "Alright," he answered warily.

"Are there different kinds of Flowers? Like there are different kinds of eagles and gryphons?"

The question wasn't what he was expected, apparently. His wariness left and he nodded. "As many types as you'd find in nature."

"What are you?"

The corner of his mouth quirked. "Tiger Lily."

"TL," Mal grinned. "Eagy for eaglet, Ryph for gryphon. I don't mean this to sound mean, but your names are very predictable once someone knows what you are."

He chuckled. "Yes. We keep the guesswork out."

Mal got to her feet. "Well, what next?"

"Want to spar or continue with muscle conditioning?"

"You're giving me a choice?"

He smirked. "When I was preoccupied, you went right into something else instead of waiting around for me. There aren't many people who take that kind of initiative, Sunshine. Any excuse for a break, they take it. Clearly, I was a little harsh judging you when Kav brought you to me. You're working hard and dedicated, so yeah-" he shrugged, "-I'm giving you an option."

Mal couldn't stop the grin that spread across her face. She had impressed him! "Let's spar. I feel like I've lost all skill with a blade since my dungeon days."

He nodded and headed to the room where the weapons were stored.

She didn't work with her own blade, the one Eagy and Ryph had commissioned for her. She loved her blade, but Eagy had insisted that it wasn't meant to practice with. It was for the real thing. Mal hadn't really thought it mattered, but she didn't argue. Instead, she asked TL for one similar in length and weight, so she'd be training properly.

He had rolled his eyes. "Well, of course. A blade is only successful if it is appropriately proportioned to your body." He didn't let her use the blade she'd admired in the back room.

TL was adept at blade work as well. She shouldn't have been surprised, but it wasn't fair for him to be good at everything. He should have at least one weakness. A flawless character is dull.

But he moved like he was a born fighter. When she commented on it, after having her blade thrust from her grip for the fourth time, he laughed. "I learned the same way you did, Sunshine. But proper motivation goes a long way."

"And what was yours?" she quipped, trying to execute a surprise strike.

He blocked it effortlessly, grinning. "To never be a victim again. If you're the best, no one is going to have the petals to challenge you for fear they'll lose their life. And I play for keeps outside my Marden."

Mal was stuck on the victim part. What had happened to him to make him work to be the best of the best in any kind of physical situation? What had he lost or was taken from him? It probably wasn't that hard to figure out. Kav had eluded that he was an old flower. Old enough to be present during the start of the Culling. There was no telling what he'd lost.

But the freeze had him somewhere closer to Wyat's age than Eagy and Ryph. Almost ripe for husbanding. Late 30s, if she had to guess. She was sure he could pass for a suitable husbanding age, given what he was and did. Yet, she was positive he was not involved with anyone.

Perhaps he liked men but couldn't tell anyone. Given what she knew about society and how they thought of anyone who wasn't solely straight, it wouldn't surprise her.

TL laying her flat on her back with her breath knocked out of her forcefully pulled her from her thoughts. "Sorry," she stammered. "Sorry."

He raised an amused brow before pulling her to her feet. "What has you so absent all of a sudden?"

"You don't want to know," she mused, shaking her arms out. She picked up her sword again and faced him.

He was frowning at her. "What you do on your own time is your business. But being so sex-obsessed is a hindrance."

"I wasn't thinking about sex, but thanks for the advice."

It was clear he wasn't convinced. And for whatever reason, that put him in a mood for the rest of the evening. She returned to her room with a large bruise on her upper arm, big enough that Eagy was irritated that TL had been so rough on her.

She waved him off, heading straight for the tub. They were kind enough that there was already a hot soak waiting for her when she came back to the inn.

Mal sighed as she sunk into the water. Damn flower was moodier than a hormonal teenager.

The Jabberwock

MAL

8

She was finally getting to the point where her skill was coming back. It was also around that time that TL started becoming harsher and more demanding in his instruction. She found herself rolling her eyes a lot. Snapping at him when she didn't immediately execute a new position correctly on the first try and he'd bark harshly at her. Once, she even threw one of the wooden staffs at him in frustration.

He was being a dick and she couldn't figure out why. They'd been getting along great. Talking. Bonding.

Or so she thought. Then one morning, he was back to being an ass. This time, she wasn't about to stalk off like she did last time.

Mal had no idea what his problem was, but she was done playing a pushover. She might need him to push her, but again, he didn't need to be a jerk just because he could.

Her men had been back for over a week now. Besides her hours upon hours of training with a dick (and not the good kind), she was blissfully happy. She had her men again.

Most of them. She was starting to get worried about Wyat's absence.

She was in the middle of being unceremoniously thrown

against the wall by TL when a horrendous roar echoed off the building outside. Her face drained of color and fear ticked up her spine. She froze where she was, not even attempting to block TL from throwing her to the ground.

He must have seen the terror in her expression because his nasty remark was cut short.

"That's a Jabberwock," she said, voice quaking.

TL frowned at her. "Yes," he said carefully. "Why?"

"The last time a Jabberwock was around, it scorched Ryph's wings and burned down the city," she whispered, trembling.

His eyes narrowed. "Really? They're usually pretty peaceful."

She looked at him in utter disbelief.

He pulled her to her feet and dragged her to the door. Thankfully, he didn't force her to go outside. She was already dragging her feet as it was. She didn't want to see.

The Jabberwock looked nothing like the one that burned down Childhood. The last one looked like it had been run over by a steam roller. Patchy scales and feathers with a scrunched, scratched wolf muzzle. It had looked sick, like it had mange.

This one was almost elegant. Its muzzle was certainly wolf-like, but smooth and scaly. Its neck and head were covered in short, fine feathers, in an array of blues and golds. The rest of it was shiny scales.

It wasn't breathing fire. The Jabberwock soared over the city like a majestic bird doing acrobatics. A colossal majestic bird.

"What's it doing?" Mal asked.

"Dancing," TL said. "It likely just had a hatchling. Happy Momma."

Mal looked on incredulously.

"The last one I saw... looked nothing like that. I mean the shape, yes. But it looked like someone had tried to skin it. Or bury it alive."

He frowned. "This is normal," he said, gesturing to the spinning Jabberwock who let out another apparently happy roar.

"There's a poem," Mal said, "from the original fairy tale. It's about slaying the Jabberwock."

"How's it go?"

"`Twas brillig, and the slithy toves
Did gyre and gimble in the wabe;
All mimsy were the borogoves,
And the mome raths outgrabe.

"`Beware the Jabberwock, my son!
The jaws that bite, the claws that catch!
Beware the Jubjub bird, and shun
The frumious Bandersnatch!'"

Those were the only two stanzas she could remember. They were the ones immortalized in other books and movies.

TL nodded and finished the poem.

"He took his vorpal sword in hand:
Long time the manxome foe he sought—
So rested he by the Tum Tum tree,
And stood awhile in thought.

"And as in uffish thought he stood,
The Jabberwock, with eyes of flame,
Came whiffling through the Tulgey wood,
And burbled as it came!

"One, two! One, two! And through and through
The vorpal blade went snicker-snack!
He left it dead, and with its head
He went galumphing back.

"`And hast thou slain the Jabberwock?
Come to my arms, my beamish boy!

O frabjous day! Callooh! Callay!'
He chortled in his joy.

"'Twas brillig, and the slithy toves
Did gyre and gimble in the wabe;
All mimsy were the borogoves,
And the mome raths outgrabe."

"That's the one. Why would Carroll write about killing the Jabberwock if they're peaceful?" Mal asked.

"They aren't always peaceful. Perhaps this Carroll ran into one like the first one you met."

That made perfect sense. If she'd run into the rampaging Jabberwock and no others, she wouldn't be as accepting of them. This one, screaming her joy, was marvelous. Beautiful.

"I'm relieved they're not all burning cities down," Mal said.

TL nodded and turned away. "So am I. Would make for a rough world."

Mal watched it for a few more minutes. As she was getting ready to turn back, Kav walking down the street towards the Marden caught her eye. She waited for him.

"Hello, Princess," he said, planting a kiss on her lips when he stepped in the door.

She smiled and moved out of the door to let him in.

"Where's TL?"

Mal turned to look. He hadn't walked away that long ago. She shrugged.

"You two getting along better yet?"

She rolled her eyes. "No. He's back to being a jerk because he can. This time, I'm too happy to care. Though, I preferred when he was pleasant to be around. It made the days shorter."

He nodded. His eyes scanned the room. Maybe it was his lack of finding TL, too, but he took her hand and led her to the back through one of the doors. When it shut behind them, he had her pushed against a wall, her feet already off the ground as his lips crashed into hers.

It had been a while since they'd been physical. Since before they arrived in Wabe. Since she had realized that she was, in fact, alive and not in some kind of painful hell.

But she'd been thinking that Kav was one of her seven. The more she thought about it, the more she was sure he was. He'd broken her out of the Bloody Queen's palace! He'd nursed her back to health. He'd taken care of her and was planning on helping her take down the queens. How could he not be one of her seven?

She'd been talking to her men about him, too. Told them what they'd been through. How he'd helped her and risked his life for her. For helping her was risking his life.

Sure, she hadn't outright asked what they thought about him joining her coterie. And she should. She would.

His hand had already dipped between her legs where he rubbed her aggressively. Heat tore through her and she pulled her legs up to wrap them around his waist.

"We should hurry," he said against her lips. "Quickie."

He grinned into her mouth as she nodded. TL would certainly look for her eventually. It wasn't nearly towards the end of the day enough that she was allowed to go home.

She only pulled her legs back when he pushed at her leggings. He wasted no time divesting them but didn't bother with her top. In the spirit of being quick, no need to fully undress. He didn't even bother to pull down his pants. He just undid the ties and pulled it out.

Mal grinned as he picked her up once more and wrapped her legs around his waist. He rubbed against her, between her legs against her clit. It sparked a wave of pleasure through her and she shuddered.

She kissed his neck, biting a little harder than was necessary. He growled at her and thrust inside her. They both groaned.

He stilled for a minute, resting his forehead against her. "Damn, Mal. You feel so fucking good."

It had likely been a while since he had had a woman, too. Of course, she felt good. At this point, any woman might, whether they knew what they were doing or not.

The thought made her grin. She almost laughed but refrained. That might break the mood.

Despite him stating that it needed to be a quickie, his thrusts were slow and deep. Filling her until he was pressed fully inside her.

It felt good. Her breaths came in time with his thrusts, his quiet grunts exciting her blood.

Kav seemed to remember that they didn't have a lot of time and sped up. No longer fully sheathed on every thrust, now he was going for the goal, chasing his orgasm. Mal didn't care if he was selfish right then. They really did need to finish. Besides, there was plenty of pleasure to be had in the endeavor.

He did manage to give her an orgasm. It wasn't anything spectacular. If she had had wings, they wouldn't have exploded from her back. But it was good, nonetheless.

"I'll make it up to you," he grunted, still keeping time with his quick, shallow thrusts. "Promise."

Mal nodded as he released with a groan, his body pressing hard against hers. It reminded her of how TL always pinned her when he slammed her down on the floor or against the padded wall in the Marden. It had always *felt* sexual, even though he insisted it wasn't. She was sure it must look that way, too, since she hadn't caught him sparring with anyone else in that fashion.

The thought of TL made her shudder. Her heart skipped.

Too bad he was such an ass. And that he wasn't even remotely interested in her, as he was so keen to remind her at least once a day. Minimum. Sometimes, it felt like once an hour.

They cleaned up with towels that were stacked on a shelf. When they emerged back into the Marden, TL met her eyes immediately.

For some reason, shame flooded her, and she blushed. Turning away, she went to the weights again. They seemed to be her escape when she had time from his drilling her or when he was busy with another client.

Kav stopped to talk to him for several minutes. She was working on her core muscles, doing a variety of crunches. Crunches were the bane of her existence thus far. She sucked at them. So, she pushed herself harder.

TL stayed far away from her for the next several hours. When he did finally call her back to sparring, he was quiet. When he spoke, it was nastier than normal.

Mal sighed and ignored anything he said except the instruction. It was going to be a long evening.

WYAT

His stone body was freeing. There was nothing stronger than him in this form. He wasn't even convinced another gargoyle was stronger than him. Especially when he was pissed.

The little fluffy rabbit was also freeing to a degree. He could fit in tight spaces. Hide, even as bright white as he was.

As he was doing then. Watching. Waiting.

They'd come eventually. They always did when he set out bait. The Sheep were predictable as fuck.

And he was pissed. So pissed, his mind was slipping into Madness at times. Welcoming it. Embracing it.

He'd lost his girl. The one he'd just gotten.

To fucking Sheep.

There would be no Sheep left alive when he was done. He'd already made it through half of them. Somehow, he'd lucked out two days ago and taken out a dozen.

And the more he killed, the more unstructured they became.

There was a reason Sheep needed flocks. They were mindless idiots, otherwise.

Actually, they were always mindless idiots. Something pulled the Sheep's strings. And eventually, when he found their god, he would end that fucker, too.

A faint bleat met his ears. An advantage to being the little fluff ball was his enhanced hearing. Sure, he never lost the big rabbit ears in any form, but his hearing was still far superior when he was this little lagomorph.

His ear twitched. He lifted his head, sticking his twitching nose into the air to see if he could get a scent. Indeed, he could. They were close, trying to be quiet.

Too bad for them, luck was not on their side.

They came, Wyat hopped out of the bushes. One hop. Two. Three. The Sheep paid him no mind. Stupid, mindless followers.

Another hop and he counted them. Five. Six, eight. There were eight.

Eight would die today.

As soon as they surrounded the target, Wyat was ten feet and growing, his body expanding in an explosion of stone and strength, claws and wings and teeth. He had dismembered two with a single swipe and beheaded another before they realized they were under attack.

Another was missing a leg as he sunk his teeth into a fifth before they managed to act at all.

Their hands weren't so strong anymore. Their blades no longer pierced his skin. He snapped a wrist, the Sheep's mindless bleating picking up to an almost frantic sound.

Panic passed through the remaining two as they scrambled to get away. In a single jump, Wyat had landed on one, crushing it to the ground. Two bounding leaps later, he'd grabbed another by an arm and tore it from its body. Blood sprayed as the stupid little fucker screamed.

"You took my girl," Wyat growled. "Your entire flock will die.

There are consequences to messing with the wrong person, you slithy piece of MutMut shit."

It was already dead when he tore its other arm from its body. The one he'd bit was still weakly bleating, thrashing around on the ground as it bled out.

Probably wasn't the best time for the short man cresting the hill to come upon him. Wyat was bearing down on the helpless thing before it had really registered the bloodbath Wyat had accomplished all on his own.

Fear blossomed in his eyes and he stumbled back frantically. "Please," he pleaded, "I have a message for Wyat. I'm a messenger, not a fighter."

The Madness had spread like a fogging blanket over his senses. Who would send him a message? What could anyone possible say to him that would warrant a message?

It took a lot of energy to push the Madness back. To find his reason. To see the helpless little man for what he was. A messenger.

"What?" Wyat growled. "What is your message?"

With a trembling hand, he handed Wyat a little sliver of paper. Wyat didn't reach for it. It would be lost in his huge stone hands.

The little man must have realized this, for he unfolded the little square. Shaking, he offered the slightly larger paper to Wyat.

He took it and brought it up to his face. Squinting, he read.

'In Wabe my big, bad rabbit. Come home. Heart, your Bunny.'

His stomach dropped. Mal was alive. She was alive and in Wabe. It took him several attempts to actually take a breath.

Looking down at the little man, he growled, "Where is she? Where was she when she gave this message to you?"

"TL's Marden. The Round End," he whimpered.

Wyat nodded and crouched, his muscles coiling. Before he sprang into the air, he asked the man one more thing. "Do you need a ride back to Wabe?"

He shook his head frantically. “N-no, thanks.”

Wyat nodded. “There’s a long blade back within the tree line, east forty paces. It’s yours for your trouble.” He didn’t wait for an answer but shot into the air.

His wings were heavy, even flying. It wasn’t a chore, per se. And it wasn’t painful. Nor was it tiring. Not really. It was just noticeable. Something he was acutely aware of.

Now that Mal was alive, the Madness retreated like a second skin no longer needed. Wabe was several hours’ flight from Garden. He’d make it by nightfall.

And he did make it, barely an hour after the sun went down. He shrunk to his normal Wyat size and figure as he walked through the city.

The Round End was the building that marked Wabe as a destination. There was no other building like it. He completely ignored the fact that it was closed when he arrived and began pounding on the locked door. He didn’t let up until a flower answered it with a brow raised.

“We open at dawn,” he said, unimpressed.

“TL?” Wyat asked.

The man hesitated before he gave Wyat a single nod.

“Where is Mal?” Wyat demanded.

TL hesitated again, studying Wyat. Protecting the little Mal?

“Wyat?” TL asked.

Wyat nodded, his anxiety picking up. If TL knew about him, then Mal had been talking about him. She hadn’t forgotten him. He wanted to pick TL up by the neck and shake her whereabouts out of him!

TL pointed to the inn down the street. “Fourth floor, I believe.”

Wyat turned and barreled down the street. He ran up the flights of stairs, taking four at a time and threw open the door.

They were all there, sitting around a tray on the bed. Chesh, Eagy, and Ryph spun with blades in hand at the ready. Then, they froze.

Mal launched off the bed as she cried, "Wyat!"

He caught her and wrapped his big body around her, sinking to his knees and burying his face into her hair.

He could feel her tears on his neck.

"That's what a reunion should be," Chesh noted.

Wyat wasn't even going to ask. It didn't matter. Mal was here. He could feel her heart beating against his.

"Why are you covered in blood?" she asked, voice filled with worry.

"I've been hunting, Bunny. There are a lot less Sheep in the world these days," Wyat growled.

She laughed. It was a watery sound. Filled with relief.

"Wyat, will you be in my coterie?"

He groaned. "Fuck yes, woman. There's nowhere else I want to be."

She squeezed him tighter with her little body. He wasn't going to let her go. Not this night. Not for a very long fucking time.

Kav

MAL

9

She had started to find excuses not to go to the Marden. Wyat was a good excuse for at least half a day. Until Eagy reminded her, and Wyat, upon learning what she had been subject to while missing, had insisted that she continue with her training.

TL had been pretty pissed when she showed up late that morning. His dark maroon eyes were hot with anger. She tried not to find it attractive. But what was a girl to do? His pants were tight, his sleeveless shirt was soaked, clinging to his taut body like another skin. Damn flower was damn brilliant to look at.

Until he snapped at her and she scowled. He demanded she spend the next hour running the track. Running! And when she paused in her mad dash, he made her start the half hour over.

Mal was about to tell him off when he relented and had her jumping through the air on the stupid pegs again. She thought he had given up on them as a training instrument. She sucked at them.

Apparently, he intended to use them as punishment for whatever he was mad at her about today. She climbed up the rope ladder and refused to meet his eyes as she sprang from one to another. The trick wasn't the jump, so much as managing her balance on the moving bars.

Her determination for him not to catch her was pretty great and she'd gotten through half of the course before falling, again, when the door opening distracted her. TL caught her as he always did. At least his anger at her didn't prevent him from making sure she didn't seriously injure herself.

"You need to stop letting things distract you," he growled at her.

Mal rolled her eyes. "When is this ever going to come up in any situation?" she demanded.

He hadn't released her yet. She was still pressed firmly against him. His arm wrapped around her back while the other had her thigh, picking her leg up slightly. He was tall enough that her feet were not on the ground. His face was seriously close to hers. His hot breath brushed her skin. The heady scent of him filled her. His anger at her wafted from him in hot waves.

"It's not the specific obstacle that you're practicing, Sunshine, but the muscle group and coordination. As well as your ability to mentally calculate distance. Keep your head in here," he said, allowing her to slide firmly down his body. He did one better this time, keeping her leg in his grip until her other met the floor.

She wanted to comment on his hands on her in such a suggestive way for one who insists he wasn't at all interested in her. The only thing stopping her was her wariness of getting him angrier and worse to be around.

Instead, she nodded. "The door is a trigger for some reason," she said, conceding. Trying to be the bigger person.

"Distractions-"

"I know," Mal interrupted. "I'll work on it."

TL studied her for a minute before nodding. Then he released her, telling her to get a drink and catch her breath before they start again. He needed to take care of something.

She did as she was instructed and drank the entire glass of water while sitting on the bench. When he wasn't back when she'd finished her break, she retreated to the weights. It was exhausting to allow her body to cool too much before starting up again. Made her feel like she'd run around the city with Lorem's burden on her back.

Mal had barely gotten through a rep of squats when TL emerged from one of the many doors. She watched him from where she'd positioned herself among the weight shelves and benches. Where she wasn't immediately noticeable but not necessarily hiding.

He spotted her after some time. His shoulders relaxed, though she hadn't seen them tense. He walked to her as soon as he found her, telling her to stop and that they would spar.

She sighed as he turned his back to her, leading their way to the mats. He enjoyed sparring with her when he was particularly annoyed with her. Something about manhandling her pleased him. Giving him plenty of opportunity to press against her while simultaneously scolding her for sucking.

His panties were certainly in a bunch as he hissed at her that she was intentionally not giving him her undivided attention. That she was thinking about getting back to her men and fucking all night. She almost bit out that the only reason he was focusing on that was because he was jealous.

Perhaps her expression had given away her thoughts because his jabs had ceased for a while. He didn't relent in his ruthless torment of constantly plowing her into the wall or floor. But his remarks had shifted to only instruction and criticism in her form.

"You ought to come clean," TL said eventually, as he slammed Mal to the ground, his body coming hot and hard on hers.

He didn't move for a moment, his dark maroon eyes capturing her will. His body was long and lithe and so solid. His lips were barely a breath away.

Then, as usual, he pulled up, dragging her with him. "You're sloppy," he demanded.

Mal stretched her back. "I hurt," she said, slowly positioning herself to try and defend against him. "Come clean about what?"

"Spend less time fucking around and more time training, Sunshine," he bit out as he flung her into the wall.

She hit violently, barely stopping herself from cracking her head on the padding (which was still fucking hard!) before his body pressed against hers, forcing the air from her lungs. She could feel everything pressed firmly at her back and ass. If she squirmed at all, he'd toss her to the ground.

"Eight hours a day in here is not enough. It'll take me months to get you back to where you were, assuming you were good at all," he hissed.

Apparently, he was back to attacking her verbally again. "Get off me," she said quietly.

Instead, his weight bore into her more and she squeezed her eyes shut. Did he know at all what he did to her? Pressing against her like this? He'd made it pretty clear he wasn't interested, but still.

"Make me," he taunted. His hands captured her wrists and trapped her.

"You know, for someone who thinks I'm a spoiled, sex driven, *weed*, you really do like pressing yourself against me."

Sure, it might not have been the best thing to say because his reactions to these comments were usually borderline savage, but there was no way she could get out of the hold he had on her. She might have been able to earlier in the day, but she'd been at this for hours. She hurt. She was exhausted. And she was still too weak to take the beating he always gave her.

He was off her in a second. To her surprise, he didn't toss her to the ground. He didn't touch her at all.

"Get out," he said, voice hard.

Mal unstuck herself from the padded wall and looked at him. The wariness in his eyes didn't match the harshness of his voice.

"We're not-"

"We're done. You're putting little effort in." TL turned and strode to the other side of the room.

She glanced outside. She couldn't see the sun through the window yet. It was too early. "I'm sorry. I'll try harder."

He ignored her as he picked up the wooden sticks they'd been using earlier.

"Please," she said when it was clear he wasn't going to acknowledge her. She barely caught the stick that came flying at her.

His long strides brought him to her within seconds. Mal brought the stick up to defend herself when he grabbed her wrist harshly and pulled her to him. His face was within inches of hers. "I'm not playing games with you, Mal. I'm not interested in any part of you. Understand?"

Mal nodded, swallowing a lump in her throat.

"If you want my help, put some fucking effort in."

"I'm sorry," she whispered.

Despite himself, his severe expression softened. After a moment, he let out a sigh. The grip on her wrist loosened, his fingers rubbing where he'd grabbed her so roughly. "Take a break. Come back after you eat something, and we'll try again." His voice was soft and lilting once more.

She nodded.

TL let her go and turned. Mal watched him before setting the stick down and turning towards the door.

"Mal," he called to her as her hand rested on the handle. She turned to face him. "Tell them you're fucking Kav. Your harem should know what - *who* - you're doing."

She flinched. Bowing her head as a properly whipped dog, she turned again.

"Be prepared to stay well past dark, Sunshine. We have work to do."

Mal trudged her way to the room. All four of her men were there, gathered around a giant tray of food. Since Wyat had joined them again, their food intake had nearly doubled. It took a lot of calories to be a gargoyle the size of Wyat.

They all grinned at her in greeting. She collapsed on the bed between Ryph and Chesh. After a minute of quiet munching, Wyat knelt behind her and started rubbing her shoulders. She could have melted right there.

Telling them now seemed too strenuous. She didn't want to fight, and it would cause a fight. They'd be upset. And this time, they had a right to be. But TL was right.

"I need to tell you something," she said, examining the little puff filled with some kind of meat jelly in her hand.

Perhaps it was the tone in which she said it. Everyone stilled. Wyat's hands froze for a moment before he continued his ministrations.

She took a deep breath and blurted it all out as fast as she could, not allowing anyone time to interrupt her. "I've been having sex with Kav. Only once since you got here but still, I should have told you. I should have talked to you about it. I'm sorry."

Wyat's hands remained on her shoulders, but he had stopped massaging. No one said anything.

"Oh, come on," Eagy said with irritation. "Mal, we just-"

"I know, I know. I swear to you it won't happen again." She continued to stare at her hands.

Ryph's hand on her chin forced her to look up, to meet his eyes. She swallowed hard. His golden eyes were irked. A frown marred his beautiful face.

"I'm sorry," she whispered. "I swear-"

"I heard you," he said, voice low and vexed. "Why?"

She tried to shake her head, but his hold on her chin was firm.

"If you tell me again 'because you wanted to,' I will break him in two," he growled.

"I don't know why," she said. "I was scared and stressed and panicky. He was helping me and-"

Ryph's eyes narrowing made her stop speaking. "Why were you scared? TL-"

"No, no. I mean back at the palace. I-"

"I thought you said you were chained the whole time you were there, until Kav snuck you out."

"I was."

A heavy silence filled with slowly increasing anger filled the room. The door slamming shut behind her made Mal jump. She wasn't sure when Wyat had taken his hands off her, but he'd apparently left.

Ryph let her chin go but pulled her against him. "What else haven't you told us?"

She shook her head. "That's it."

"Why-"

"I don't know. It didn't seem like the right time before and since then... I guess I've been scared of telling you. I didn't want to fight or want you to be mad. I had a coward moment."

Ryph snorted.

"That's all?" Chesh asked.

Mal glanced around Ryph to look at him.

"Anything else?" he clarified.

She shook her head. "No but to be fair, I don't recall much of when I was at the palace. Most of the time, I think I was unconscious."

Chesh scowled, his fiery eyes piqued with teal flames as his ears flattened.

The door flung open again and Wyat tossed Kav to the floor like a rag doll. If his already crushed, bleeding nose was any indication, Wyat had hit him at least once.

Ryph's embrace tightened around Mal. She felt the growl in his chest a heartbeat before his wings erupted from his back, shredding his shirt to escape. His newly released tail lashed in anger behind him.

Kav looked up from where he crouched on the floor. Smart man that he didn't try to make any move. There was no way he could get by all four of the men. One, maybe. But apparently not if that one was Wyat.

"You best have a really fucking good explanation for touching our Mal while she was chained," Eagy said.

Although he sounded calm, his voice was as cold as his icy eyes.

Kav's dark brown eyes met hers a moment before Wyat kicked him over with a foot to his shoulder, knocking him painfully onto his side and breaking their eye contact. "Keep your eyes off her," Wyat warned.

Kav didn't move for a minute. Slowly, he got to his hands and knees, spitting blood.

"I swear to you, my intent is to help you kill the Bloody Queens," he rasped.

"That's not what he asked," Chesh hissed. "What made you think you had the right to touch her at all?"

Kav tilted his face up but stopped short. "I'm sorry."

Mal absently noted that there were a lot of apologies flying around Laddenworn since she'd arrived. It was too easy to hurt someone. Too easy to misunderstand and fuck up. Words were as dangerous as weapons here.

Even so, she never got the impression that apologies came easy to anyone. Not least of all, the men she surrounded herself with. And yet...

"Well, that fixes it," Chesh quipped.

Kav pushed himself back so that he was sitting on his heels. He gingerly touched his ribs. With his head bowed, he said, "Look, I didn't know she had a harem. She-"

"Was chained and helpless," Wyat growled. His body tensed, as if preparing to assault him again.

"I only had her restrained because she kept pulling the tube out of her arm when she'd wake up."

"None of what you've said so far comes even close to excusing your actions," Eagy said.

Kav picked his head up a little, his eyes meeting Eagy's. He carefully did not look at Mal. "No," he said quietly. "It doesn't. I didn't think I was forcing her. I'm sorry if she thought I was. That was never my intent."

His eyes left Eagy and looked at Chesh.

"Why did you release her, Knave of Hart? Your actions and words seem a little treasonous to me," Eagy said.

He bowed his head again. "They killed my family. I've been waiting for the Right One to arrive."

Eagy glanced back at Ryph, a strange look on his face, before looking down to where Mal still sat folded in his Ryph's. Eagy sighed and turned to Wyat.

"I suppose we should take a vote-" he began.

"Just let him go," Chesh said, flicking his hand. "But you should know: I've been dying to see if Wyat could crush a man with his bare hands. If you touch her again, I think we'll find out."

Kav nodded, lips pressed firmly together. He pulled himself to his feet and left the room. A moment later, Wyat was kneeling in front of Ryph and Mal, pinky-red eyes staring intently at her.

"Did he have your permission?"

"He didn't *not* have permission. I admit I was a little groggy and pretty sure I was dying, if not already dead, but I didn't tell him no," she answered. She left out the part where she'd been gagged initially. Her screaming would have called too many people to investigate his room. And she was pretty intent on screaming every time she came to.

But these four men were more important to her than Kav. Yes, she liked Kav. He'd certainly helped her escape. Actually, if she was honest, he broke her out. And he'd nursed her back to health as they made their way to Wabe. He'd put her up in an inn. And put her in touch with TL to get her strength back.

Still, these four men were her life. They were the life she'd have after her fairytale fix. She never saw Kav fitting into that. Everything about it had been a mistake. Thinking he was one of her seven had been a mistake.

"I told TL I'd go back to practice more today," she said.

Chesh lept from the bed. "I'll walk you."

Reluctantly, Ryph let her go. Quietly, the two of them left the room. When they were down on the street, far enough that the men couldn't hear them through the balcony, Mal said, "Chesh-" at the same time he asked, "Is there anything else to tell?"

"No," she said, shaking her head. A few steps later, he wrapped his arm around her waist, pulling her against his side. With it came his long, furry tail.

"I know you revolt at the idea that you should ask us before you invite anyone else into your harem, but really, to keep us all sane, you need to, Mal. That's not saying you don't have the final say, but you've got a harem full of strong, short-tempered animals who are insanely possessive."

Mal nodded and blew out a breath. "I didn't keep it from you because I wanted him in our harem. I... I don't think I do. I really did think I was dead, or dying, or... I don't know. I thought I'd never see you again. I thought my life was over. It was a mistake, Chesh."

He kissed the side of her head as they approached the gym.

"Should we talk about TL?" he purred.

Mal snorted. "Hardly. Pretty sure he hates me."

"Hmm," he answered, pushing the door open for her.

When she looked at the course he'd set up, Mal let out a long breath. TL did not intend it to be an easy evening. He stood against the wall in the back with his arms crossed against his hard chest, face set as he watched the door. Waiting for her.

"I hope you brought your Wabe game, Sunshine. We're done playing around."

The Madness Bait

MAL

10

She managed to get into the washroom alone this morning. It was nice to have a soak by herself. To just relax and decompress.

They were leaving the next morning. There was a lot they needed to do and Mal could continue her conditioning while they traveled. They would plan extra time in the evenings for at least an hour's worth of practice and strength training.

There was just too much to do. It was clear that she needed to step up her game. Find more friends and supporters. See what she could do about amassing her own army. Failing that, establishing allies and followers.

On top of the list was looking for kid gloves. They were debating tracking down the Duchess and taking hers – by force, if necessary. She was only using the magic to torment others. And attempting to eradicate the Serpents.

And, Chesh had informed her, they still hadn't heard from Wally. It didn't appear that he was in Wabe. He'd done some digging while Mal continued to work with TL. The place Wally had holed up in last time he was in Wabe was empty. Completely.

When she got out of the warm water and drained the tub,

extinguishing the fire beneath, she dressed in clean clothes. She'd miss clean clothes. After spending so long in a single set of clothes dried with dirt and blood while in the dungeons, she would never take for granted something as simple as clean clothes again.

She emerged to find the four of them deep in a hushed conversation. They were so intent on their discussion, they didn't so much as indicate they'd heard the washroom door open. Mal raised a brow.

"She's going to hate it," Ryph argued, his voice hushed.

"She still needs to see it. They frightened her," Eagy insisted, voice equally hushed.

Mal narrowed her eyes.

"The queens need to go first," Wyat stated. "We can't get sidetracked anymore. They took her, damnit. I won't lose her again."

"They don't deserve this, though. And she needs to see it!" Eagy said.

"It's going to upset her," Ryph said. "You know how she is."

"How am I?" Mal asked. She was amused to see the four of them jump. A blush tickled Eagy's cheeks.

"Caring," Ryph said.

"And what are you trying to keep me from seeing?"

None of them answered. She crossed her arms and waited.

"The Madness Bait," Chesh told her.

That didn't at all answer her question, even if it was the answer.

Ryph sighed. "We're outnumbered, now," he said to Wyat. "We might as well go."

Wyat frowned. "The queens-"

"Are my first priority," Mal said. "Nothing will change that."

He was not at all convinced.

"YOU'RE GOING TO HATE THIS," Ryph said as they took a passage that brought them under the streets of Wabe.

Mal wasn't going to argue. Anything underground couldn't be a great thing. So many illegal activities came to mind. Gambling. Fighting or wrestling. Trafficking.

Still, if they were trying to keep her from seeing it, it had to be up there in the heinous scale.

They came to an arena with seating all the way around. Mal started to make her way to the bottom, close to the ring, but all four men agreed that they would stay closer to the top.

"Safer," Chesh said.

To their credit, none of them looked particularly enthusiastic.

Mal looked around. The arena itself was empty. The floor was mulch or sawdust. Hard to say from as far away as she was. Others were starting to pile in.

Everyone else looked excited. Laughing. Anxious for the show to begin. Some held beverages as if they were at a sports event. Others held food platters like it was a show. One even held a little handmade banner.

A door she hadn't seen in the sides of the arena wall opened and a man sauntered out. He looked confused. Lost. Vacant.

She leaned forward, as if the few inches would give her a better look.

The man scratched his head, eyes flitting around anxiously. Fearfully.

"What is this?" Mal asked, frowning. Nothing good was going to come of this, she was sure.

"We already told you," Eagy offered.

"There aren't enough words for this," Ryph said. "Just watch the horror unfold."

She really hoped they were being overdramatic. She hadn't

known them to be, but suddenly she was internally begging them to be exaggerating.

The first indication that it was truly beginning was when the audience started stomping their feet on the floor in rhythm. Whether they did it for themselves, as a sort of outlet for their excitement, or to get the man in the middle worked up, she didn't know. But the man in the arena was certainly getting upset. He was shaking, his head whipping around at everyone. The noise made him cringe with every footfall.

He gripped the sides of his hair and grit his teeth.

Mal wanted to jump down there and pull him out. No one deserved that kind of torment. No matter what their crime.

When a door many, many times bigger than the one the man came out of started to creak open, the crowd lost all rhythm to their stomping and sped it up, cheering. The man in the middle fell to his knees.

The door stopped when it had opened completely. Silence fell. The man looked up and around him. A smile grew on his face and he climbed to his feet.

Someone in front of Mal and her men sniggered. Another behind her coughed.

A snarl came from inside the large open door. The man spun and stared.

The shadow on the ground caught the man's attention. As it grew, the man took several steps back.

"A Savage?" Mal wondered out loud. Would it turn into a shadow beast?

Her men didn't answer.

Then, it came out. Slinking slowly. Stalking the man with its giant head bowed.

There was nothing that came to mind for Mal to relate it to. It was a dusty gray with a white and black spattering of spots. It was perhaps the size of an elephant. Its front paws looked remarkably hand-like but its back paws were all canine. It had a tail that was maybe medium length. It wasn't short haired, nor necessarily longhaired.

Its head was... almost cute. Both cat and rhino-like. A strange, yet adorable, combination.

Except the teeth. The teeth were big and poked out of its mouth.

A low rumble of a growl echoed through the air.

"What is it?" Mal asked.

"Bandersnatch," Wyat said.

"And what is it supposed to do?" She was one hundred percent sure she did not want to know. She could already guess.

"To the death," Chesh whispered.

Mal shuddered. She shook her head. "Why? What did he do to deserve that?"

"Nothing," Chesh said. "But catch the Madness."

Her heart thundered. "We need to stop it." She tried to bolt to her feet, but Wyat on one side and Eagy on her other prevented her from moving so much as an inch.

"We can't," Eagy said.

"We can't just let it happen," she pleaded. "He doesn't deserve death because he's sick."

"He's not sick," Wyat said. "He's mad."

"Mental illness. Yes, that's what I said. He's sick. He needs treatment, not to be torn apart by that thing."

"This isn't the Outside," Chesh reminded her. "There is no treatment, no cure. The Madness cannot be undone once it takes root."

Fear must have fully settled into the man in the arena, for he no longer looked like a man. He was almost a shadow with grotesque claws and burning yellow eyes.

"I can't watch this," she whispered and turned her head away as the Bandersnatch lunged.

The crowd erupted in cheers. Bile rose in her throat.

It was a surprisingly long battle. She hadn't thought they'd been evenly matched. Both things screamed, the animal and the mad man. There was the unmistakable sound of bones breaking, flesh tearing. Cries of pain from both. Fear filled the air.

As the round ended, her men took her from the arena. She couldn't stop herself from looking, no matter how hard she tried. The man was dead. There were body parts all over the place, including the Bandersnatch's tail.

She managed to make it out of the arena before she vomited. Chesh rubbed her back while Eagy held her hair away from her face.

"You okay?" Eagy asked.

"Who sets those up?" she demanded, voice shaking.

"The Queens," Ryph said. "The Mad are dangerous. If they chose to rise against the Queens, they stand a chance of winning. So, the Queens made a sport out of disposing of one of their bigger seen threats."

"And there's an audience!" she exclaimed. "Who enjoy that!"

"Not everyone in there is from Wabe, Mal," Chesh said. "There are people from all over Laddenworn. These are held twice a year. They draw in a big crowd."

Mal was so overwhelmed by how incredibly furious she was, she couldn't speak. Who did she punish for this? The queens would already get theirs. But what of the audience?

"Take me home," she insisted. "I can't be here anymore. I won't be returning to Wabe unless absolutely necessary."

Eagy

Mal was still upset several hours later. She'd insisted they tell her about the Madness. Unfortunately, even Chesh wasn't sure what to tell her.

"Madness has been a part of Wonderland from the beginning," he said, frowning.

"When did it make the Mad morph into monsters?" she demanded.

Chesh shook his head. "I haven't the slightest idea, Kitten."

She growled at him. Literally growled. It was adorable.

Like Eagy, the others didn't dare laugh right then.

"When can we leave?" Mal asked, instead.

"First thing in the morning," Eagy said. "We'll meet TL at his Marden and be on our way."

She looked at him with another frown. "Why are we meeting him?"

"You'd rather see if he can find us later?" Wyat asked, laughing.

"He's not coming," she said.

"Well, of course, he's coming," Ryph said. "He's definitely one of your seven. He-"

"He's not coming," she insisted. "I asked him, and he said no."

The four of them looked at each other.

"So, let me get this straight," Wyat said, "Kav intends to come with us and we aren't feeling him. But TL refuses. For what reason?"

"Doesn't matter." Mal flipped her hand in the air. "He's been nothing but a tool since just after you got here and I'd rather him not be around."

"We need him around," Eagy said. "He's not Wally, but he's a trainer. Trainers train in other things besides muscle, you know."

"I don't know, but it still doesn't matter. He said no. And I sure as hell will not beg for someone to join us who has no interest in doing so of his own freewill."

Eagy didn't argue. He hoped when he dropped it, the others would, too.

He waited until everyone was settled that evening, Mal tucked within Ryph's wings and the both of them wrapped tightly in Wyat's big arms, before he dressed again and left the room. He had no idea where Chesh always ran off to.

TL not going was just unacceptable. Why spend weeks working with Mal to up and walk away?

He felt Chesh drop next to him before the cat became visible. "What?" Eagy asked.

"Where you headed so late, Birdy?" he purred.

"Where have you been, Demon Cat?" Eagy countered.

"Do you think I should hang around and watch you three fuck her?" Chesh asked.

"She didn't ask for you to hold off, you know," Eagy said, glancing at him.

Chesh shrugged. "It's not all about sex, youngling."

Eagy's feathers bristled. "I know that," he snapped.

Chesh's too wide grin climbed up the sides of his face. Eagy shook his head. "Seriously, what do you want?"

"Where you sneaking off to?"

Again, he bristled. "I'm not sneaking. I-"

"Waited until everyone was asleep..."

Eagy huffed a breath. "Fine. Because I'm irritated that TL doesn't want to go. I'd like to talk to him myself."

Chesh nodded and continued in step as Eagy made his way to the Marden. There weren't any lights on but then, TL lived around back.

"If you're coming, you best be useful," Eagy snapped.

"Don't get your feathers in a twist, Eagy," Chesh said, knocking his shoulder into Eagy's. "I didn't actually think you were sneaking around."

Eagy glanced at him. "You just felt like being a... what did Mal call it... a tool?"

Chesh laughed. "Yeah, that was a new one to me, too. I assume it's a negative metaphor since she's been calling TL a tool for days in a very unpleasant tone."

"Maybe I shouldn't talk to him," Eagy said, hesitating. "He has been pretty harsh towards her lately."

Chesh nodded. "Yes, but we need him. You're right on that. And I think the four of us will be pretty focused on Mal.

Having someone not interested around to watch Kav would be helpful."

That decided it.

He knocked loudly on TL's door. When the flower didn't answer, Eagy took it up again and continued until the he did.

His short hair was ruffled in a way that it shouldn't have been able to with how short it was. He was frowning as he swung open the door before concern lit his eyes. "What's wrong?" he asked.

"We need to talk," Eagy said.

The concern flitted away, and TL frowned once more. "Now?"

"That depends. Are you really staying behind when we leave in the morning?"

"Yes."

"Then yes, now."

TL sighed heavily and opened the door for them.

The room was small, barely big enough for a bed and a small kitchen. A door in the wall led to what Eagy assumed was a washroom.

"I'd offer you a seat, but as you can see, there isn't one," TL deadpanned.

"We need you," Eagy said, ignoring his comment.

TL started to shake his head.

"We don't trust Kav and after losing Mal, there's no way we're going to be able to focus on anything but her. We need someonc to watch Kav."

"Why don't you trust Kav?" TL asked.

"Why would we? He's the Knave of Hart."

"He broke her out."

"He fucked her while she was chained and delirious," Chesh offered, rocking on his heels.

TL's eyes widened. "I... didn't know that."

"Yes, well, he'd have you believe it otherwise. But from what Mal said, it wasn't until she was two days outside the palace that she was finally convinced she wasn't dead. He admitted to keeping her in chains, even when he retrieved her from the dungeon. He also admitted to taking her while she was restrained in the chains."

"And, frankly, he's a little sneaky," Chesh added. "He's constantly snooping around, sneaking in and out of places when he thinks he's not being watched."

"Sounds like you manage to keep an eye on him just fine," TL said.

Both Eagy and Chesh shook their heads.

"When she's here with you, we know she's safe. Within your Marden, with you to keep her alive. Then, we're free to do our own thing," Eagy said. "But we lost her once while we were deep within Silence. We won't make that mistake again."

TL stared at them. Eagy couldn't guess what he was thinking. His face remained impassive. Unimpressed as his arms crossed over his chest.

"I have no interest in her," TL stated.

"We aren't offering you her body," Chesh hissed.

His eyes flashed hot enough that the room illuminated like lightning.

TL sighed. "Make it noon. If I go, I need time to make arrangements here."

Eagy pursed his lips. "This isn't just a game? You really had no intention of joining us?"

TL rolled his eyes. "I don't know what kind of games you all play, but no, I don't want to go. But I will. Because I do want to see the queens dead. When that's accomplished, I'm leaving."

Eagy nodded. "After noon tea. We'll meet you at the front of the inn."

TL jerked his head in a nod and moved to open the door again. Eagy and Chesh left without another word. They continued to walk away in quiet until they were on the other side of the Round End.

"I truly thought he was just messing with her," Eagy confided.

Chesh nodded. "I did, too, actually."

"Honestly, how can anyone living in this fucked up world not jump at the chance to help change it?"

"Maybe the idea of losing their life when the Next One fails isn't worth the risk."

Eagy considered this. Twenty-seven had come before Mal. Twenty-seven had failed. A few, quite spectacularly.

"I mean, how many before Mal did you jump in to help?" Chesh asked.

"Point taken," Eagy said.

"Even Wyat made her prove herself before he agreed to join us."

Eagy sighed and stopped outside the inn, where he stared up at the window where their three others were.

"This time," Eagy said, "if we're about to fail, we take Mal and get out. I won't lose her, Chesh. Not again."

Chesh nodded. "I don't disagree. I think she will, though."

"Then it's a plan she doesn't need to know about."

"It would be useful if I could evaporate with her," Chesh said. "I should have been able to save her from the Sheep. I was right there. I had her in my arms."

"Not your fault. We're all blaming ourselves but really, no one has survived the Sheep. They had to have been expecting you. Wyat wasn't even able to change."

"That's some strong magic," Chesh observed. "Maybe we need to make the kid gloves a priority. The magic already works the way it does within us. It's settled. We have all the magic we are ever going to get. But Mal is an open book."

"Highest possibilities," Eagy mused. He nodded, thoughtfully. "Since we don't have a solid destination until we hear from Lepa or Wally, we have time to search."

Noli's Trap

EAGY

11

"I've been thinking," Mal said, almost as soon as she opened her eyes.

"Yeah?" Ryph asked, amused. "You were asleep three seconds ago."

She shrugged. "I am a master multi-tasker."

Ryph cocked his head to the side.

"About what?" Chesh's little cat body asked.

"If the Queens are truly working on a second Culling, and they're targeting anyone who isn't a pure human, we can visit every Village and Patch and Colony, etcetera-" she waved a hand in the air "- and simultaneously warn them and gather support."

"If we lead with the warning, we might get a better show of support," Eagy said, musing over the word 'human'.

"There isn't really an 'if' about it," Wyat said. "They either get on board or they can defend themselves."

Mal looked at him with a brow raised. Ryph and Eagy glanced at him as well.

"You mean like you did?" Mal asked in a sweet voice.

Wyat rolled his eyes. "Things are different now. When I asked for proof, the Queens weren't trying to kill entire races.

We were still living in relative peace. That's not an option anymore."

"Stand up and fight or lay down your life?" Chesh offered.

"I refuse to accept these terms," Mal said as she sat up, disentangling herself from Ryph and Wyat. "Just because someone doesn't want to fight, doesn't mean they deserve death."

"But maybe the unconditional protection should have limits," Chesh countered.

Mal looked at his little kitty eyes warily. "Meaning?"

"Those who voluntarily treat others like dirt, they can defend themselves if they choose not to stand up to the Queens."

She looked at Eagy, a smile tugging at her lips. "I like that."

Eagy fought to smile in return. It meant everything to him that she wanted to protect him, but it was unnecessary now. No one else mattered other than those in this room.

"These are the things we need to think about eventually," Wyat stated, sitting up as well. "When the Queens are gone, the bloody terror ends. But that doesn't mean society is civilized outside of their rule, either."

Mal nodded and headed for the washroom. "I agree. Although, I did not sign up for that. I'm here to fix your fairy tale. Not rule a kingdom once the fairy tale is fixed."

"When you depose a queen, you take the throne," Eagy said.

She paused at the door. When she turned, she was frowning. "We will come up with another solution when the time comes. I have no intent on being a queen or ruling Laddenworn. Do I have time for a soak?"

Eagy nodded. "We're leaving after noon tea."

"Oh?" she asked, brows puckering again. The many expressions that flitted across her face made his chest ache. He would make sure he looked at that face every day until the end of Laddenworn.

"Slight change of plans. No big deal."

She looked at him thoughtfully before giving a nod and

retreating into the bathroom. He loved how much she trusted him. She should have asked, but she didn't.

"What's the change?" Wyat asked as the water started.

"I spoke with TL last night. He needs time to get his affairs in order before he takes off with us."

"You convinced him to go?" Ryph asked.

"I convinced him that there's no way we'll be focusing more than 10% of our attention anywhere other than Mal. And we need someone to watch Kav since we all agree there's something going on there." 10% was probably a little generous. 2% was likely accurate and only because Eagy couldn't help himself but pay attention to what was going on around him.

"He agreed?" Wyat asked.

"Not readily," Eagy said, frowning. He sighed. "Still, my intuition says to trust him more than I do Kav, which is not at all. So, there's something. Unless you disagree?"

He wasn't exactly hopeful that Wyat would disagree. But he had a weird feeling that he couldn't explain. Kav put him on alert. TL, not as much. That didn't mean TL was a good guy, though.

Chesh grew into his person form. It was a strange sight. His body lengthened and stretched in a very uncomfortable way. Somewhat disturbing. His fur grew backwards into his body, leaving his skin bare, revealing the dark, jagged stripes in his skin. Eagy thought the stripes were much like his etchings, revealing something about him as Eagy's delineated his bloodline. But with Chesh being the only demon cat, and completely unlike the other cats in Laddenworn, it wasn't the same.

Eagy shuddered. He much preferred his transformation. It just seemed to happen. Nothing came out of anywhere, really. He called it on. Like magic.

"Where had you been when the messenger found you?" Chesh asked Wyat.

"Garden," Wyat answered.

"Did you find their Field?"

Wyat nodded.

"Nothing useful there?" Eagy asked.

Wyat shrugged. "I wasn't looking for useful. I was looking for Mal."

"I know. I'm asking if it's worth raiding."

Wyat frowned. "I don't know. I was this close-" he held his finger and thumb and inch apart like he was ready to pinch something, "- from losing it. I was already slipping when I found it. When I didn't find her, I started hunting them. I'm quite good at it."

Ryph patted Wyat's arm. "I think you were more successful than we were."

Eagy nodded. He'd had them running around in circles for who knew how long.

Oh, wait. He did know how long. Three fucking months!

"You got us to Wabe," Chesh told Eagy, as if he'd read Eagy's mind. "We gathered loads of information on our way."

Eagy smiled and turned to look out the window. He appreciated Chesh's vote of confidence, but it didn't change the fact that they hadn't come anywhere close to finding Mal. In fact, they had been heading in the wrong direction. Either queen's dungeons hadn't even been on the list of possibilities.

Stupid, really. The Sheep were assassins. And suddenly, one day, they abduct instead of kill. Why else would they except to turn Mal in?

The knocking on their door had all four turning. TL was to meet them out front in several hours.

Only Chesh was dressed, lounging on the head of the bed where he'd been stretched out as a cat. Wyat and Ryph hadn't left the bed yet and Eagy had removed his clothes again when he came back last night. Just in case Mal woke up and wanted to play some more.

Ryph left the bed, pulling his wings tight to his back. His tail flickered. Eagy grinned. The damned beast was gorgeous in any form, but there was something about his hybrid half-form that made Eagy hot. He was already starting to feel his cock hardening.

Kav stood on the other side of the door. He frowned at Ryph. "I thought we were leaving early."

Ryph shrugged. "We changed our minds."

"Would have been good to know," Kav deadpanned.

"Would have been good for you to keep your hands off our Mal," Ryph growled.

Kav didn't answer.

"I'd say 'call it even', but we're not even close."

"I told you," Kav said, his voice gentler now, "I didn't know she had a coterie."

"Tell me," Chesh said. Eagy got the distinct impression there was a threat in that tone, even as low and even as he spoke. "How many grown women have you come across without a coterie?"

At Kav's silence, Eagy knew their point was made.

After several long breaths, Kav nodded. "You're right. I won't defend my actions anymore. I was wrong."

Was that supposed to make them like him better? He was in a room with four animals. Kav couldn't possibly think that admission would change their opinion of him.

"Front, after noon tea," Ryph said, shutting the door without waiting for an answer.

THEY HADN'T TOLD Mal that TL would be joining them. Why Eagy had kept it from her, he couldn't say. Then again, he told himself, he wasn't really keeping it from her. It hadn't come up.

TL was outside the inn with Kav and his tove when the five

of them exited the front door. Part of Eagy hoped that Kav would have lost track of time and not shown up. He was keeping a lot of secrets and omitting many truths. This much, Eagy knew for certain.

Mal looked at TL with surprise. TL met her gaze reticently. She didn't say anything to him. When she turned away, it was with a mask of indifference as she placed her hand in Ryph's, though she smiled at the tove who returned the gesture.

Ryph grinned, liking Mal's affection. Eagy grinned, liking Mal's dismissal of TL.

She'd spent almost all their time together in contact with someone since they'd rejoined. Many times, Eagy was sure she was trying to figure out how to touch them all at the same time. As if they'd disappear if she couldn't keep them within her grasp.

Eagy understood the feeling. He always tried like hell to keep from wrapping her in his arms. Just to be sure she was safe. By the way Wyat, Chesh, and Ryph were always brushing a hand, or tail, lightly across her, he knew they suffered from the same fear.

TL walked most of the day with Kav and his ride. Eagy remained close, between them and Mal with her other three coters. He wanted to hear what Kav was saying. So far, nothing of interest.

They had known each other a while, by the sounds of it. Catching up on others they knew. Talking about the Marden.

Ryph tugging on Chesh's tail distracted him from his intense concentration of Kav. Eagy narrowed his eyes as Ryph wrapped Chesh's tail around his palm. He had to fight to restrain himself from ripping them apart.

He was distracted again when Kav mentioned something about the Queen. Whatever it was, Eagy missed it. Ryph messing with Chesh was too irritating.

Catching up, he pulled Ryph out of the group, frowning at him. Waiting for an explanation.

Ryph grinned hugely and planted a kiss on Eagy's lips. Eagy rolled his eyes.

. . .

Mal

Mal was actually glad to be traveling once more. She didn't even care that she was sleeping on the ground again or missing being clean with clean clothes and warm meals.

She had her men. They were hers for real. Intentionally and all!

It was a remarkable feeling.

What was weird was having Kav and TL around. They seemed like different parts of her life. Kav represented the time she was dead (not truly dead, but it sure felt like she was being tortured in hell) and TL for that span of time that she was so weak, she was all about welcoming death to end the struggle.

She'd gathered that they didn't have a true destination in mind. A little bit of following Silence. Some of tracking down the Duchess with her magic kid gloves. Searching for Wally. And hoping to stumble across the settlements of flora and animals.

The days were pretty uneventful, thankfully. For the first few, anyway.

On their fifth day in Silence, they stumbled upon some footprints that Kav recognized too late. He jumped away, backing into their larger group surrounding him. Ryph and Wyat stumbling backwards tripped whatever held the trap at bay.

Before anyone had time to react, a woven mesh of fire surrounded them like a net.

Mal backed into the nearest body, Chesh, whispering "What fresh Hell is this?"

"Indeed," he hissed.

Wyat pulled Eagy and Ryph into the middle of the group, keeping their readily flammable wings away from the fire. A second passed before he pulled Rival in as well, running a smooth hand down the tove's neck. Rival stared at him silently and Mal wondered what he was thinking.

"Can you fly out?" Kav asked Wyat.

Wyat frowned at him. "If I changed in here, with all of us huddled together as we are, I'd shove each of you into the fire."

"You're made of stone," Kav said. "Surely the fire doesn't hurt you."

"Stone still burns," Eagy snapped. "Glad to see you're willing to offer him up and not yourself."

"That's not-"

The snap of a branch made them all turn. It was loud enough to be heard over the crackle of the magical fire.

A man stepped out from behind a mushroom. Or had he been in the mushroom? It was hard to tell from the angle they were watching from.

Sweat dripped down Mal's back. Magical fire or not, it was hot.

"Noli," Kav said.

The man grinned widely. His hair was long and bushy, surrounding a strangely shaped face and golden brown, round eyes. He was tall, languid. A little underwhelming.

"What have I caught?" Noli purred.

"If you don't release us, you're about to find out," Wyat growled.

Noli cocked his head to the side, lowering it like he was stalking his prey. "Do you think?"

The fire flared up, closing the circle tighter.

"He's mad," Kav murmured. "He will burn us alive."

"The fuck he will," Chesh hissed.

Mal could feel her face burning. She glanced at Ryph to see barely concealed panic. A beast of fur and feathers should not be surrounded by fire.

"You are minions of the dark," Noli said. "And I have captured you." He puffed his chest out proudly.

Chesh narrowed his eyes. "I wonder how much hell I have

left in me?" he murmured. "I think now is a good time to find out."

He held his hand out in front of him. A moment later, a burst of teal fire covered his hand.

"Do you suppose," Ryph whispered. "Your help fire is stronger than magical fire?"

"Hellfire," Chesh corrected. "Hell. Not help. And we're about to find out."

Ryph reached out and snagged Chesh's tail. Eagy batted his hand away, baring his teeth. Ryph turned his head to bury his face in Mal's neck as she brought the two feathery beasts closer to her.

"Last warning," Chesh said. "I'll burn this entire forest down to get to you."

Noli studied him for a minute. It was only then that Mal saw that he was, indeed, mad.

There was a reason those who are not of sound mind usually get off in a court of law. The insane cannot be held accountable for their actions.

But if it meant being burned to death, Mal was all for taking him down. If it was them or Noli the Mad, she was choosing them.

"Do it," she said.

Chesh wrapped his hand around one of the rungs of woven fire. At first, nothing happened except Mal being filled with intense anxiety that he was being burned. But then the teal flames licked from his hands and rapidly consumed the magic fire.

"You best run," Wyat said, looking at Noli with rage in his eyes. "I do enjoy the chase before I tear you apart."

Noli didn't move or speak. He watched the teal fire consume the fire netting. When it burned a bright teal, it fell away.

"Get down," Wyat said, under his breath.

Mal was pulled down without hesitation by Ryph and Eagy. Chesh, TL, Rival, and Kav joined him as Wyat-the-stone-gargoyle erupted above them. As he shot up, it was clear that he would have pushed them into the fire as he'd said he would.

Noli looked at him wide-eyed, fear finally penetrating his absent, amused gaze. He stumbled back, falling to his ass, before turning and trying to run.

"Is he mad enough to turn into that yellow-eyed thing the maddest do?" Mal asked.

"Let's find out," Wyat said as he made chase for Noli.

Trees came down with loud, screaming crashes. Branches snapped. Mushrooms puffed up like balloons before exploding in dust.

With as big as Wyat was, and as fast as he was, it was no time at all before they heard Noli's screams.

"I really hope he doesn't kill him," Kav stated.

Mal and the other five men stared at him while Rival wandered off into the trees, nibbling on bark. It was at this moment that she was sure Eagy was going to draw his blade on Kav.

"Why?" TL asked.

"The trap was set for someone. And he mentioned 'minions of the dark,' something I'm not familiar with. I'd like to know what he's talking about."

"It seems the consensus is that he's mad. Would he even know what he's said?" Mal asked.

Kav shrugged. "He's not *that* mad, Princess. Not quite Hatter mad."

Wyat came plowing through the trees with Noli being dragged along by his thick, golden hair. Noli was howling. Whether it was from pain or the promise of pain, Mal wasn't sure.

He dumped Noli in front of Kav. His red eyes were intense, deep, rusty red like a brick. "You have ten minutes to get your answers before I skin him alive."

Noli's eyes widened and he jumped to his feet. Wyat slammed him back to the ground a heartbeat later, where he landed with a thud and the unmistakable sound of bone breaking. Or at least, fracturing.

With his foot now on a tail Mal hadn't seen before, Wyat folded his arms. Noli began to howl again.

"Ask your questions," Wyat said. "My patience is on a short leash."

Kav moved to crouch in front of Noli. With a fistful of Noli's hair, he forced the man to look at him. "What are minions of darkness?"

Noli bared his teeth. "You will not have me. You will not. Will not. Not. Not."

"Are they who you set the trap for?"

"Minion," Noli yelled, eyes flashing to Chesh. "Will not have me!"

"Do you want to die?" Kav asked, his voice more conversational.

Noli looked at him. Mal was sure, with the clarity in which he met Kav's eyes, that at least some of this performance was for show.

"I really don't have a problem with Wyat killing you. He has been murdering Sheep, you know. Do you want to be next?"

Mal narrowed her eyes. How had he known Wyat was killing Sheep? Glancing at her men, none of them seemed overly concerned. But TL frowned at him.

Noli sat quietly, appearing to ponder his question. When he glanced up at Wyat behind him, Noli shuddered and turned back.

"Who is the trap for?" Kav asked again.

"Nobody," Noli answered, eyes darting around. "Nobody is coming."

Eagy stiffened.

Noli and Ornicun

CHESH

12

He'd forgotten about Nobody. It had been a long time since Nobody had been mentioned. Even Chesh, as pretty immune to fear of Laddenworn that he was, felt a tremor of unease creep down his back.

"What makes you think that?" Kav pressed.

"There are whispers," Noli said, whispering himself. "All around Silence."

"It's true."

At the new voice, all but Wyat spun to face their intruder. Chesh frowned. It wasn't often he was snuck up on. Only because he'd been so focused on the damned lion in front of him did he miss the unicorn. Quite the pair, these two. They all should have known the unicorn would be close by.

Mal stared at Orn wide-eyed.

"Orni," Noli cried, reaching out his hands as if he were a child asking to be picked up. "They want to kill me."

Ornicun pressed his lips together. He and Noli had been lovers since they were children, much like Eagy and Ryph. They were also of the same mindset that they didn't need a wife if that wife wouldn't have them both in equal standing.

"You really ought to be more selective on who you trap, my dearest," Orn said.

Mal tilted her head to the side, curiosity bright in her eyes.

The two couldn't be more different. Where Noli looked like a person already on his deathbed, Orn was a god. Night dark skin with long silver hair and deep purple eyes. He was tall, broad, and a sight to behold. There was also a long, twisted horn in the middle of his head.

Chesh had heard that the horn was his hybrid form. But he'd never heard of Orn without it. Nor had he ever heard or Orn changing to his animal. This was Orn's only form, as far as Orn was concerned.

"Nobody is coming!" Noli wailed.

Orn nodded thoughtfully. "I'd appreciate it if you didn't kill him," he said, looking at Wyat. "He's a bit mad, but he's my heart and soul."

Ryph glanced at Eagy. Eagy met his gaze, the corners of his lips twitching up.

"He didn't mean anything by it," Orn continued.

"Perhaps not," Kav stated. "But when we told him to release us, he refused. Three times."

Orn sighed. He didn't advance to Noli. Shame, really. The little bit of hellfire Chesh had used had made his fire burn and he ached to pull on more. He'd forgotten what it was like to be a demon. To torture and burn and punish until his heart was content. He was so long in Laddenworn, he'd almost forgotten he was a demon.

Just a cat. That's what this damned world had made him. Until Mal came along and gave him something to care about.

But Orn was one of the more intelligent animals. He knew when he was more than outnumbered.

"Perhaps you'll allow a trade," Orn suggested. "Tell me what you want in return for my lover."

Kav pressed his lips together. It was clear that he wanted information. Chesh hadn't realized that Kav had known that

Mal's men weren't the biggest fans of him. By the way he pursed his lips, he knew that he was by no means a true member of this group. His opinion didn't really matter. In order to get what he wanted, he needed a good reason to convince the others to agree. And now, in front of Orn, he couldn't make his argument.

Chesh couldn't stop his grin from climbing up the sides of his face. Excellent.

"You start talking and if we're satisfied, we'll release your pathetic cub," Eagy said. "If not, you best think of a Plan Tea."

Orn nodded. "What did you want to know?"

Eagy looked at Kav. The surprised look Kav returned was almost comical. But he stood from where he was still crouched in front of Noli.

"He's mentioned 'minions of dark' and clearly this trap wasn't meant for Nobody. And since he's brought up Nobody, you might as well add that," Kav said.

Orn studied Noli for several minutes. He met Kav's eyes before looking at Wyat. "Is he hurt?"

"No, we're not hurt after he trapped us in a net of fire, but thanks for asking," Ryph growled, a hand absently rubbing his shoulder where it had been burned the worst last time.

Orn nodded. He glanced at Ryph before looking back at Noli.

You can say what you want about the unicorn, and there was a lot to say about the psychopath, but he loved his lion.

Maybe Eagy realized this, too. "He's not hurt," he said. "Just whining."

"I hadn't made it to the 'hurt' yet," Wyat growled. "But I'm certainly getting closer the longer I stand here."

"He's hunting the Poachers. The queens have offered a hefty reward for their heads," Orn said. "So, I suppose, the net was made for you." A dubious smile graced his lips as he met Eagy's eyes.

Chesh chuckled. He had forgotten the silly name the queens

had dubbed Eagy and Ryph when they had first begun to hunt the queens' soldiers.

"Although, your numbers have grown," Orn added, his strange eyes shifting over their group.

"I haven't heard anything about a reward for the Poachers," Kav said, frowning. "Not in many years."

"It's an old Call to Action, but we checked. It's still active. And we're interested in the reward." Orn shrugged.

"Fine. Next," Ryph prompted. "Minions or Nobody. Choose a topic."

"I don't know anything about either," Orn said.

Wyat reached down and grabbed a large fistful of Noli's hair, dragging him to his feet. Noli let out a howl, grabbing at Wyat's hand. This time, Wyat had caused pain.

Orn's face contorted as he took a step forward. Ryph and TL both pulled out blades and Orn stopped.

"Stop," Orn begged. "I'm telling you; I don't know."

"Your boy does, though," Wyat growled.

Chesh wasn't sure what Wyat did, but Noli's yeowls changed to something that was filled with agony.

"Please," Orn begged. "Stop hurting him."

Eagy bit his lip. Glancing at Ryph, he moved to Noli's side. After a thorough search and divesting him of all weapons, Eagy convinced Wyat to release Noli to him. Wyat was not in the least pleased about it.

Noli was bigger than Eagy by at least a hand. But there was no question that Eagy was stronger and more skilled. It would not be anywhere near an even match. Eagy could be an assassin himself.

Noli gave Eagy a smile, but Eagy shook his head. "I'm not releasing you." He pulled out his blade, pressing the tip firmly into Noli's neck. "I want answers and you want to live with your unicorn, right?"

Noli swallowed. His eyes flickered to Orn. "Yes," he

whispered, not shifting his gaze. "We're not so different in that, eagle."

Chesh wondered if Noli had intentionally left the 't' off the end of eagle. Appeal to the one thing Eagy couldn't change about himself. The thing that bothered him every day, that he was ridiculed for. The lion was calculating. Not as mad as he'd been making himself seem. Interesting.

"No, we're not," Eagy agreed. "That's the only reason you're not in Wyat's claws right now. But you best start talking because like you, I will do what I need to protect mine. And 'mine' has grown considerably. And *you* threatened that."

Noli took a breath. "The trees are talking. The flowers, too. Nobody stirring, and rolling, and stalking. He has put his fingers out. His minions. As he tries to get a grip. The dark is rising, the Beasts are retreating, he's preparing for his trip." His gaze flickered to Orn before meeting Eagy's ice blue eyes once more. "The Ten are moving, dancing, tasting. For what, they will not say. But Nobody moves, growing stronger, growing, growing, every single day."

Mal frowned, her pretty face puckering. Chesh smiled to himself, knowing she was now filled with a whole new set of questions. At least she had held off asking them.

And thus far, if they knew who she was, they hadn't given any indication. Since her imprisonment, she hadn't given them any arguments about being safer. More prepared. Not calling attention to herself. Chesh thought she'd readily wear a sack if it meant they could stay together.

"Tell me more about the traps," Eagy said. "How many are there? Who else are they set up for? Where are they?"

"If I tell you, I don't trap you," Noli whined.

"If you trap me again, I'll make sure Wyat tears you apart," Eagy countered. "And I won't lose tea over it."

Noli clearly struggled with the request. He didn't want to die. He didn't want to leave Orn, otherwise, Chesh wasn't sure he'd be as docile as he was.

"Answer him, Noli," Orn said, quietly.

Noli's face turned into a pout. "Ten, one for each. Designed for each. They catch the Poachers and carve out the Steele. Always at the M."

Eagy nodded.

"What do you know about Twenty-Eight?" TL asked.

Chesh was impressed that every member of their group managed to act like it was a casual question, just falling in line with the rest. Even Mal managed to look uninterested.

Noli's expression scrunched. Frowning, he said, "Nothing. I'm not tracking The One, Right or Wrong or Next."

"Orn?" Eagy asked.

Orn's attention was still fully locked on Noli. "According to the papers, she's still in Hart's dungeon."

"And what do *you* know?" Ryph pushed.

Orn glanced at him. "Don't you think if I knew something about anything, I'd tell you?" he snapped. "You have my lover. There's nothing else you can take from me that will make me talk to get it back!"

Ryph looked at Noli as if seeing him for the first time. His gaze traveled to Eagy and lingered for several minutes. Then, he was looking at Mal, at Chesh, at Wyat.

"Tell me something worth telling," Eagy said, "And you can have your lion back. Alive and mostly unhurt."

"I don't have anything to tell," Orn said. "You know what we know about Nobody. We told you about the traps."

"Gossip will do," Wyat suggested, taking a step closer to Noli and Eagy.

Orn sucked in a breath and started rambling anything he could think of. "There are troops in Childhood, digging through the rubble, searching for something. They're not allowing the residents to rebuild. There's a Patch moving around. The Duchess is trying to kill the Serpents but failing, quite spectacularly, actually. The Ten are underground or silent. Silent.

The queens want Steele taken out, but they're too big. That's all the gossip I know. Please."

"Nothing useful," TL said.

Mal frowned at TL. "Let him go, Eagy," she said, her voice low and indistinct.

Eagy looked at her, brow raised. Noli's eyes flicked to her as well. He stared, as did Orn, as if seeing her there for the first time.

"Angel," he said, "he would have turned us over to the queens."

She shook her head. "Maybe. But-"

"There's no 'maybe,' Bunny," Wyat growled. "They're a lot like the Sheep."

That was enough to make Mal look at Orn and Noli again. She inspected them, considered Wyat's words.

No one had argued Wyat's accusation, including Orn and Noli.

"Assassins for hire," Mal said, quietly. She hooded her eyes. "Let him go."

Eagy stared at her for several long heartbeats. They all did. All waited to see if Eagy would comply with her request. With her demand. He scrutinized her for a very long time.

Surprising them all, he pulled his blade away from Noli's skin, though he didn't pull it away completely. "I'll compromise, Angel. I let Noli go this time. But if there's ever a next time, we'll be having lion for dinner."

She frowned but nodded, nonetheless.

"Orn?" Eagy prompted.

"I agree," Orn said.

Eagy still didn't drop his blade. Over Noli's shoulder, he met Orn's gaze. "Not allowing Wyat to hurt him any longer was a courtesy. Not a weakness."

"I know," Orn said. "I am appreciative."

Eagy dropped his blade to his side, flipped it in his hand so the blade faced behind him, giving him a good grip if he needed to plunge it into someone's chest in close range. Noli didn't move, his honey brown eyes watching the hand the blade was in. Wide. Fearful.

"Go," Eagy said.

Noli didn't say anything or meet anyone's eyes. He turned and ran to Orn, flinging himself in Orn's arms. Orn held him close, a hand going to his lover's head.

"He hurt my hair," Noli whimpered.

"Don't play with gargoyles, baby," Orn tisked.

"He broke my fire," Noli whined, burrowing himself further into Orn's embrace. Orn nuzzled him, cooing soft assurances before answering.

"Best we find another hobby, hmm?"

Noli nodded. "Away from Nobody?"

"Of course." Orn glanced up. His eyes lingered on Mal.

Chesh couldn't tell what passed through his expression. Appreciation, perhaps. Gratefulness.

He gave Mal a nod and turned with Noli still in his arms.

The seven of them didn't move or speak for several long minutes, waiting for Noli and Orn to get away.

"That was a unicorn?" Mal asked eventually.

Eagy chuckled. "Yeah." He reached for Ryph and held him close for a moment, resting his forehead against the beast's. "You're not singed, are you? Burnt at all?"

"No," Ryph said, voice hushed. He trailed his hands up Eagy's arms, pushing at his sleeves. They weren't loose enough to push back, but it was enough to convince Ryph that Eagy was whole as well.

Wyat finally shrunk back down into his normal giant self.

"And Noli's the lion?" Mal asked.

"Yes," TL said. "N O L I. L I O N. Same letters, just twisted. As is he."

Mal's eyes widened. "Twisted!" she exclaimed under her breath. "The letters of the characters' names are twisted. As is all of Laddenworn. Which, if you rearrange the letters, *is* *Wonderland*! Damnit, Ache."

Chesh raised a brow. The others looked at her in confusion, as well. What did Ache have to do with anything?

Before anyone could get sense out of her, she turned on Wyat. "You're the white rabbit, aren't you?"

"I am a white rabbit, yes."

"But are you *the* white rabbit?"

He hesitated, considering her words. Finally, he nodded stiffly. "I suppose."

"But Wyat is not a twisted bit of white rabbit." She turned to Chesh and the others in the group. "Actually, none of your names are twisted."

"We're not very far along in the Madness," TL said.

Her eyes lit up. "Ohh. The maddests' names are a reflection of how mad they are! So, when you said Ache was quite mad, his name reflects that. Though, to be honest, I didn't find him that mad. Horny, sure. But he seemed pretty sane to me."

"Quenching the Absence gives you a limited reprieve," Kav supplied.

"He wasn't mad when he walked into the room and found me in his kitchen, drinking his tea and eating his biscuits, unannounced and uninvited."

"Trust me," Eagy said, "he's more than a little mad. He and Ahdem are long gone, especially when they're together. Ache can push it off for a time, give himself a bit of clarity in small bursts, but it comes roaring back and plunges him further. Deeper into Madness."

It was clear Mal wanted to argue. She shook her head but didn't say anything concerning Ache anymore. Instead, she moved on to a slightly different angle concerning madness.

"Okay, so, the madder they become, the more their name changes. So, of the lot of you." Mal paused and looked around her. She broke out into a glorious grin. "I have the sanest bunch of men in all of Laddenworn."

Ryph and Wyat laughed loudly. Chesh grinned.

It was true, to an extent. There were a lot of people who had managed to keep the Madness at bay, even with the Absence. But to find six men, equipped with the oddities and specialties that would serve Mal well in her endeavor to fix Wonderland back to its original state was pretty impressive, if Chesh did think so himself.

"And that means, your weird friend Lepa is all kinds of mad," Mal declared.

Eagy smiled. "Yes. That doesn't mean he doesn't know what he's talking about, or that he's unhelpful."

"He is a bit slow to answer," Mal deadpanned. "What are we at, four months now?"

Chesh grinned and turned towards the path. Lepa really did not hit the right buttons with her.

Rival came sauntering back into the part of the forest they were in before the lot of them headed on through the path again. He was still munching on bark, his dark eyes watching Wyat. Wyat had shown compassion bringing him furthest away from the fire with those who could burn easiest. Rival wouldn't burn easiest, but the gesture was not wasted on him, apparently.

"We have food," Mal said, watching Rival. "If you're hungry."

Rival looked at her for several long moments, still crunching the hard back. "It sharpens my teeth," he said, voice smooth and deep. "Being kept like cattle does not bode well for keeping my teeth healthy."

Mal nodded, watching him hesitantly now. "Are we feeding you enough?"

Rival's lip lifted, displaying those teeth. It was a smile. Chesh recognized it for what it was. Mal quirked her lips in return, so she must have been privy to the expression, as well. "Quite."

She nodded. It was clear she wasn't quite interested in turning her back on him, but she did so. His lips lifted again, head tilting to the side. Kav pet his neck, running his fingers through his mane, before turning them both back on task.

It was time they got out of this part of Silent. Away from the M's and Noli's traps. And away from the lion and the unicorn.

The Ten Children

MAL

13

They followed the invisible path for several more days. Mal spent a lot of time either searching for the so-called path or considering all she learned from Noli and Ornicun. She'd filled several pages of her Memorandum Book with all of their weird ramblings.

Nobody, which they spoke of as if it were a person. This also led into 'minions of the dark' in some way. Trees and flowers were talking, etc. All very odd.

Eagy and Ryph, AKA the Poachers, who the queens had a reward for. It was a "Call to Action" by the queens. Much like The Hunt for Twenty-Eight had been.

Ten traps. One of each and to catch Steele. Always at the M. Yep, sounded like a bunch of mindless rambling.

Troops in Childhood, digging through rubble. Not allowing anyone to rebuild. Now *that* was suspicious.

Patches were moving.

The Duchess was trying to kill the Serpents. At least she was failing.

The Ten were silent and/or underground.

The Ten.

"What are the Ten?" Mal asked.

"The Ten Children," TL answered from behind her.

"I need a little more than that."

Chesh grinned.

"The Queens' ten children," Eagy supplied.

"They have *ten children?"* Mal asked in disbelief. "How is that possible when the fertility is so low in Laddenworn?"

"There is Luck and Consequence. Mingle and Blend," Kav said.

Mal shook her head. "They have ten children together? How many for each?"

"No, it doesn't work that way," Kav said. "They're a remcule, the two queens and the two kings. The children are all of theirs. I couldn't even guess which child shares parents. Especially since I wasn't part of the palace when they were carried."

"Explain to me a remcule," Mal said. "It's the same as a harem? As my coterie?"

"More or less," Eagy said. "It's your family unit."

"Whereas a harem or coterie is...?"

"Your coterie is solely dedicated to you. They're your men are not committed to your family yet. It's a time to see how your dynamics work as a couple and as a family. Harem covers both the coterie and the remcule. Your family."

Mal nodded. If she understood him right, she had a coterie, not a remcule. But she was sure they were coming to care about each other. Eagy and Ryph obviously already did. But she was sure the four of them, Eagy, Ryph, Chesh, and Wyat were trusting each other. Looking out for each other.

"So, tell me about the ten. Who are they? How are they involved and why are they silent?"

"There's not much to tell," Kav said. "Even from within the palace, they're rarely seen and never heard. They were likely just tools."

"They used their children as tools?"

Kav nodded. "From what I understand. As I said, they're

rarely seen. Hardly ever spoken about. It's as if they don't exist, most of the time."

Mal looked at Chesh. "Thoughts, Cheshy-Cat?"

Chesh grinned. "My beautiful Kitten, I'm afraid the knave is right. Even when they were doing their parents' bidding during The Culling, they appeared as figureheads."

Mal sighed.

"Don't let them lead you to believe they weren't cruel," TL said. "Just because they were recruited to do their parents' bidding, didn't mean they didn't do it. Even if silent."

Wyat began to mumble a rhyme that Mal's ears barely picked up.

Children ten from Queens of Blood hear they doth declare
They shall seek and eradicate all that is quite fair
Then they ask, "Why should their land not be shaped to
please?
Time and Tym again, I mean, we've been in a freeze."
Although to clear it up, they did not have a choice
The Queens, they say, "rally up or you lose your voice"
So the ten rise up to meet the Queens greedy need
Get, strangle, quid and mangle, all have done the deed
In garden of hearts the children enjoy their pie
"This was quite gory," said Lily with a loud sigh.
Child Five and Four nod, as they enjoyed the treat
"Too bad that they're all dead. One was rather sweet."
Nine leaned in to whisper, "I hear that One comes near
That Boy Sheep, lover you know, I await to hear
But we should consider this new One a warning
And lay low until next -

"Are you sure that's how it goes?" Chesh asked, interrupting.

Wyat tilted his head. "Fairly sure."

"No, Chesh is right. I think you have a few lines mixed up,"

Ryph said, turning around and walking backwards as he studied Wyat.

"They've since not spoken," Kav said. "After the garden pies, only Lily has spoken."

"Who are the others?" Mal asked. "Their names?"

"I don't think they were named, except Lily," Ryph said thoughtfully. "That's the only name I've ever heard."

Kav nodded his agreement. "They're referred to by their birth order. Lily, Two, Three, etc."

"That's..." Mal shook her head. There just weren't words. Did not naming them mean they were conceived just to be tools?

Mal sighed.

WYAT

MAL HAD BEEN quiet since the discussion about the Ten. Which part had bothered her more? That the queens had been able to have ten children or that they used them for their own ill purpose? Or maybe it was just that they weren't named. Mal had gone on about Laddenwornians' twisted names the other day.

They were deep within Silence now. Wyat wasn't sure what they were looking for this far from the edge of the forest. The things they'd find would get more and more odd as they traveled.

Perhaps that was the point.

Were they still looking for magical objects? They'd be coming up on the Cravat Mountains if they continued along this trajectory for too much longer.

Actually, now that he looked around, they were close to the mushroom groves. Any moment now...

"Wow," Mal breathed, her footsteps faltering as the glow ahead of them got brighter. "What are they?"

Yep, mushroom groves.

"Mushrooms," Ryph said.

"Magic," Wyat offered.

A stream cut across their path, trickling over rocks that glowed, making the water itself look it was alight. The glow sent rivulets of light dancing through the air, only to be outdone by the mushrooms themselves.

The mushrooms were deep blue or bright red, the ribs giving off a soft glow. But because there were so many of them, the entire place was lit like it had its own personal sun. The mushrooms in the grove didn't tower over them as those in the rest of Silence did. They were still tall. Taller than Wyat in his stone body. But they didn't soar like the trees.

There were others, too. Little ones, about the size of his palm. The small green ones made the eater shrink. The gray/blue ones made the eater grow. He pocketed a few of them. Never know when they could be useful. In the grove, the ground was no longer covered in moss but smooth, round stones.

"Who lives here?" Mal asked.

"No one. Why?" Chesh asked, his nose lifted as he sniffed the air.

Wyat smiled at his inability to deny his cat's curiosity.

"The ground looks landscaped," she said. "The way the stones travel around the mushrooms. And look-" she stopped and pointed. All sets of eyes moved to follow where she indicated. "There are doors in the trunks of some of the mushrooms."

"Of course, there are," Ryph said. "How else would you harvest them?"

"But who put them there? No, wait. How do you harvest them? Do you eat them?"

The men laughed. Her curiosity was only ever outdone by her desire to right what was so wrong. It was humbling. And made Wyat want to hold her to him forever.

"No, no," Ryph said. "You don't eat them."

"Come here," Wyat said, offering her his hand. "I'll show you."

She placed her tiny hand within his, smiling up at him.

Her smile did things to him he really thought might be inappropriate right then. No one had ever looked at him the way she did. With trust. And affection.

He brought her to the nearest mushroom. A tall blue one with a door. It took Wyat using the sharp blade of his dagger and running it between the door and the jam for it to become moveable.

The mushrooms grew the doors. There was a theory that the mushroom grove used to be a town. A small settlement, where the denizens were using nature to make their homes. As Silence overtook this part of Laddenworn, it swallowed the town, as it was doing Wabe.

But the story says that the town that Silence overtook was filled with magic masters. Some say that they refused to leave and so they became the enchantment within the grove. Others say that when they abandoned it, they cast their magic into the grove. In doing so, they extinguished themselves.

Whatever the reality was, the mushrooms were overflowing with magic.

The door finally released; a wafting woodsy aroma filled the air. It wasn't overwhelming, but enough that it tickled his nose. Mal sneezed.

With a gentle push, Wyat opened the door.

The inside was illuminated with a soft lilac light, glittering and shimmering from the walls.

"It sparkles," Mal said, stepping in.

Wyat nodded. He didn't follow her in. Squeezing himself into the door would be comical. He'd take up most of the room inside, as well.

The shine from the walls played off Mal's hair and skin. She looked like she had been wrapped in a rainbow. Kissed by magic.

"This might be a good way for Mal to start working with magic," TL said. "She can use the residue here to learn the feel of it. How to call it and manipulate it."

Mal nodded eagerly. “Yes, teach me to use magic,” she said, looking at TL with a wide, excited grin.

TL put his hands up, taking a step back. “I teach physically. Not magically.”

Her smiled widened and she tilted her head. “I’m fine with your methods.”

Turning away, TL rolled his eyes. “You know what I mean, Sunshine.”

Mal’s playful grin lingered but she conceded, and her gaze moved on, seeking out who she thought might be the best candidate for a magical teacher.

Wyat watched TL thoughtfully. He was awfully hesitant where Mal was concerned. Staying as far away from her as he could. His bedroll was always directly across from her at night. He walked in the group either lead or caboose, so he could stay out of her reach.

“Come on,” Chesh said, stepping past Wyat in the door and joining Mal inside the stalk of the mushroom. “Run your hand along the wall, Kitten, and join me outside.”

Mal did as Chesh requested. Her hand came away covered in powdery, shining residue. She looked upon it with glee as she carefully followed him outside.

“Let’s try something simple.” Chesh reached down and plucked a nightshade flower from the ground. “These only bloom under the moon. We’ll see if you can make it bloom with magic.”

“I don’t know what it looks like when it’s in bloom. Does that matter?” she asked.

Chesh considered this, one ear shifting. “If you think you’ll work better that way, I’ll show you a bloom.” He held it in the palm of his hands and the deep blue petals opened. Slowly at first, gently laying out one after another as it spread wide for them to enjoy.

“Oh, it’s beautiful,” Mal breathed. “Truly.”

“In the night, they give off little songs of light,” TL said, frowning at the bloom. "I'd prefer if you didn't kill a bunch of them."

Chesh shook his head. "One more, Blossom. Promise." He handed over the bloomed flower to TL before plucking one more from the ground.

TL flinched and turned away once more.

"Rub your hands together," Chesh said. "Spread the magic between your palms and fingers. There you go. Now, cup your hands together."

As she did, Chesh placed the closed blossom in her hands. He surrounded them with his and purred, "Concentrate on what you want it to do. Visualize it. See it. Will it so."

Mal stared determinedly at the blossom. Her cute little brows puckered. Her delicate lips pinched together. When she scrunched her nose, Wyat grinned.

She didn't succeed. At least, not then.

Chesh spent the rest of the afternoon trying to teach her how to use the magic.

Wyat left them to it and sought out TL. TL was supposed to be on their side. Helping them to get Mal back where she needed to be. The farther away from Wabe they got, the more on edge he became. Trying to keep as much distance between he and Mal as he could.

Should that bother him? One less man to share her with.

That wasn't what put him on edge, though. There was something else. The way he wouldn't meet her eyes bothered him. He didn't even like to talk to her when no one else was around. Like she'd bite.

Personally, Wyat enjoyed her bites.

There was no accounting for taste, apparently.

Wyat wandered the bank, keeping TL in his sight as he walked aimlessly. Eagy falling in step silently next to him made him glance away from the Flower to meet Eagy's ice blue eyes.

"He's not working out as well as we'd hoped," Eagy said.

Turning his attention back to where TL paced by the river, Wyat nodded. "You feel it, too? Like he's hiding something?"

Eagy nodded. "Though I can't tell if I'm bothered by it or curious as to why he's keeping such a remoteness between him and the rest of us."

"Like he doesn't want to be associated."

"Or attached," Chesh said, coming up on Eagy's other side.

When they both looked at him, Chesh grinned. "Ryph's giving it a go." He shrugged. "Perhaps the beast reaches the magic a different way than I do."

"Attached to what?" Eagy asked, accepting Chesh's explanation as to why he left Mal.

"Us. Mal." He shrugged again. "He's keeping an eye on Kav, as we asked him to. We didn't specify that he needed to be companions with us."

Eagy sighed. "You think we shouldn't worry about him, then?"

Chesh raised a brow. "Do you actually want my opinion, Birdy?"

Eagy didn't meet his gaze for several strides. When he did, it was just a flicker of his eyes meeting Chesh's. "Yes," he said simply.

The demon cat's smile grew unsettlingly disproportionate. "I think we don't need to worry about TL and that you made the right choice in convincing him to join us."

Eagy nodded, his shoulders relaxing some. He glanced up to Wyat. "You?"

Wyat studied TL for several minutes. He thought about his animal intuition. Something bothered him. But was it a threat to any of them? To their mission? To Mal?

He didn't feel the prickling of warning. The accompanying dread. Not like he did when he observed Kav.

Though, perhaps, that was because of Kav's actions to her while she was in chains. Even then, the thought sparked a kindling of fury in him.

"No," he said, eventually. "I feel like he's hiding something. Like he's keeping something from us. But I don't think we need to worry about him. At least, not in the same sense that we do the knave."

Eagy nodded. "Okay, good."

Wyat was surprised to find Eagy stayed beside him and Chesh instead of returning to Mal and Ryph. He appeared deep in thought, dipping his fingers into the water. Once in a while, an image would swirl to the surface, but never solidify. As if Eagy couldn't focus on anything in particular.

A shout went up behind them and the three turned. Mal was jumping up and down with a ribbon in her hand.

"I did it," she shouted, spinning with the ribbon above her head. "And it's pretty, too!"

Ryph was grinning, clapping, beaming at her.

"What did she do, exactly?" Wyat asked.

Eagy and Chesh shrugged, but were smiling, nonetheless. They remained where they were, watching Mal celebrate. A few minutes later, TL joined them as Mal turned the ribbon into one of the long vines that hung like hair off the largest of the mushrooms.

The four watched silently as she tried again with the closed flower.

"Where's Kav?" Chesh asked, his fiery eyes remaining locked on Mal's efforts.

"Tending Rival," TL said. "He's being a bit whiny."

"Kav or Rival?" Chesh asked.

TL smiled. "Frankly, both. But I was referring to the tove."

"What's Kav whiny about?" Wyat asked.

TL shrugged. "I suspect he knows that I'm here to watch him, but he hasn't said anything."

"He might not think so if you weren't the only one acting like Mal was a disease," Chesh offered.

Stiffening, TL turned his gaze away from Mal's concentrated efforts on the blossom.

"You want me to fawn over her?" he asked, voice like a storm.

"No," Eagy said, looking at him. "I want you to sell the role you agreed to take."

"I agreed to watch Kav. That's what I'm doing."

Wyat looked at him. He was frowning. Defensive. His voice dark and cloudy.

Yes, he was hiding something.

Perhaps TL knew what Wyat was surmising for when he met Wyat's eyes, he frowned. "Look," TL said, "I don't want her getting any ideas. She's already a flirty little thing and if I make it look like I'm the least little bit interested, she tends to take ten more steps in that direction. I don't want her."

"You've made that perfectly clear," Eagy said. "And while I'm actually quite relieved, if we are to catch Kav in whatever scheme he's up to, it will only happen if he thinks he's free to do it."

"*If* he's up to something," TL said.

"You don't think he is?"

"You must have had a suspicion since you agreed to join us," Chesh added before TL could answer.

TL stared at them for several long minutes. "Fine," he snapped. "Make sure she understands this is an act."

He stood and walked back across the little rocky stream.

"He is hiding something," Wyat said. "But I agree with Chesh. He's not a threat to Mal or what we're doing. I trust in that."

Eagy went back to swirling the water. Again, faint images danced and undulated. Chesh and Wyat watched in almost a trance as the colorful pigments came together and burst apart over and over again. They were so deeply invested in the nonsense that Mal plopping down at Wyat's side startled him. Not enough to make him jump, but enough that he snapped his eyes to her.

She smiled up at him in that way of hers, making his heart flutter and his stomach leap.

"The water is magic, too?" she asked.

Wyat nodded.

"Put your fingers in," Eagy said, removing his.

Mal dipped the tips of her fingers into the cool water. A face appeared. A face that looked remarkably like hers but masculine, with short hair and sad eyes.

Wyat glanced at her to be sure he knew what she looked like. Yes, they were the same face. Mal's eyes were filled with tears, though none fell down her cheeks.

"Who is it?" Ryph asked gently.

"My twin. Reth."

"You left him behind in the Cold Lands?"

She nodded, whipping at her eyes. "He was at DeadEnd, too. He entered his own fairy tale the day I came here."

The image swirled away, disappearing into a rainbow of colors that danced and twirled until they coalesced again. This time, into ten faces.

They were grouped together as if they were sitting for a family portrait. Their hair varied from raven black to pearly white. Their skin ranged from olive tones to mocha.

But their eyes were all the same pools of darkness.

Around the ten faces, words appeared. It wasn't until one read "Lily" that they realized who they were looking at. The Ten Children. And as Kav had suggested, only Lily had a name. The others were called by the number that was their birth order.

And more horrifying than seeing their faces was that their lips were sewn together.

Wildflowers

MAL

14

The haunting image of the ten children made Mal truly reconsider them. Sure, they had been instrumental in the Culling, from what she'd been told. But they surely didn't sew their own lips together! But did that excuse them from their actions?

There was a fine line deep within this world dividing the cruel and the victims. Which side someone was on was never really clear. Often times, they tended to overlap.

The group stayed within the mushroom grove for several days while Mal attempted to work on magic wielding. Some things she was able to get quite easily, like changing the vines into ribbons and back. Others, like making a damn flower blossom, was not one of them. It was a constant frustration. Since she didn't think that making a flower blossom would make or break her career as a Fixer, she decided to let that one go.

Mal spent several hours throughout the days trying to conjure more glimpses of the Bloody Queens and their offspring. She wasn't specific with she wanted to see. Anything having to do with them was welcomed.

But besides the one image of the two sisters and their eight brothers with their mouths sewn shut, she hadn't been able to make any other images form. Seriously, nothing. Not even of Reth again.

"Do you think that reflected their current state?" Mal asked.

"Ornicun did say they'd been silenced," Kav said.

"No, he said they were 'underground or silent. Silent'," Eagy corrected.

"It doesn't matter," TL said. "Whatever cruelty they suffer at the hands of their parents does not excuse their actions. They were willing participants."

"There was a rhyme Wyat just recited that said if they didn't fall in line, they'd lose their voice," Mal noted.

"There was no knife at their neck forcing them," TL stated.

Mal didn't argue. Clearly, one of the children had wronged him. He had been their victim in one way or another. She nodded, since he'd been not quite so aloof lately. Like a smidgen less.

They hadn't left the mushroom grove far behind when music flitted through the air. Just a note here and there for a while. Then, bouts of laughter skipped to them.

"Great," TL said, rolling his eyes.

"Lorem?" Mal asked.

"No," Ryph said, crossing his arms. "He doesn't leave Tulgey, thankfully."

Eagy tried to hide his smirk behind his hand and a cough.

"Wildflowers," Wyat said, studying TL.

"And they're bad because..." Mal prompted.

"They're not bad," TL said. "Just a little... eccentric."

Mal made a face. Everyone in Laddenworn seemed a tad eccentric. But then, perhaps they thought that about her, too.

"Aren't you a kind of wildflower?" Ryph asked.

TL glared at him. "No," he deadpanned.

Chesh's grin reached his temples. Wyat hid his smile behind a hand. Mal couldn't stop hers before he saw it. TL rolled his eyes.

The wildflowers were eccentric. Their hair ranged from sunflower yellow to daisy white. Purples and reds and oranges and blues and pinks. Every color of the rainbow. Their eyes were just as varied.

Their way of dress was somewhere between the Songbird and Raptor villages. They wore long, flowing skirts – everyone, male and female. But their skirts were made of strips of cloth – or petals if you looked at them right. So, while they provided some kind of modesty while standing still, something they didn't appear capable of, everything was on display when they were moving.

And boy were they moving. There were four metal carts that held tall fires. Around the fires, the wildflowers danced, sang, and laughed.

As with every other place Mal had been to, there were few women. She counted maybe a dozen, which actually seemed like rather a lot. But there were easily nine dozen men. And no children. Not a single one.

Their dancing was rhythm-less for the most part but every few minutes, something would change, and they'd fall into perfect choreographed steps, completely in sync with each other. It was intricate and screamed of meaning. There was a language in each step, but it was foreign to Mal.

Rival came up beside her. His dark tongue poked out as he licked his lips. Mal chose not to ask if the tove ate wildflowers. She went back to watching their strange dance.

"What does it mean?" Mal asked, awed.

"It means there's darkness they're warding against," TL said, frowning.

Then, the steps broke apart. The seriousness left their dance and they spiraled and laughed and skipped about.

"I feel like we're spying," Mal said.

As if she were heard, an older man, perhaps the oldest man she'd met thus far in all her time in Laddenworn, approached them. Unlike the man who immediately wanted them to leave the un-Birthday party they'd stumbled across and needed to be bribed to be allowed to eat (and consequently groped on their way out), this man smiled widely as he neared.

"Hello, travelers. Care to join us for some tea?" he asked.

"Please," Eagy said, offering him a kind smile. "Thank you for your hospitality."

He was as tall as Eagy with bright yellow hair and dark brown eyes. "Sunny," he said, bowing his head. "Please join us."

The dancing didn't stop as Mal and her men joined the wildflowers. TL was very stiff and rather annoyed that they agreed to join them. Every now and then, someone would break off from their dancing to introduce themselves and sit for a chat.

After half a dozen had come and gone, Mal looked at TL expectantly. "So far, I'm not seeing why you're so uncomfortable."

"Wait for it," he said.

Mal missed when and who made dinner but before long, two large trays were set in front of them, piled high with a vast array of foods. Sunny and another older man with blue hair named Forgy sat with them. Three more joined sometime later, two women and a man, perhaps a little older than Mal. Late twenties.

Age mattered to women, considering it seemed to be solely what they based their husband-prospects on, so Mal made a point of trying to guess.

When they introduced themselves as Adde, Onnli, and Saydi, she thought that perhaps she'd overestimated. The girls were giggly, huddling together to talk quietly to each other. The man looked on protectively. And, if she had to guess, Adde and Onnli were siblings. They looked near identical, save the gender difference.

The three stayed with Mal and her men when Sunny and Forgy left. Their giggling and whispering died down and they sat back, relaxed.

"So, where you headed?" Adde asked.

"We don't have a set destination," Kav said. "Looking for someone." He tossed the nearby lounging Rival a few large scraps. Rival plucked them out of the air with a loud snap of his jaws.

"How long have you been here?" Wyat asked.

Saydi shrugged. "Days. We're on our way to Tulgey."

She sounded rather sad about it. Her eyes dropped to her hands. Adde appeared to mirror the sentiment.

"You want to stay in Silence?" Mal asked.

Both girls nodded. Curiously, Mal looked at Onnli.

He was a rather quiet man, with his puffed-up yellow hair and almond colored eyes. She didn't think she'd heard him talk yet. And shaking his head, he still didn't speak. But whether that 'no' was that he didn't want to go or that he didn't care that they were going, Mal didn't know.

A loud drum began beating in rhythm, echoing off the trees. There was an excitement that mixed with the beat as flowers abandoned what they were doing to gather around the fires again.

"Come on," Adde said, getting to her feet. She pulled her probable-brother and Saydi up, as well. "Come and join the dance."

"I'm afraid I don't know the dance," Mal said.

She laughed with Saydi. "You don't need to, silly. It'll teach itself to you."

"What are we dancing for tonight?" TL asked, like this question made a lick of sense.

"There's a darkness rising in Silence. We're dancing to make sure we have safe passage through," Saydi said.

Mal exchanged looks with her men.

"Come on," Adde repeated, holding her hand out Mal. Saydi did the same to Chesh. Onnli to Wyat and Eagy. Whoever they were closest to.

What harm could there be in trying to ward off darkness? Mal placed her hand in Adde's, allowing the girl to pull her to her feet. On her cue, the others did the same.

Mal took her place with Ryph, whom she somehow managed

to get paired with. He grinned his golden smile that always warmed her body to her core. With a glance back, she found Saydi with Chesh, Adde with Eagy, Onnli with Wyat. TL was with another flower who hadn't introduced himself, as was Kav.

"They don't seem too hung up on gender," Mal said quietly.

Ryph looked around before meeting her eyes, confusion coloring the beautiful brown. "Meaning?"

"Meaning, men are dancing with men and no one cares."

Ryph smiled. "There's a lack of women, Mal. And the dance is important."

"So, it's a show."

He tilted his head to the side, another question in his eyes. Before he could answer, Mal clarified. "Meaning, they do care about gender here as much as everywhere?"

He looked around again. "Yes and no. But I don't have much experience with flowers. You'd have to ask TL."

The dance started with a crescendo of drums. When the beat stopped to just a whisper, other instruments picked up. And before she could get nervous, her and Ryph were moving.

She didn't know the moves. Nor did she have any idea how she was successfully pulling it off. She felt like she was in a pornographic dance, the way their hands slid over each other, their legs wrapped here. A mouth there. Bodies pressed tightly together and spun apart.

Mal was sweaty under her long-sleeved shirt. Her heart jumped, skidded, stuttered with every touch Ryph laid on her. With the look in his eyes. With every sensual movement of her hands on his body, feeling the hard planes and muscles contract.

It wasn't soon enough when they turned in for the night. She was led to a tent, barely big enough for two. They made it hold three when Eagy joined them, soon after they had been stripped of their clothes.

Ryph was eager, as he always was, but Mal wanted him below her this time. He was an animal who preferred the top. Unless it was Eagy, in which case he took bottom. The thought made her smile. Her smile was swallowed by his mouth when he yanked her down to him.

His body was strong and hot. Not hot as in gorgeous, though that he was. All their dancing had him feeling like he was a good five degrees hotter than normal. She ran her hands up his chest to his shoulders, kissing him with as much heat and enthusiasm as he gave her.

When he tried to sit up, she shoved him back down. A low growl vibrated through his chest. She smiled into his kiss. "It's okay, beasty," she said in what she hoped was a solid purr. "I want to ride you this time."

Ryph groaned and allowed her to push him onto his back. A little scooching around and he was lying flat where he pulled Mal's leg over his hip. She settled, straddling what was more than ready for her.

Then, Eagy pushed the flap open and stopped. "Oh, good," he said as he started pulling his clothes off before he managed to get inside.

Ryph was already reaching between them, adjust himself to line up with her heat. He was not much on foreplay. Actually, she didn't recall him once getting into foreplay. She'd always meant to ask him about it, suggest it maybe. But by the time the thought had formed, he was already pushing deep inside her and her mind was a blur of pleasure.

Luckily, she was a very horny girl.

Now was no different. Ryph wasted no time pushing into her. He wasn't slow about it tonight. Sometimes, he fully sheathed himself in four or five thrusts. This time, it was one. His hands on her hips had him pulling her down as he thrust his hips hard. Mal cried out, gripping his forearms.

"Ryph," she moaned.

His answering grunt sent a heat through her that turned liquid between her thighs. He chuckled. Mal guessed he noticed the difference when he next shifted them for a repeat.

Eagy finally finished ripping his clothes off and pressed

against her, his chest firmly to her back. He shifted forward, bringing his cock to her ass cheeks.

"Can I?" he asked, breathing into her ear. His hands slid around her waist, washing slowly up her stomach to cup her breasts.

Unlike Ryph, Eagy was gentle. He performed the same motions Ryph did, but there was a bit more care to his actions than impatient and eager Ryph. When he pinched her nipple and pressed his hips into her ass, she groaned.

But she wanted something different this time. Still both of them. At the same time. But she wanted to try something different. Something new.

Mal pressed her hands to Ryph's stomach, trying to still him. He was not easily stilled. But his thrusts were distracting. Especially in this position, he hit that spot like a hammer on a nail head. Over and over and it drove her crazy.

"Inside with Ryph," Mal said, having managed to get Ryph to slow down. Just a little.

"Yes," Eagy said, reaching between them.

She was almost positive he hadn't caught her meaning. She was certain when she felt his head start to push into her ass.

Mal shook her head. "No, Eagy," she breathed, shuddering. He pulled back immediately. "*With* Ryph. Same place. Both of you at the same time."

"Can we?" Ryph asked, breathless. His hands tightened on her waist. "Really?"

"I don't think we can both..." Eagy trailed off.

"Have you seen Wyat?" Mal asked, glancing back. "Trust me, as wonderfully full as you two are, you can."

Eagy smirked and leaned his head against her shoulder, hiding his expression. Ryph laughed. She was immensely glad they weren't easily offended or threatened. She didn't always remember when to hold her tongue until she'd already spoken.

"Okay," Eagy murmured.

"Fuck, this is going to feel good," Ryph said, enthusiasm dripping from his voice.

Eagy nodded against her shoulder. After a moment, in which she felt his hand stroking himself (ugh, as if she could get anymore turned on), he gently pushed her down so she was hovering over Ryph, her face inches from his.

Aroused excitement made his brown eyes liquid gold, his smile wide with anticipation.

Eagy's head pressed against her, pushing to make room between her walls and Ryph's cock. She kept her eyes locked with Ryph, trying to relax her muscles. Damp down her own enthusiasm to have them both. She loved one on one. One right after one. But together, Mal couldn't get enough. Nothing made her hotter than having them both at once. Nothing was more satisfying than both at once.

Nothing.

His progress paused, his hand running along her thigh and hip.

"I'm good, Eagy," she said.

He chuckled behind her. "I'm not. Too soon to finish yet."

Ryph nodded, groaning. "Tell me about it."

"Fill me," Mal said in, again, what she hoped was a successful purr.

When they both groaned, she figured it had to be close. Or perhaps it was just her words.

Eagy did fill her. His pause ended and he pushed in with more force than he had been. Her body flexed around him, hugging him tight. Strangling them. That was probably a pretty accurate euphemism, since they both made strangled sounds of pleasure.

Their thrusts were out of sync, their rhythm leaving a lot to be desired. But it almost didn't matter. With Ryph pushed against her g-spot the way he was, each eager, hunger-filled move he made sent her tumbling towards her climax. The noises they made, how they moved against each other and with each other. Their hands on her body, holding her, holding each other. It all went straight to her libido and she came crashing with a cry of undiluted pleasure.

Eagy and Ryph seemed to have followed in unison. Eagy's hands on her hips tangled with Ryph's, giving him leverage to keep his grip and momentum up, dug into her and he stilled. Ryph's roar counteracted Eagy's quiet gasps as Ryph's wings fought to release from wherever they were hiding. They were rocked up, Eagy and Mal almost toppling off him, before he wrapped his tail around them both, keeping them anchored in place.

Who knew a tail could be so strong?!

Their last thrusts sent tendrils of heat racing through her before her body's strength finally waned completely and she lay on Ryph's chest. Both of them pulled out of her at once. Intentional or because of her collapsing, she didn't know. A moment later, Eagy lay on top of her.

Ryph wriggled under them. "Damn wings," he grumbled.

Mal grinned and Eagy chuckled.

"Need to switch?" Eagy asked.

Ryph nodded. "You'd think I could contain them since I've only had them my entire fucking life," he grumbled. His hand left Mal's side. He reached beside him and pulled his wing by way of a fistful of feathers. "Fun fact," he said, "Wings are useless when you're lying on them. Can't even get them to move themselves."

Mal laughed and wrapped her arms tightly around his chest. She dug her fingers into his feathers. He stilled, sighed, and wrapped his arms back around them both.

After several long minutes, in which she enjoyed feeling both of their hearts against hers, Eagy said, "Can we do that again?"

Mal grinned.

Chesh

HE WAS tired and worked up. Mal, Eagy, and Ryph had had an insatiable appetite last night. Not that he was at all surprised. The dance was always stimulating. Once upon a time, the dance led to many offspring conceived.

That was far before the queens. Before the freeze.

At least someone was getting some.

It felt like Wyat dropped to the ground with a thud when he sat next to Chesh that morning. His eyes, redder than pink in the firelight, were bloodshot. He looked rumpled. Chesh grinned at him. At least he wasn't the only one suffering from last night's voyeurism. The rabbit was just as worked up as Chesh was.

They spent the morning around the coals of a small fire with Adde, Onnli, and Saydi. The three told stories of wildflowers come and gone. Stories of old legend that even Chesh hadn't heard.

"Fireweed crept along the banks of the cliff, reaching for the fire in the sky," Saydi said. "But no matter how high he reached, he couldn't touch the fire. He crept up the cliff, higher and higher, until he was at the very crest. He stretched, lengthened his body, grew taller still. Until his body transformed into something bright and beautiful. Still he stretched on, his heart pining for the fire."

"He never managed to touch it, the sun," Adde added. "Still, it's said that fireweed only reproduce at the tallest elevations in their never-ending endeavor to reach the fire in the sky."

"I don't know if that's sad or endearing," Mal said.

Adde laughed. "It's not sad. Flower stories are mainly to entertain."

"Some tell our histories," Saydi said. "Of our vain existence."

Onnli rolled his eyes. "Not all are vain," he said.

His voice surprised Chesh. It was a deep whisper, chilling him as if it swayed in an early summer breeze.

"We are vain, but we're hindered in our preening," Saydi insisted.

Onnli sighed but didn't argue. He met Mal's eyes, his holding a hint of humor. Indulging humor.

"Flowers are beautiful, and we know it. We're bright and wild with the most intoxicating scents. Our lesser brethren are the pride of many gardens, you know," Saydi said.

She was referring to planted flowers. Not people flowers, of course. Details that seemed a little fuzzy to Mal, if her furrowed brows were any indication.

"But we can no longer preen without a reflection to perfect our petals," Saydi continued sadly. She raised her hand to her white gold hair and twirled a strand around a finger. "The best we can do is rely on each other to tell us how to preen."

"Or the watery image within the rivers and streams," Adde added. "But they lie."

Mal was immediately interested in this comment. If images in water was a lie, then perhaps the image of the ten children had been a lie. Perhaps they had names. Perhaps their mouths really weren't sewn together.

But then, what about her brother's image had been a lie?

"Why don't you have reflections?" Mal asked.

"We have reflections, silly," Adde said, laughing. "We don't have reflective surfaces. What are they called?"

"Looking glass," Onnli said.

"Oh," Mal said. She reached for her messenger bag over her shoulder and dug out her little pocket mirror. She handed it over. "It's small, but that's all I brought."

Adde accepted it with a hesitant smile. She flipped it in her hand a couple of times and thanked her, reaching out to hand it back.

So, pocket mirrors weren't a thing. Good to know. Mal grinned and popped it open, turning the mirror to Adde.

Adde's eyes went wide. She reached greedily for it and stared. For several long minutes, she stared silently, scrutinizing the image looking back at her. "Is this what I look like?" she asked, voice hushed.

Saydi leaned over to peer in, just as enthusiastically as Adde had. She backed away slightly to try and see Adde in the mirror. Finally, she said, "Yes. That's you."

"I'm..." she paused, looking at herself. "I'm.... beautiful."

Saydi nodded, grinning. "Can I have a turn, Adde?"

Reluctantly, she handed over the little mirror. Saydi was just as taken by her reflection as Adde had been. She didn't have to be coaxed to give up the mirror, though. Mal got the idea she rather preferred to look at Adde or Onnli. She offered the mirror to Onnli who shook his head, closing it and handing it back to Mal.

"How did they manage to get rid of all the mirrors?" Mal wondered out loud.

"Only one mirror was to exist in Laddenworn," Chesh told her.

"Let me guess, the prophetic one?"

Everyone around the fire nodded.

"So, I assume it's kept in one of the palaces, yes?"

"There's a verselet about that," Adde said. "I don't remember it, though."

"You never did pay much attention to your rhymes," Saydi said, grinning.

Kav sat forward, his voice smooth and soft as he repeated the rhyme:

"Inside the room, down the longest hall
Looking glass, looking glass, on the wall
Who in this land is fairest of all?

"The looking glass it doth reply
Willing ear and eager eye
All be fairer far and nigh

"The Queens paled the sunny sky
Echoes fade and Memories die.
All maidens slain in July.

"Still words haunt me, to take my prize
Moving under midnight skies
Never seen by waking eyes.

"No children, no maidens to hear
Eager eye and willing ear
Death took all far and near.

"Inside the room, down the longest hall
Looking glass, looking glass, on the wall
Who in this land is fairest of all?

"It is you, the mighty queen
All else life drifts on the stream
Life, what is but a dream?

"And we're back to Snow White," Mal murmured.

"The what?" Adde asked.

Mal shook her head. "Never mind. I'd like to get my hands on the mirror, though."

"Do you think it shows reflections or just tells you things?" Adde mused.

"Dark, evil things," Saydi said.

"Actually, according to the little ditty Kav repeated, all the mirror did was answer a question. What the queens did with it was what was dark and evil," Mal said.

The two looked at her, their heads tilting to the side as if caught in a wind. Onnli grinned.

Their talk turned to lighter things for the remainder of the day and into the evening. Once again, they joined the dance to ward off the spreading darkness.

And, once again, Chesh was left frustrated in the morning. This time, Wyat didn't join him in his frustration. He'd had their Mal last night while Eagy and Ryph enjoyed each other. That left Chesh alone, still hard and irritated.

They awoke to an empty camp. A place where it looked like nothing had ever been. No traveling wildflowers with their erotic dances and tall fires. Their drums and songs and an abundance of food.

Chesh missed the food.

They hadn't packed the tents Chesh and the others had used. That meant they'd acquired three tents.

And three lingering wildflowers.

Adde, Saydi, and Onnli were gathered under a mushroom, gingerly picking apart some bread and cheese. The two girls were scratching Rival between bites while Onnli pleated his mane down the length of his neck. Adde looked up when they approached with a huge grin on her face. She offered them her food. "Want some? We have more."

"Where'd they leave to in such a hurry?" TL asked, suspicious.

"You don't feel it?" Saydi asked, placing her hand flat on the ground.

A moment later, all but Mal bent to feel the ground. Ah, there it was. The steady rhythm of marching feet. A very large group was traveling. And since the wildflowers had taken off, they must have been heading this way.

"That was a little rude," Mal said. "You'd think they'd be decent enough to wake us and warn us if something was up."

"It's not Bloody Soldiers," Eagy said. "No need to worry."

He was frowning, though. Annoyed. Worried, no. Wary, absolutely.

"Who is it, then?"

"Steele," he answered. "A warning really would have been appreciated."

"Sorry," Adde said, bowing her head.

"Not from you," Wyat said. "But why are you here? You know we're Mal's coterie, yes?"

Adde laughed. "We're not interested in you," she said, waving her hand flippantly in the air. "No offense, but you're just not my type."

"Any of you," Saydi added, though she eyed Mal for a moment.

"Then...?" TL prompted.

"I know we should have asked first, but we'd like to accompany you. You haven't been very forthcoming with what you're up to, but it has to be more meaningful than wandering around endlessly and without purpose," Adde said.

TL sighed. "Great."

Steele Warriors

MAL

15

Mal was actually pretty psyched to have a couple of girls around. It had been so long since she'd been around any. Months. Had it been a year yet? No, perhaps half a year. It was hard to tell when she didn't have anything to keep time with. The watch from Wyat that he made her start again told time, but it seemed to tell time on a different scale.

Some days, it was slow. Others seemed to skip whole hours. But at six o'clock every night, it told the correct time.

She couldn't get much out of her men about Steele. Just that they were annoyed they'd be running into them. Not annoyed enough to get back to walking, though, apparently.

Chesh and Eagy moved the tents closer to the tree Adde, Saydi, and Onnli were under while Mal built a fire. Ryph and Wyat went to gather more wood. The three wildflowers had been left with an abundance of food. While they stored most of it away and out of sight, they prepared enough for breakfast.

It was mid-morning by the time the front of the contingent came into view. Mal still couldn't see a path of any sort, but they seemed to be following a natural bend within the trees. One that took their whole line about fifty paces in front of their little encampment.

They wore a mismatch of armor. She recognized the Bloody Soldier pieces, as well as the Collectors of Madness. But there were others as well. Black and copper. Charcoal and pearl. Crimson and blush. Bone and ivory.

Their weaponry was an array of strange pieces she'd never seen before and blades of all shapes and sizes. For the first half hour, they marched by on foot. Then, animals popped in here and there. A tove. Some weird bird thing. A flamingo.

A cart pulled by something massive came creaking through next, breaking up the neat rows of men in arms. It was a closed cart. Mal assumed it carried provisions. How do you feed a large army?

More men followed a second cart.

When that cart had cleared, Mal thought the army had passed. There was a break in bodies. As she was sitting back, ready to go on about her business of internal debates on how to fix Laddenworn, more men came along.

These weren't dressed in armor. Not metal armor, anyway. They wore something Mal thought resembled older armor. Leather, maybe. Thick hide.

They were cleaner, better groomed. Their weapons looked newer and shiny. She wondered if they'd ever been used. Each one rode on a tove.

She didn't need to guess who they were. These were the 'officers' of Steele. Those who considered themselves more important and therefore were allowed more luxuries than those who actually did all the work.

Behind them came more men. All marching on foot. Wearing the mishmash of sullied armor and carrying a hodgepodge of weapons.

Mal also didn't need to guess who was in charge. He sat stiff backed on the back of his rusty tove, conversing quietly with another. Unsmiling with dark hair and darker eyes. His hair was on the longer side, a strand falling into his eyes, which he casually brushed aside with the back of his hand.

He must have felt Mal staring, for he looked up and met her eyes as they passed.

That had been a mistake. He broke from the group and strode into their little camp. Two others broke off behind him. One was the man he'd been speaking to. The other looked exactly like him, but with shorter hair.

Well, they were beautiful. Shocker.

The longer haired brother (twin?) stopped a few feet away and continued to stare at Mal. He didn't speak. None of Mal's men spoke, nor did they move.

When he swung his leg over and landed on his feet, the man he'd been conversing with waved at the contingent behind them. A holler went up and passed down the ranks as the company came to a halt.

Finally, the staring man looked away. His dark eyes scanned Mal's men, the lounging tove, and the three wildflowers.

Likely making a guess, he settled on Eagy. "I hadn't realized you were extending your ranks, Poacher."

Eagy shrugged. "You're getting louder, Meddul."

Meddul made an annoyed face. "Hard to teach animals how to walk in silence."

"Since animals hunt in silence, maybe you're just not fit to encourage them to continue to move silently," Eagy countered.

"Poor leadership," Ryph agreed.

Meddul glared at both of them. "I hear you had a failed run in with the Sheep. I wouldn't be bragging if I were you."

"True. But we've recovered what was stolen, gained a few more friends, and destroyed over half the Sheep. I say we're ahead, if it's a competition," Eagy said.

Men and their pissing contests. Mal rolled her eyes. She tuned them out and looked at the man Meddul had been talking to while they marched.

He was nothing spectacular to look at. Blond hair, green eyes.

Scruffy around the edges. There was an arrogance in his posture. Meddul had the same arrogance, but it was creepier in the blonde man. When he met Mal's eyes, he smirked.

Yep, he thought he was something special.

Mal casually looked away, hoping it would bother him. Petty, sure.

The brother sat on Meddul's other side but where blondie was a few paces back, the brother was in line with Meddul. The only difference in this man was that his hair was cropped shorter. More military-like than wannabe model.

He was looking at Mal. His gaze was not like blondie's. When Mal met his eyes, he smiled. It was amused, kind. He glanced between his brother and Eagy and rolled his eyes before meeting hers again.

Mal grinned back. She was going to like him.

"That's Lede," Chesh whispered in her ear, leaning in close enough that his breath tickled her neck. "Twin to Meddul. Not quite such a slithy mome."

She'd suspected 'slithy mome' was an insult. Having never heard that particular phrase, she assumed it was something worse than their usual 'daisy'. Mal tilted her head toward Chesh. "The blonde?"

"I think his name's Itle, though I don't know for sure. Meddul's favorite changes at least once a week."

Meddul must have heard him because he left off his pissing contest to glare at Chesh. Lede grinned again but tried to hide it behind his hand. Blondie scowled.

"Just a little, Cheshire puss," Meddul deadpanned. "Talking too much."

Chesh's eyes flashed. "Bait me, Lesser-of-the-twins." His tail flickered behind him as a sudden heat filled the air, bringing with it a surreal teal glow. The toves stepped about nervously. Even Rival picked his head up. "You lost your muchness when you traded it for your army."

Meddul glared, pressing his lips together.

"And now they barely follow," Chesh continued. "Don't think I can't feel their desire to desert you. I might be stuck here, but I am what I am. And *you* are close to losing it all."

Lede slid off his tove in time to catch Meddul from lunging at Chesh. "Easy," Lede murmured. "Our men are watching."

"Yes, a pity that," Chesh purred. "You almost showed them how truly weak you are."

Wyat grinned. "Truly a pity."

Somehow, and Mal completely missed how it came about, Steele set up camp around Mal and her men and friends. Since Meddul insisted that his tent be set up in the clearing that theirs were, he would have his army surrounding them for greater protection.

Eagy refused to allow them to be surrounded. "If you're worth anything, you can protect yourself."

Meddul growled, "The leaders must remain standing to give orders, even if the others fall!"

"Or they could lead by example," Mal suggested.

Meddul barely glanced at her. In that glance was a clear dismissal.

Lede hid another grin.

It seemed that Meddul was all about arguing when he didn't get his way. Eagy didn't give him an inch, though. He maintained that if he insisted on joining them, they'd be abiding by how they'd set camp.

"Since you invited yourself, you can compromise," Wyat said.

"There's no compromising happening," Meddul insisted. "You're simply refusing me my preferences."

"You're one man. You don't need two tents."

"One is for conferring with my men away from prying eyes," Meddul insisted. "It's necessary."

"Necessary for hiding something. Why would you hide your plans with the men who have chosen to follow you?" Chesh asked. "What are you hiding from your men?"

"I'm not hiding anything," he growled back. "They don't need to be involved in everything. It would take ages to make a decision. And frankly, there are few who are qualified to make decisions for the whole."

"But you are. Naturally," Ryph drawled.

Meddul pressed his lips together, his shoulders stiffening.

"Aren't you self-important?" Mal commented as she stirred the fire.

Meddul stiffened. The look he gave Mal was scathing. She felt quite proud of that accomplishment. Before he could make his cutting remark, Wyat wrapped an arm around Mal's shoulders. His sexy accented voice was deep and threatening. "Careful, Lesser-twin. She can cut your throat without pause, but I will simply tear it out."

Meddul didn't respond. Wyat's assertion made him study Mal a bit more thoroughly. Still, he dismissed her.

In the end, Meddul was allowed one tent, which he was forced to share with his brother. Blondie, Itle, was not allowed a tent within the little clearing. In fact, the 'officers' weren't allowed to sleep in the clearing at all. Nor were they allowed to circle the perimeter.

"Who do you think is here?" Eagy insisted, rolling his eyes.

"No one yet, but there could be. The queens have been trying to take us out for years," Meddul answered proudly. He even managed to puff up his chest.

Mal mused that he really deserved to be taken down a peg. Even Rival snorted at the comment.

While the men bickered – and by men, she meant Meddul – with whichever of her men denied his ridiculous demands, Lede had moved his way in and sat next to Mal.

"You're a Tweedle," she said as way of greeting.

Lede grinned and nodded. "I'm the rational one. Lede," he said, offering his hand.

Mal noted it was the first time someone had offered to shake. Was he from the Outside? She took it, but he didn't shake it. He closed his fingers around hers and brought her hand to his lips, pressing them against her knuckles.

Heat rose to her cheeks, simply because she hadn't expected it.

She extracted her hand and glanced away. Wyat and TL were both watching her with Lede. She smiled and turned back to the show in front of them. At the moment, it was Meddul versus Ryph to see who would be able to build a fire. A redundant point, perhaps, since Mal had been tending a fire all morning. One which was still burning. Meddul was insisting on bringing over a smoker and grate. Ryph was refusing.

"Is he always a jerk?" Mal asked.

Lede shrugged, chuckling. "He doesn't mean it. It's been a long time since he was challenged."

"You mean outright denied," she pointed out.

He laughed this time. "Absolutely. Maybe it'll make him remember why we started Steele."

"He's forgotten?"

Lede sighed. "Not quite so drastic, but he has lost his focus. The good he's done... well, it was long ago. Our men have forgotten and now look upon him as not much better than the queens."

"He's going to lose them."

He nodded. "Sooner or later. And when that happens, the queens will have him. He likes the perimeter because he'll be alerted before any Bloody Soldiers have penetrated the camp enough to get near him."

"Their lives are expendable," Mal spat.

Lede bowed his head. "You and I both know they're not. Med knows he's about to lose them. He's got this crazy idea that if they know The One is out there, they'll rally again."

"The One is out there. In the queen's dungeon," Mal said.

He looked at her, meeting her eyes and holding her gaze. "So the paper says," he said softly.

"You don't believe it?"

Lede shook his head. "Not anymore. Seems my brother was right about that, at least."

"Meaning?" she prompted, her heart kicking up a beat.

"Meaning if she was still in the dungeons like the papers claim, she'd be dead. Her body would be on display as all the Wrong Ones before her. Med theorized that they don't have The One."

"And you believe him? He is kind of a pompous asshat."

Lede tilted his head to the side. The telltale look of not understanding what she'd just said blossomed on his face.

Great, she thought. If she hadn't given it away before, she had now.

Mal rolled her eyes. "So, say you find this One. Then what?"

"Med thinks all they need is a little encouragement. Something to remind them that they have a mission and the time is coming to act. The One's presence seems like that sign, no?"

"And that will just make everybody fall into line?"

"Yes."

Mal and Lede looked up. She hadn't realized they'd gathered a crowd. The bickering and arguments had stopped as Mal's men, the wildflowers, and Meddul and Itle had gathered in front of Lede and Mal.

"Say that were true," Mal said, eying him warily, "You think The One's existence in Laddenworn is really enough to what? Bring their spirits up?"

"It's been a long time since we've had any hope," Meddul said. "They don't have the confidence that they're able to win. When you're already convinced of your failure, you give a little less, so if things go bad, you can still escape with your life."

"But their lives are expendable," Mal said.

Meddul nodded. "I know you're trying to make me look like a daisy-"

Wyat snorted.

Under his breath, Ryph mumbled, "You do that all on your own."

Meddul continued as if not hearing them. "- but lives will be lost. If it means I lose all my men but kill the queens, it will be worth it."

"As long as you survive," Mal deadpanned.

He shook his head. "I don't think my life is worth more. But if I'm gone and we don't kill the queens first, who is left to take up my mantle?"

"Because you've been so successful thus far."

"I have done good. What have you done?"

"Gathered some strong-ass men to help me take down the queens."

"You believe you're The One, then?"

"I believe I'm a better person than you. Unlike you, I don't value my life over theirs. Unlike you, I value theirs more than my own. Unlike you, I'd lay down my life to make sure they survive to see another day. I don't give a flying fuck if that makes me The One. At the moment, I'll consider being better than you a giant feather in my cap."

When everyone around her looked at her in confusion, she knew she'd used a few too many metaphors that they didn't understand. But by Meddul's reddening face, he understood enough.

Her men and her wildflowers were grinning ear to ear, triumphant in her win. Even Lede fought not to smile. For many long minutes in which Mal savored the fact that she had put him in his place, Meddul remained silent.

He remained subdued throughout dinner. He didn't speak to anyone. If Mal had known any better, she would have been prepared for the after-dinner sequel to Asshat of Steele, episode one.

"With your woman as a figurehead, we could take out the queens next week," Meddul said, eyes locked on Eagy.

"I am not a figurehead," Mal said.

Meddul ignored her.

Eagy shook his head.

"I have the numbers. We need a unifier. If your girl is The One, that will be the catalyst to get them back on in the right place," he continued as if she'd never spoken.

"If your numbers were so great, you'd have succeeded long ago," Chesh said.

Meddul shook his head. "Every story, every ballad, states that we need The One. Without The One, we can't win. But with her, we can. It would have been a fruitless endeavor. But we can win, now. All we need to do is borrow her."

"Fuck that," Mal spat.

"Just for a week," Meddul told Eagy. "She won't be in any danger. The troops need to see her. Need to see that we have The One among us."

"I'm not-"

"Maybe not even a week. You can join us if you'd like. Officers. Generals. Knights. A gargoyle and a gryphon would certainly be welcome."

Ryph growled, his golden eyes darkening. Perhaps he didn't like to be talked about as if he weren't there, either. As if he belonged to someone. Even if that someone was Eagy.

"I won't even let anyone touch her."

That was it. Mal stood suddenly. Meddul looked at her as if just seeing her there for the first time. With her still hot tea in hand, she threw it in Meddul's face before taking her blade and putting it to his neck. He was surprised enough that he stilled, looking at her wide-eyed.

"Let's set this straight, Lame-twin, or whatever it is they call you," Mal gritted through her teeth, "I am not an object for you to borrow and use how you please. I don't belong to-" she cut herself off, having a brief flash of memory. Last time she'd said something about not belonging to anyone, she'd canceled all her coterie out. With frustration, she looked at Eagy. "Can I say it?"

Eagy smiled humorously and bowed his head. "We will fix it later if we need to. Say what you want, Angel."

Satisfied, she faced Meddul again, digging her dagger a little deeper. She didn't miss the drop of blood trailing down his neck. "I don't belong to anyone, fucker. If you want me, you can ask me."

She turned, dragging her dagger harshly across his neck, and left their little group. Crouching inside her tent, she stripped away her outer layer of clothing and lay down. It wasn't late. Not nearly late enough to sleep. But she couldn't stand to look at that arrogant jackass for another minute.

The Dream Child

MAL

16

She was irritated when Steele was still there the next morning. Mal was secretly hoping that they'd disappear in the night, like the wildflowers had.

Speaking of wildflowers, the three that had hung around were surrounded by a group of Meddul's officers. It looked like Onnli was trying to field their attention, but the girls were definitely not going unnoticed. And neither looked like they were happy about it. Saydi even looked a little fearful.

By the looks on the officers' faces, they were much like Itle. Arrogant. Entitled? Sure, she was judging, but by their expressions and laughter, she didn't think she was far off the mark.

Mal found Wyat at their campfire, stirring up the coals for their tea. Can't have tea without hot water. Can't have a morning without tea.

"Will you do me a favor?" Mal asked, leaning on her toes to give him a kiss on his cheek. Luckily, he was crouched over the fire so she could actually reach him on her own.

He smiled, giving her lips a peck back. "What's that, Bunny?"

"Rescue our wildflower friends from the assholes, please."

Wyat looked over her shoulder where the three were

cornered under a mushroom. His head cocked at 'assholes', but he didn't need a further explanation. With a nod and a severe grin, he stood and made his way to the group.

Mal sat where she had a nice view of Wyat. Before he'd reached them, Lede sat next to her.

"About to be a show?" he asked.

She nodded. "I don't like the people you hang around."

He chuckled. "I don't choose the Inners."

"Let me guess. Your Lesser-brother does."

With a wide grin, Lede nodded. "It's Lesser-twin, I think."

She shrugged. "Shocker."

Whatever Wyat said to the group of Inners made them all take steps back. Mal was pleased to see, and also sorely disappointed, that none of them found the gumption to actually challenge the big man.

"Pity," Lede said as the first slinked away.

Mal laughed, amused that he had thought the same thing. Or at least she thought that was what he was talking about.

Wyat gestured to the edge of their clearing, a clear command that they stay out. One had the nerve to look defiant. Wyat's cuff on the side of his head sent him sprawling and knocked the look off his face.

He turned with the three wildflowers in front of him as they made their way to Mal and Lede. Eagy and Chesh had taken up seats in the moments that Mal was watching Wyat's confrontation.

"I think I missed it," Chesh said. "Perhaps we can request a do-over?"

Lede grinned. "Please do. Would you ask Meddul? I'd love to see his face."

Ryph joined them as Wyat and the flowers arrived. "Whatever I missed, I think we're going to hear about it," Ryph said.

Sure enough, Meddul had just stomped his way into the clearing.

Mal sighed. He was such a tool.

The flowers sat, one on each side of Onnli. Wyat remained standing, his arms across his chest. Sitting as they were, he looked even more imposing than usual. Seven-foot forever must have that affect.

"What makes you think you can put your hands on my Captain?" Meddul demanded.

"What makes you think your piece of trash has the right to put his unwelcomed hands on my Flower, here?" Wyat countered, gesturing down to Adde.

Meddul didn't look. "He wouldn't do anything that wasn't welcomed."

"It wasn't welcome," Adde said. "He didn't seem to care when I told him 'no'."

Meddul, again, didn't spare her a glance. "She's unhusbanded in a group of available men. What do you expect-"

"You forced your company on us," Eagy snapped. "Keep your cocks in line or get the fuck away from us. End of discussion."

Meddul stared at him. Before he could say anything, his gaze moved to his brother sitting next to Mal. "You allowed this," he accused.

"No, you did by letting them get away with their behavior. I'm not your toady, Med, and I never will be."

Meddul was fuming. He turned on his heel and stomped off, flicking the hair that fell into his face away with a rough jerk of his hand.

"There aren't many who can get under his skin quite like you, Eagy," Lede said, chuckling.

"How do you stand him?" Ryph asked. "As Mal says, he's a tool."

Lede sighed. "He's my brother."

"Too bad," Eagy said. "You're really too good for all this." He waved his hand in the direction of the troops gathered around.

"Aww," Lede cooed, "I had no idea you liked me as much."

Eagy rolled his eyes. "Don't flatter yourself, Tweedle." He reached for the kettle and made himself some tea.

"I wouldn't dream of it."

"How long has this Steele thing been a thing?" Mal asked.

Lede looked at her, tilting his head to the side.

"When was Steele started?" Chesh clarified.

"The Culling," Lede said, studying Mal with scrutiny. "Not that I didn't believe you before, but your strange phrases certainly emphasize you're from the Cold Land."

"I'm not exactly hiding it," Mal said. "And at what point in the Culling did your misogynistic brother decide to gather a group of incels and pretend they're the good guys?"

"I don't know what half of those words mean," Lede said, frowning. "But I'm assuming you're not singing his praise."

She rolled her eyes. "Not in the least."

He smiled. "I swear to you, he's not always a... misogynistic brother of incels."

Mal laughed at the way he tried to string the words together. And the expression on his face when he contemplated the words.

"Although," he amended. "Since I'm not really sure what those things are, I don't really know if he is or was or isn't one."

"Tell me when Steele started," Mal said. "Never mind the rest. Trust me when I say he is this and those who are his favorites are, as well."

Lede nodded hesitantly. "About the time the rivers flowed red with blood."

"That's not very clear."

He nodded. "Listen to The Culling, then:

"I am bored, old friend of mine," the Hart Queen said,
"And what's more, the worlds ugly afright;
And yet we sit here, staring out, my dear Redd
Do you want to spice it up, tonight?"

"Queen Redd nodded, pond'ring, staring at the sun
A wicked smile did curl her lips vain
She replied heartily, "We should have some fun,
"Do tell me, how shall we make our reign?"

"'Twas a tale brought forth by a child before
I recall, do you remember that?"
"Dream Child told of those that hearts adore
But, do tell, what do we do with that?"

"In my youth, I was quite fine, with curly locks
I kept my limbs and vessel supple
Oh they came and begged with mighty hungry cocks
I divulge, I enjoyed a couple

"Alas my youth has gone; my looks are quite weak
For be nothing better than suet;
But my mind is clever, there is more to seek
What say you, shall we look into it?"

"Redd smiled slowly. "We make and write the law,
Proclaim our change by word or sharp knife
And with our strength, we will eliminate flaw
With their hearts and blood we will gain life."

"With the glass, we'll weed them out, I do suppose
Not one fairer maid will live; ever!
We'll cull them, Far and near, right beneath their nose
My dearest, you are awfully clever."

"Pawns lined up, small and tall, covering the sky
To purge the land, make it thick as mud
All maidens, fair and not, prepare yourselves to die
For now all rivers flow red with blood.

It was premeditated," Mal noted. "This isn't the first time I've heard about the 'Dream Child.' Who is it? Or is 'what is it?' a more accurate question?"

"My guess is a 'who', but I couldn't begin to know," Lede said.

Mal looked to those around her. Her men and the flowers.

"In our stories, the Dream Child is called Alice," Adde offered.

"The Alice?" Mal asked.

Adde looked at her with question. "Opposed to?"

Mal laughed. "No one, I suppose."

She let the conversation drop for a time while she pondered this. Did Alice think she was dreaming when she was here? Was that why they referred to her as the Dream Child?

Did Alice call herself the Dream Child or was that a name Wonderlanders gave her? So many questions and no one seemed to have answers.

Mal watched those around her converse. They were in a decent mood, despite the asshat troops just a couple hundred paces away. She was happy to see that the wildflowers were okay, too. They hadn't been cowed too much by the jerks. She hadn't seen the officers actually put their hands on Adde, which was probably a good thing. She'd have gone over herself with a blade drawn and to hell with it all.

As Lede laughed at something Wyat said, he swayed and leaned into her, bumping his shoulder to hers. She hadn't realized he was so close. A smile curved her lips as she looked at Wyat's big, white ears.

Her mind wandered back to Alice. It had been a dream for Alice. She woke up. That was how she escaped. In the second book, she stepped into and out of the Looking-Glass.

Was that the real reason the queens broke all the mirrors?

No, wait. The Looking-Glass brought her to another place entirely. The Looking-Glass house. And if her theory was correct and another fairy tale had infected this one, the Snow White looking glass had to come in from Outside. And if Alice was really here and left, she had to leave from somewhere. A different looking glass than Snow White's?

But what if there was a leak? Something streaming in keeping the infection strong?

"Maybe that's why the Culling, Round Two was starting," Mal murmured.

Around her, the men's chatter stopped, and they all looked at her. "Sorry," she said. "Thinking out loud, apparently."

"What Round Two?" Lede asked.

Mal opened her mouth to answer when Meddul caught her attention in the distance. She met Lede's eyes and pressed her lips together. She actually liked Lede, but he was his brother's man, wasn't he?

Lede bowed his head, guessing what she was thinking. "Look," he said, quietly. "Despite having different methods, our objectives are the same." He met her gaze. "We want the queens destroyed. If this is pertinent to that, sharing information will go a long way."

"What information have you shared?" Eagy asked.

"I don't get involved in that. Not in planning, strategizing, researching." He shook his head. "You want that information, you'll have to get it yourself. Sorry."

"Useless," Ryph said, grinning.

Lede smiled back. "I like to fight. Not so unlike you."

"Okay," Eagy said, getting to his feet. He sighed, looking at Meddul and his cronies warily. "Let's do some investigating. TL, Kav, Ryph, want to join me?"

The three got to their feet, leaving Wyat and Chesh with Mal and the wildflowers.

"I'd really love to see Eagy use his talons," Chesh mused. "He doesn't use them enough."

Mal was sure he was speaking metaphorically, but Mal agreed. He didn't sink those in nearly as often as he should.

EAGY

"THEY OKAY ON THEIR OWN?" TL asked, glancing back to where Mal sat.

Eagy frowned at him. For someone who had no interest in Mal, he sure was concerned about her safety and their ability to keep her from harm.

"You think they can get by Wyat and the demon cat?" Ryph asked, looking back and considering his own question.

"I suppose not."

"At least not without us hearing it," Kav said.

Eagy walked through the Inners without giving them much thought. An eaglet might not be all that imposing, but a gryphon was. A tiger lily wasn't anything to scoff at, either. Kav? Well, Eagy just didn't want him hanging around Mal. It was easier to keep an eye on him when he was in the same vicinity.

Meddul was standing over a table with maps littered over the top. There were marks all through it, making it almost illegible. Was that even of Laddenworn?

Meddul looked up when the four of them stopped. "What?"

"Start talking," Eagy said. "You can begin with why you bothered to stop at our camp."

"You think you can come among my men and demand an answer?" Meddul said incredulously, straightening to his not-that-impressive height.

"I think if you want to keep face, yes," Kav answered before Eagy could. "You've already had your ass handed to you several times since you arrived. Might as well tell us why you're still hanging about."

Meddul's face heated. From anger or embarrassment, Eagy wasn't sure. Either was fine.

"You have The One," Meddul said. "We need her."

"First off," Ryph said, "her name is Mal. And the more you

refer to her as an object, the less likely she's going to be willing to help you."

"Regardless of the fact that you're on the same side," TL pointed out.

"Second, we don't own her. If she wants to join you, it's her choice. You will ask her," Ryph said.

"And before you get any ideas, she is ours," Eagy said, holding Meddul's dark eyes. "And we will not hesitate to tear you all apart to protect her."

"We won't put her in danger," Meddul insisted. "I really only need to borrow her."

"Again, you... misogynistic incel... she's not an object we own," Ryph growled.

"What does that even mean?" Meddul said, anger coloring his voice. "I'm not trying to buy her from you."

"It means you're lower than scum," TL offered, though Eagy was sure he didn't know what the words meant, either.

"I wouldn't put it past you to try and purchase her," Kav said, crossing his arms. "So, let's talk. If you have anything worth offering, maybe we can talk to Mal about teaming up."

Eagy looked at him, lids drooping. He was sure Mal would not team up with Steele. She was pretty hateful of them and how they treated the wildflowers that morning. Not to mention the way Meddul had treated her all day the day before.

Then again, he didn't really think Kav meant that.

Meddul blew out a breath. "Fine," he said, moving closer to the table. He pointed at the map, indicating several red marks throughout Laddenworn. "There are Bloody Soldiers amassing around the outer towns. We think they're recruiting."

By recruiting, he really meant forcing Laddenwornians to join their army.

"There's also talk of the queens training animals as troops."

"What animals?" Kav asked.

"Borogroves. Toves. Flamingos. I've even heard rumors of a few Jabberwocky, Bandersnatch, and Jubjub birds. I haven't actually seen any evidence of this, but the talk has been pretty consistent."

"That might explain the Jabberwock in Childhood," Ryph said, absently rubbing the back of his arm.

"The one that burnt it to the ground?" Meddul asked.

Ryph and Eagy nodded.

"We were there when the Jabberwock attacked. It was... rough. Ravaging. Frenzied," Ryph said. "It looked like it had been in a fight with multiple Jabberwocks."

Meddul frowned.

"That's the second one reported like that," one of his Inners said. "There was one outside Vile half a year ago in similar shape."

Meddul rubbed his face. "I'd hoped those were rumors."

"What else?" Eagy asked.

He shook his head. "New armor is supposedly being made, though I haven't found evidence of that, either. But, again, it's a consistent rumor."

"For the animals or the soldiers? And what is it supposed to offer them?" Kav asked.

Meddul shook his head again. "No idea. As I said, I haven't found evidence. No forges. No excessive mining." He shrugged. Looking at the map for a while, he paused in his conversation.

Eagy could see how tired he was. Perhaps he did think he was doing good. If he wasn't such a daisy and allowing his Inners to be worse, Eagy might actually encourage teaming up with him.

Or not. A group that large drew attention to itself. The queens always knew where Steele was. But they would make decent allies. If they were decent people.

"Go on," TL prompted.

"There's not much else to tell. The Ten are apparently silent or underground. I heard that the Soldiers burned a Patch to the ground. Otherwise, nothing new." He met Eagy's eyes. "I really think you should join us."

"Your backwards attempt at Mal is wasted on me. I told you, ask her," Eagy said.

"You know she won't agree," Meddul said.

"After you've been such a gentleman," TL said.

"I'm trying to free our world, not play in a sandbox."

"And to think" Ryph said, "had you not gotten off your tove with a tea bag up your ass, Mal probably would have been all for this. She's more than determined to fix our world, Meddul. You have no one but yourself to blame for her refusal to go along with your demand."

"Ryph, we need her more than you do," he said.

"And if you ever so much as lay a hand on her, I will personally sink my talons and my claws, and my very sharp teeth into your flesh. Are we clear?" Ryph growled.

Meddul had the intelligence to be frightened of Ryph's threat. Because it certainly was a threat.

"Mark my words, Meddul. If at any time you touch her, it won't just be me you answer to. And I won't rest until I shred you into tiny ribbons."

Meddul turned away, looking at his map. "I have an army. We have the strength. All we need is... Mal."

Eagy was impressed that he actually used her name. He was not convinced Meddul saw her as a person. She was a tool to him. An object for him to exploit. And still, he refused to simply ask her. He might have been surprised.

Then again, after he defended his Inners actions against the wildflowers, probably not.

"You need a lot more than Mal," Kav said. "You need to get your Inners in line. Give your army someone to actually look up to instead of disgusting toads. Show your men that you're worth something. Instead of wandering around thinking you're better than the rest of Laddenworn, make yourself beneficial and do something for the people you're actually trying to free from the queens. Then, perhaps you can convince Mal you're not a tool and worth her time."

"We don't have time-"

"There's time if you make time," TL said. "Right now, not even your Inners would follow you in a real fight. Only your Muchier-twin would, and that would be just to keep you from dying."

The anger that rose in Meddul was pretty spectacular to witness. His face was almost purple, he was so mad. It really set off his eyes.

"The world has been crumbling for centuries," Eagy said. "You want to get Mal's favor? Prevent the Soldiers from burning anymore Patches. Stop the Duchess from trying to murder the Serpents. Actually do good."

"I don't want her favor," Meddul grit out. "I want her presence."

"And that is exactly why you'll never have either," TL said.

Eagy shook his head, disappointment thick in his chest. It would have been nice to have an army behind them. That could certainly increase their chances of keeping Mal alive. But at the cost of having to put up with Meddul and his Inners.

Not a damned chance.

They returned to the campfire where Mal was laughing, huddled close to Lede as he showed her something in his memorandum book. Her laughter filled the air again.

Eagy would be surprised if Lede left with Steele when his brother finally gave up and moved on.

The Hatter and the Hare

MAL

17

"No," Mal said, her arms crossed.

"I need-"

"No," Mal said again, interrupting Meddul.

It was the third morning Steele had been there. At least this morning, it looked like they were packing up. Meddul was leaving all the heavy lifting to everyone else while he insisted that Mal join him.

"You're The One. I have-"

"No."

"I-"

"No!" she insisted, drawing it out. Emphasizing the sound of each letter.

His face started to change colors as he looked at Eagy. Mal really enjoyed making him angry. Especially when he was acting like an entitled jackass.

"You have to understand," he told Eagy, "we can win this together."

Eagy shrugged. "I told you. She isn't a piece of property. If you can get her to agree to join you, we will."

Lede leaned his weight on one leg. His arms were crossed,

but he brought a hand up to cover the grin as Meddul turned almost purple with fury.

"Let's go, Med," Lede said, taking Meddul's arm and gently urging him toward the tree line.

"It's not fair," Meddul told him. "She's being obstinate and condemning us to failure."

"Not wanting to be a part of Steele does not mean she's being obstinate," Lede reasoned. "Come on. Maybe some time to think about it will work in your favor."

"Work in my favor?!" Meddul stopped and spun on him. "I'm the good guy!"

"Right now, you're just a jackass who might have at one time been a good guy. But finding yourself more important than those who fight under you doesn't make you a good guy. Doing a couple of good deeds many years ago doesn't give you a lifetime pass as a good guy," Mal said. "You want to be the good guy? Why don't you help the Patches rebuild in a protected environment? Or support the Serpents in defending themselves from the Duchess. Because right now, I have less than no interest in helping you or getting your help. I'd rather try it on my own."

Meddul stared at her, a vein throbbing in his neck. "You'll regret this," he growled. "I swear you will." His gaze was hard as he spun on his heel and stomped off. Lede grinned at her, mirth bright in his dark eyes.

She was a little sad to see *him* go, at least.

Mal watched as Meddul argued heatedly with his brother before jumping onto his tove and taking off down the line to catch up to his officers.

Lede shook his head and turned back to Mal. She smiled at him. He sighed as he made his way back. Her heart did a little dance.

Chesh nudged her towards Lede. She glanced back at her men. She was surprised to see even Eagy had a hint of a smile. They approved of Lede?

When she faced Lede again, her lips parted, but no words came out. How do you ask someone to be a part of your coterie? Or even to join her? She hadn't had a problem asking TL. Certainly not Wyat or Chesh. But then, she hadn't really been asking Chesh or Wyat to be a part of her coterie when she'd asked for them to join her mission. And somewhere inside her, she'd known TL would say no.

But Lede was different. She genuinely liked Lede. He was the first person she'd met where she didn't only want his help in her endeavor to right Laddenworn, but she wanted him to be a part of her life. Intentionally.

Her lips moved again but, foolishly, she couldn't find words. Her cheeks reddened and she closed her mouth.

Lede smiled, bringing his hand up to the side of her face. His thumb rubbed her cheek, his calloused finger sending tingles through her skin.

"I can't," he said. "If I leave now, my brother is going to get himself killed."

Disappointment flared in her stomach like a lead ball and she tried to turn away. He didn't let her, though, bringing her closer with his free hand on her waist.

"I promise, Mal, the next time we meet. And there will be a next time. Let me get him straightened out. He might be a... what did you call him? A misgonist inctel?" She laughed despite herself but didn't bother to correct him. He didn't know what it meant, anyway. "But he's my brother. And believe it or not, he was a really good guy at one point. I need to remind him of that before I leave him for you."

Mal nodded. "Alright," she said, her voice quiet. "Next time we meet."

Lede grinned. He kissed her forehead, his lips lingering for several heartbeats, before he released her and returned to where his tove waited. Mal could see the tove's mouth move as Lede climbed on its back. Whatever it said made Lede smile. He waved and disappeared among the marching men and trees.

Mal watched for several minutes. "Tell me, *was* Meddul a good guy at one point? Truly?"

"He was," Chesh said. "As the rivers ran red, he and Lede began hunting the soldiers. He saved many families from their blades. He rebuilt villages and towns. He helped supply the newly homeless or bereaved with essentials. It's how he amassed a loyal following."

"What happened to him? Absence?"

They laughed behind her as Mal continued to watch the Steele men march on.

"Disappointment. Once, they thought they had The One. Steele made a gutsy move to dethrone the queens. He failed and the Wrong One died. He's had several plans since then, all of which end in failure. With each failure, he becomes a little madder, and those who once would have gladly followed the Hero-twin to his death, now aren't quite as confident in him."

"Is he mad? Is Lede?"

"Hope is a drug and when hope begins to die, the Madness begins to take root," Wyat said.

"Lede never held much hope. He enjoyed the fight. He relied on his anger to lead him right. Meddul was the Justice-Bringer, while Lede was the Truth-Teller. The death of hope has caused Meddul's Madness to rise and his sense of right and wrong to blend. He tries to fight it off, but he's not as successful as he'd like to think he is," Chesh said.

"What's a Justice-Bringer and a Truth-Teller?"

"Justice-Bringer has the ability to determine who is truly at fault and what the right punishment is for their exact crime. He was quite good at it. Bringing balance to the lawful and the lawless. A Truth-Teller has the ability to know if what you speak is the truth. He also has a hard time telling an untruth because of it," Eagy said.

Both very useful talents to have.

It was late afternoon when the last of Steele marched on,

before evening tea, when they could no longer hear the steady march of their feet. "They really aren't quiet."

"It's their size alone that keeps them alive," Eagy said. "The queens have their soldiers spread too thin around Laddenworn for them to actually be a threat to Steele."

"That is likely the only reason the men of Steele remain with Meddul," Chesh added.

They spent another night in the clearing, giving Steele plenty of time to get out of the area and assure that they wouldn't run into them again.

After a quick breakfast the following morning, Mal, her men, and the three wildflowers set off again. Still, with no real destination except to look for Wally and wait on Lepa's reply.

It felt good to have so many around her, supporting her and believing in her. Though TL was only there in a strange capacity with his hesitation to be around her. Or even talk to her, some days.

His focus in the evenings had been teaching Adde and Saydi basic blade work so they would be in a better position to ward off unwanted advances. He gave Mal reps to do until she couldn't feel her arms.

They walked most of the day until they came to a very familiar house. Since Mal still couldn't distinguish any trail within the trees or moss, she had no warning they'd happen upon the house with two rabbit ears.

She was happy to see Ache had added the additional support beam needed for the roof. It was level now, even if the hole wasn't completely patched. The chimney on the one side was once again smoking. Faint laughter reached them from behind the house.

Ache wasn't alone this time.

Her heart jumped at the sound of his deep laughter. Part of her still wished he'd joined her. He'd make a good addition to her group. He was a big gargoyle. Surely, two gargoyles were better than one.

Except that she recalled that Wyat was one of the gargoyles who did not work well with others. When it came down to it, she would choose Wyat. The big bad rabbit had hopped his way into her heart.

They paused on their way by, listening to the clink of porcelain and bursts of laughter from the back.

"Would it be rude to say hi?" Mal asked.

"He'll recognize you this time," Chesh said, a hint of a smile reaching his lips.

It was probably his big rabbit ears that had picked up their voices. The laughter in the back stopped and a moment later, Ache wandered around the corner with Ahdem at his side. Ache was only slightly more dressed this time than the first time she met him. His sweats hung low on his hips. Real low. Low enough that that enticing V of his stomach lead straight down to the base of his barely hidden, half hard cock. She thought his tail was likely above the waistline, too.

Ahdem was dressed similar, his pants just as low, revealing just as much. Except he wore the same hat he'd been wearing at the Mad Tea Party she'd attended months ago. A dusty, feathered thing, with rich purple ribbon over a worn maroon. Sticking out of the ribbon was the sales tag, 10/6. Ahdem was that classically handsome mixed with model gorgeous. The vacancy in his eyes did nothing to take away from it. If anything, it added to it.

Ache grinned as he made his way to them. "Well, my beautiful little girl, you did stop by next time you were in the area, as I asked you to."

Mal grinned, her cheeks reddening before she could even try to stop herself.

"Although, I hadn't expected quite so many additional guests," he mused, dark cocoa eyes passing over the nine others and a tove with her. She couldn't tell if he was upset about it or not.

"Perhaps we should invite them to tea," Ahdem said, his deep, smooth voice oddly hypnotic.

Ache's ear twitched, a brow rising. "Yes, yes. Of course." The smile he gave Mal was nothing short of sensual. "Would you care to join us for some tea?"

If rabbits could purr, that would have been a purr.

Mal looked at her men. Eagy was studying Ahdem and Ache with squinting eyes. Wyat and Chesh seemed amused.

Eagy's gaze met hers. With a slight raise of his shoulders, Mal turned back to Ache and agreed.

The corner of Ache's lips quirked up. He took a step to the side in time with Ahdem, as if they planned it, and they both gestured towards the side of the house.

There was a stone path leading around the side of the house Mal hadn't noticed the last time she was there. It was well manicured, large slate stones with moss weaving around them. She followed them back to the cutest garden she'd possibly ever seen.

A white picket fence with arched arbors on either end circled the quaint yard. The fence was covered in flowering vines. The vines climbed up the arbor and hung over like a waterfall. Around the inside perimeter of the fence were elaborate flower gardens. Dominating the yard was a long table.

Unlike any version of Wonderland she'd read or seen, the table wasn't a mismatch of furniture and porcelain. A single white, wooden table was surrounded by matching chairs with cushions. The table was set with more than a dozen places, pristine tea sets in front of each.

"This is beautiful," Mal said, stopping at the gate.

Ryph reached in front of her and unlatched it for her. Apparently, she'd been standing behind the gate, staring. Stepping through felt like she was entering a magical world. A different world, far removed from Silence.

"Should I sit anywhere specific?" Mal asked.

Ache pulled out a chair for her next to the head of the table. "Right here."

This time, she was sure that was a sensual, suggestive smile.

Mal returned it with her own as she took a seat. Ache sat next to her and Ahdem across from her. On her other side, Wyat sat. The rest of her men and the wildflowers circled the table. Rival laid in a flower bed to nap.

"We have been card plays," Ahdem said, holding up a set of very large cards. "Care to card?"

His silver eyes seemed to penetrate somewhere deep within her, even if it were an absent stare and only vaguely in her direction. The slight tilt of his head and barely half a smile was damn sexy. Why did he have to be mad?

"What's the pay per round?" Wyat asked.

"Lowering beats the highering drink," Ahdem said as the cards shot from one hand to the other in a waterfall.

Mal really hoped someone planned to explain.

"The drink?" Eagy asked.

"Sense Switch," Ache said.

Her group made a variety of agreeing motions. She trusted they wouldn't have her playing something too mind dulling.

Ahdem nodded curtly and tossed the cards in the air. They soared through some acrobatics, sending lightning bug lights blinking in the air before each person had a card set face down in front of them. A single face up card landed in the middle, along with the remainder of the deck in a perfectly neat pile.

With a gesture of his hand, Ahdem had each teapot raise in the air and spin in circles as they rounded the table. As they came to a stop above a new spot, they poured a cup of tea and lowered to the table with a light clink.

He had an impressive amount of magic, for sure. She wondered if he was too far into madness to teach her.

"Flip," Ache said.

As everyone else did, Mal reached for her card and flipped it. They weren't cards like any other playing cards. There weren't suits or numbers, but they were filled with varying degrees of color. Hers was perhaps three-quarters purple.

Mal glanced at Wyat's. A little more than half filled with orange. The one in the middle had hardly any gray.

"What a soaring last card for hand," Ahdem said, reaching for his teacup. He raised it, his absent gaze directed towards Mal with a damn sexy grin lighting his lips. "Tea down." He raised it into the air in her direction as if to clink glasses.

Around the table, everyone picked up their teacups, raising them as Ahdem did before bringing them to their lips and sipping. Mal did as everyone else.

The tea was warm and sweet, the aroma going straight to her senses. For a moment, she felt like she did a spin in her seat. Or perhaps just her head spun on her shoulders. Placing her hands on the table to steady herself, her ears were filled with soft bells of tinkling porcelain.

"Oh," she said. As soon as she spoke, the smell of musky woodsmoke filled her lungs.

Wide-eyed, she looked at Ahdem. His silver eyes met hers as the brush of a feather whispered up her arm. She shivered as heat rushed through her. Damn, he was beautiful. The smile on his face suggested he knew he was.

Before she could get a grip on what was happening, her senses returned to normal. The vagueness in his eyes had dulled as the wooden table beneath her hands no longer filled her ears with bells.

A deep, steadying breath later, Mal looked at Eagy next to Ahdem. "What the hell was that?" she asked.

He grinned. "Your senses switch for seconds of ten with each sip."

"Is it the same for everyone?" She refused to look at Ahdem. By the smirk that tilted his lips, she could only guess that, perhaps, they were.

"Not necessarily," Ache said. "Some teapots hold the same brew, while others are different."

"Are we going again?" Saydi asked with a wide grin.

Her men's eyes were on her. "I don't have to be the one to make decisions for us, you know."

"We weren't sure if you liked it," Eagy said.

"Oh. We can go again," she said, feeling her body heat up in anticipation.

Ahdem didn't appear to do anything to make the cards gather in front of him, but they flew through the air as if he called them. Two seemed to fight over which would be on top of the pile. Ahdem tisked them. Subdued, they put themselves within the middle of the pile, several cards between them.

Mal vaguely wondered if they were the playing cards turned warriors within the stories. Or was it strictly Ahdem magic?

They went through the same motions again. Ahdem tossed them into the air. They danced and twirled before one fell neatly in front of each person. A gesture later, new teapots of different teas filled their cups. At Ahdem's command, they each flipped. Mal's was filled with green. And once again, they cheered their drinks and sipped their tea.

This one was clearly a different kind of tea than the last. Her head didn't spin on her shoulders, but the world felt like it tipped on its axis. Mal closed her eyes. The tilt had made her feel nauseous.

She hadn't meant to touch the table this time, but her hands automatically reached for it to help her ride out the dizziness. No sound accompanied the touch. Instead, she tasted strawberries and cream cheese spread, making her mouth water.

It was so strong, she 'mmm'ed. The sound filled her with the scent of cedar. It shouldn't have complimented the strawberries, but it did in a very intoxicating way.

Before she could open her eyes, her senses righted, and the world settled.

She wasn't sure if that one had been more pleasant than the last.

As she was going to comment, a noise filled the air that set her teeth on edge. A sour note filled her lungs as her brain rattled in her head.

Chesh stood abruptly as everyone with animal ears covered them and cringed.

"Fucking whiskers," Ache growled.

"What was that?" Adde asked, voice filled with fear and trepidation.

"It sounded like..." Chesh trailed off.

"Like what?" Eagy asked.

"Hell."

The Goatman

MAL

18

"Hell?" Ryph asked, his head tilting like a curious animal.

"Think the place where bad people get tortured for the rest of time," Mal offered.

Chesh glanced at her. A bemused smile flickered, but he was distracted trying to hear the sound again. It was so loud, he didn't really have to strain to hear it. They'd all hear it if it happened again.

"I feel like we might already be in Hell, then," Ache said, leaning back in his seat.

"No, this is worse. I mean, you're physically tortured continuously for eternity."

Ache looked at Ahdem. A thoughtful, sad expression lingered as Ahdem absently looked his way.

"I maintain my assertion," he said quietly.

Glancing at Ahdem herself, Mal wondered if the madness was painful. Did they feel it? Or was it painful to watch someone you care about lose themselves deeper to it all day? Which would be more torturous?

She didn't argue again.

After several long, quiet minutes in which they waited, the

sound did not come again. Chesh frowned. Except that, as he was sitting down, it filled the air once more.

This time, it was worse. Her eyesight blinked in and out of focus. It felt like a static shock; every hair on her body stood on end. This time, everyone put their hands to their ears as it shrieked and wailed.

"We need to go," Chesh said when it ended.

"Must we?" Adde asked. "I don't wish to be tortured for eternity."

"Then stay here," Eagy said. "We'll come back for you when we've found the source."

Both girls looked nervously at Ache and Ahdem. Maybe not nervous about being left behind. Nervous about being left with them.

"Will they be okay here?" Mal asked Ache.

Ache waved a hand flippantly in the air. "Here or not, I care less."

Mal frowned at him. He was a lot more attentive when she was here last. Had he fallen that much deeper into madness since she'd been here?

His dark cocoa eyes looked up into hers. They were clear. There was none of that vague, absent look the others lost to madness had. It made her wonder. Was it an act?

He tilted his head slowly, a whisper of a smile spreading across his lips. His ear twitched.

No, he wasn't mad. He was uninterested.

"You don't mind?" she asked him, a little more quietly. As if she were having a private conversation with him instead of a public discussion.

He leaned forward, reaching his hand towards her face. A gentle brush of his fingertips across her jaw reminded her of the man she'd spent the night with. "No," he said. "They will be safe and untouched when you return for them."

Mal sighed. Smiling, she thanked him.

"As will you, if you wish to stay," he offered. "Safe, I mean. I do not promise untouched."

This time, she grinned widely. "I need to see what it is. This is my story to fix, you know."

"I don't know. It is our story that you walked into," he countered.

Mal looked at her men around her. Eagy with his fierce protection. Ryph with his big heart. Wyat with his soft nature hidden under all those watches and stone. Chesh with his happy knowledge and sincerity. TL and Kav were harder to place in her heart, if they belonged there at all. But her coters...

"I'm invested now," she told Ache when she met his eyes again.

He bowed his head.

As the sound filled their air again, Mal got to her feet with her hands over her ears. She was at the gate with the others when it had passed. Looking back, she assured the wildflowers they'd be okay. Rival heaved himself to his feet, brushing his body against Adde's as he joined Mal and her men.

Neither Eagy nor TL looked convinced, but Mal trusted Ache. He'd had a pretty open opportunity to prove that he wasn't to be trusted when she was there last. He didn't. And he'd sent her off with food and drink.

They walked for a long time. Quite regularly, that gods-awful sound filled the air. It didn't seem to get louder or quieter, no matter which way they walked. Mal wasn't certain they were walking any which way in particular. She thought that they were just walking. Paths did not make themselves known to her.

Mal was quite sure they weren't going to find the source. She was proved wrong when they came across the first tree that looked like it had been burnt from the inside out. Its leaves looked the same. Its trunk was twisted like a candy cane.

"Treachery," Chesh said.

After the next bout of torturous sounds, they came across a

second tree. This one had branches sticking out of it like a pincushion. A dark liquid oozed around each spear-like branch.

"Violence," Chesh said.

A third and fourth tree were still bubbling as if they were boiled in acid. The odor supported this theory, although their roots were still firmly in the ground

"Heresy," Chesh said.

"Levels of Hell?" Mal asked.

The others looked between the two, lost and wary.

"No. Punishments."

It was then they found a man. Chesh sucked in a breath, his steps faltering when he came into view.

His back was toward them. The only thing they could see was his hand on a tree because he was covered in a black cloak, the hood over his head.

"It can't really be," Chesh whispered, his voice awed. His fiery teal eyes were dancing.

The man turned and Mal's heart almost beat out of her chest. He had a goat head. The sign of Satan. She swallowed and very subtly, took a step back.

"Good evening," the goatman said.

For several breaths, no one said anything.

"Hello," Eagy said eventually. They'd all been waiting on Chesh to speak, but Chesh was stunned into silence. "I don't suppose you're the one making that horrible screeching?"

"It's not coming from me," the goatman said, clasping his hands in front of him at his waist. "But I am afraid I'm causing it."

"Why?" Eagy asked.

"The sinful need to be punished, don't you think?"

Chesh let out a breath.

"What is 'sinful'?" Ryph mumbled in her ear.

She shook her head subtly. Now didn't seem the time to answer when the possible devil was standing in front of them.

"There are worse sins than the trees can commit," Mal said quietly. "The queens, for example."

"But that is not my responsibility. I punish the already committed. Not the committing or yet to commit," the goatman said.

That might as well have been the equivalent to 'not my job', in devil speak.

"What could the trees have done?" Eagy asked. Glancing at him, Mal thought he was speaking to himself more than anything.

"Treason. Heresy. Violence."

Eagy looked at Chesh. His lips twitched, as if he meant to smile. But he looked too starstruck to smile.

To a demon, the devil must be like a god.

"How are you here?" Mal asked. "Not that I mean that to be rude," she quickly added. "I mean... were you summoned?"

The goatman looked at Chesh. "No," he said. "I'm looking for the vein. It felt strongest here. One's work is never done."

Mal frowned. Even another from the Outside was incredibly vague when answering. Why was she even surprised?

"They are not all bad," the goatman said. "Some are even redeemable."

This seemed like a waste of time. Not that tea was a particularly a good use of time. But really, what were they to glean from this goatman who may or may not be the devil?

"It runs deep," the goatman said. He tilted his head as if listening. Chesh's ear swiveled outward. "Very deep from very far. I must chase it."

Then, he was gone.

Mal looked around, startled. He simply was not there anymore. Not like Chesh's evaporation, but like a light switch turned off.

"Was that your devil?" Mal asked Chesh.

He was still staring at the spot where the goatman had been. He met Mal's gaze after some time and shrugged. "Hard to say,"

Chesh said. He glanced back at the trees that had been tortured. "How could he be here if that was him?"

"I need an explanation," TL said.

"What is 'sinful'?" Ryph repeated.

"Someone who does things that are considered wicked or immoral," Mal said. "Cruel or evil. Corrupt, blasphemous, or... criminal."

"There are a lot worse than the trees," TL noted. He looked around the forest. "I'm not even sure trees could be any of those things."

"It doesn't matter," Chesh said. "If he was Satan, he wasn't really here to punish trees. It was probably just something he was doing while looking for the reason he was here."

"The vein?" Eagy asked skeptically.

Chesh shrugged. He looked at the spot where the goatman had been unsurely. "I've been stuck here for... too many forevers to count. Not once has the real he been here."

"If not the devil, who else walks around with a goat head?" Mal asked.

"There are those who walk around with sheep heads," Wyat pointed out.

"Fair," Mal conceded. "Still."

Chesh shrugged. After several minutes, he turned away from the spot. "Whatever the case is, he's moved on."

Mal waited to hear the rest of that thought. 'And I'm still stuck here.'

"It's too late to get back to Ache's now," Eagy said. "We'll have to find somewhere to camp for the night."

"The word hovels are close by," Kav said.

"I'm sorry, what?" Mal asked.

He smiled. "Word hovels. You'll see. We can at least find a number of beds. I don't particularly care for sleeping on the ground, if there are other options at hand."

"Can't have the knave lowered to our standards," Ryph mumbled, turning away and walking.

"Don't tell me the ground is your first choice," Kav countered.

Ryph shrugged. "It's the company I bed with that matters most. Wouldn't you agree?" he asked, giving Kav an accusatory look.

Kav sighed. "I've already apologized."

"That makes it better," Chesh said, wrapping his arm around Mal's shoulder. "So sorry for possessing you while you were little more than comatose."

Kav didn't answer. It was probably wise. Mal wasn't sure why they decided to bring that up again, but it was best left alone. Looking back on it, she wasn't sure how she felt about it anymore. At the time, and the weeks following, she hadn't been upset about it. He saved her life, after all.

Then again, she had clearly not been in the right mind. And she knew she had talked about her men. She certainly wasn't a single woman. Even if she had been *technically* single at the time because of her words spoken in anger. The memory now left her uneasy and a bit creeped out. Especially since she'd let him take her into TL's back room later on.

She had been convinced that he was one of her seven. But then, it wasn't like she had to be involved with all seven of her seven. Right? Four seemed a perfectly good number. Manageable, even. Any more than that and she was sure she'd be forever trying to manage equal quality time with each individually and together. It seemed too complicated. She had a headache just thinking about it and it wasn't even a thing right then.

The word hovels were little more than small, square structures with thatched roofs. They were leaning against trees or against each other. Some looked like they weren't really standing at all but tipped on their sides.

There were dozens of them littered throughout the trees. All the same shape. All in various states of disrepair.

"There's barely enough room for one person," Mal said. "Never mind a bed."

"There's plenty of room," Kav said, stepping close to one. He nudged open the door and angry mumbles immediately filled the air.

"The verbs are in a temper," TL said with a sigh.

Mal looked at him like he'd lost his mind.

"The adverbs are passive, though," Kav said, shutting the door and cutting off the angry mumbles. He moved on to the next hovel, which was quiet, if not welcoming.

Whispers floated out the door. Ryph stiffened, his face falling into a grimace. It was then that the notes in the wind met her ears. They were vaguely familiar. With Ryph's curse, Mal knew who it was.

Lorem.

As she recognized that it was him, he came into view as he flitted through the trees and around the hovels. A song was always on his lips, but the words were not logical this time. Though, were they logical last time? *This time*, they weren't in a language she recognized.

The burden on his back shouldn't have allowed him to dance as gracefully as he was. He glided across the ground as if he were a ballerina, used a tree as a pole, and performed an elegant turn that brought him face to face with Mal and her men.

He stopped, the music stopping with him as he stilled. The burden on his back made him hunch over with his head bowed. Long, white hair that looked like it hadn't seen a comb in a decade covered most of his face. A single grass green eye peeked out.

With a heavy sigh and a rock as if caught in the wind, Lorem sunk in on himself. When only the burden was left, a click echoed off the trees and Lorem stood without the load this time.

He was every bit as breathtaking as she had remembered. Tall and big like Ryph, but strangely light in color. And when light hit him right, iridescent scales glittered along his skin. His shiny, white hair shimmered. And, of course, he was naked. Because, why not, apparently?

Lorem stretched, reaching his arms high above his head and arching his back. Several audible cracks reverberated in the air. The way he twisted his back drew your eyes directly to his abdomen and down to what could only be described as impressive. Even when not quite hard.

"Hello, Lorem," Eagy said with a sigh when Lorem had finished stretching. Showing off, probably.

"Pet," he said. This time when he looked around their group, his gazed skipped right over Ryph. His strange green eyes settled on her. "The one who finds being small offensive. How do you do?"

"I don't find it offensive," Mal said. "I find your greeting a bit offensive if I'm looking to be offended about something."

"Are you now?" he asked.

She found it hard to concentrate on his words when his scales glittered just so. And his voice was unsettlingly compelling. Compelling to what, she wasn't sure.

"No?" she said, the word coming out like a question.

He smiled and it was something sultry. "Good. I mean not to offend such a tiny thing."

Again, she bristled at the reference to her size.

"Easy," Wyat murmured close to her. "He means it in the same way Ache does."

Mal glanced back at Wyat. With his assuring smile, she urged her irritation away. Besides, by the look on Ryph's face, they might all have to devote their efforts to keeping him calm. Beside them, Rival sniggered before biting into a tree and tearing free a piece of bark.

"Will you be joining me tonight?" he asked, eyes once more locked on Eagy's.

Mal got the feeling he wasn't at all asking everybody.

"No," Ryph snapped, grabbing Eagy's hand and jerking him

to his side. "He will be with me tonight. As he is every night, reptile."

"Hmm," he hummed. His gaze lingered on Eagy for a time, unmistakably filled with hunger, before it moved on to Mal. "And you?"

To say Mal was surprised when she was sure he was being insulting earlier was an understatement. She didn't manage an answer before Ryph was growling again.

"No," Ryph barked. "She's with the gargoyle tonight. The flower or the knave. Or your hand. Those are your options."

"I'm not an option," TL retorted with a frown. "But thanks for offering me up."

Ryph didn't have the state of mind to retort as he moved in front of Eagy, trying to block Mal as well.

"Neither Mal nor I are interested in Lorem," Eagy cooed to Ryph. It really did sound like a coo, too.

"Are you so sure, pet? Have you ever had the pleasure of scales?" Lorem asked, leaning against a tree trunk, his erection growing by the passing minute.

Mal was sure Ryph's wings were trying to break out. His hoodie looked like it was moving on its own. Bulging in some places before settling back down.

He bared his teeth at Lorem, the growl that rumbled through the air a clear threat.

It was a good thing that Lorem wasn't part of her seven. There was no way they could put up with a possessive, jealous Ryph *all* the time.

"Why aren't you in Tulgey?" Chesh asked.

Yes, yes. Distraction.

The flirtatious smile fell from Lorem's expression. "The Soldiers are getting abundant. The trees are growing scarce."

Eagy tilted his head. Hands on Ryph's hips, he leaned around the beast to look at Lorem with concern. "They're burning the forest?"

Lorem nodded. “Patches, too,” he said sadly. “Whole Patches. Villages are next, we hear.”

Mal wanted to ask who ‘we’ was, but that didn’t seem like the important part. “Is it too late to get a message to Lede?” Mal asked instead.

“We’ll go in the morning before retrieving the wildflowers. Silence isn’t amenable to destinations at night,” Eagy said.

Mal really hoped that wasn’t too late.

“Will they try to burn down Silence?” she asked anxiously.

“No one messes with Silence,” TL said. “Not even the queens want the Unnamed at their doors.”

The beasts without names, ancient and terrible. No, she supposed even the queens would avoid them. But, if you were believing the wildflowers, there was also the darkness growing in Silence to consider.

Before any more bickering could take place, Mal excused herself to bed, grabbing Wyat’s hand as she turned away. He didn’t argue and they found themselves a nice little hovel with passive adjectives for company.

Getting Wyat inside was comical. But he did actually fit. Even on the bed. It seemed to stretch with him.

That observation had been a little hasty. As he rolled over to allow Mal room, his elbow hit the wall. He grinned. When he rolled to his side, pressing back further to the wall, his foot hit the wall at the end of the bed. Stretching the other way, his head made a thud.

Mal giggled. “Tight fit.”

Wyat smiled good naturedly. “All good, Bunny.”

Mal reached up and ran her fingers though his platinum hair and up over an ear. A shiver ran through him. “Is this like, insta-turn on?” Mal asked as she gently scratched at the base of his ear.

The sound he made was more of a rumble than anything else. “Come here,” he groaned when she wrapped her hand around the ear and stroked it to the end. He pulled her to him, his mouth devouring her smile.

She loved his body. So very big. Everywhere. And hard like stone. Beautiful marbling. Her favorite river of veining went up his abdomen to his chest. It was a good thing they'd gotten out of their clothing before even trying for the bed. There wasn't any way he'd be able to undress her without putting his hand through the wall. Unintentionally, of course.

He tried to roll them over, his large hand wrapping almost entirely around her waist, but she nearly fell off the bed. She laughed as he grumbled. Wyat scooched back further but when she was finally under him, his leg was hanging off the side, kneeling on the floor. There was no purchase for him to really get in position.

Mal giggled again and pushed him up. "Switch with me," she said.

"You want top? Really?"

"Don't tell me. The women here are missionary only," Mal said as he shifted back onto his knees to let her move. She watched him openly as he rolled over, adjusting so he was flat on the bed. Flat except for his very large hard on.

"No," he said, grinning. "Well, I guess I don't really know that, actually. I haven't had a woman but you in ages. Hard to recall what positions she liked."

Mal nodded. "Sure, sure," she hummed as she climbed back onto him. He was like a giant log. Huge under her, between her legs. But now that she was on top of him, that gorgeous vein of gray in his otherwise pearly skin stood out. In the dim room, it was several shades darker than usual. She ran her fingers up it, tracing its winding trail to his chest. When she reached its apex, she leaned in to kiss it.

His heart was a fierce drum beat against her. She explored the expanse of his chest with her hand as she traced the river again, this time with her tongue. His muscles danced beneath her, trembling in anticipation.

She followed the river backwards, down beyond its delta, to the throbbing shaft of his cock. He was so thick she couldn't stop her smile. Wrapping her hand around him, she marveled at the fact that she couldn't touch her fingers around. This only made her grin wider. She felt like she might have a Chesh smile.

Holding him firmly, she licked up the side, bringing her tongue to flick his head. He groaned, his hand closing around the one she rested on his hip.

He was always so careful with her. Careful not to hurt her as much as he was able. Careful not to put too much of his weight on her so she could breathe. Careful not to try and coax her into anything, never mind make it feel like he was forcing her.

For such a big man, he was a softy. So gentle and sweet.

And hung like a gargoyle.

Who knew she'd end up with a pension for pain? And she loved what he did to her.

Mal wasn't convinced she really knew what she was doing with a cock in her mouth. Eagy and Ryph weren't interested in foreplay. Well, if she were honest, it was mostly Ryph who got to her first and he really wasn't interested in anything but burying himself deep within her. Eagy didn't seem to care either way.

Since Wyat had been back, she'd been with him a handful of times. Eagy and Ryph were a bit monopolizing of her. Wyat didn't argue or push. He waited his turn.

He was too big to properly fit in her mouth. If she really tried, she managed to get his head inside before her jaw snapped. She pressed the flat of her tongue along his head and moved just her tongue up and down. She gripped him tightly with her hand and stroked him as she did.

His hand on hers tightened.

Perhaps one day, she'd convince Eagy and Ryph to let her watch them do this. Then, she could get a good idea of what she was supposed to do.

At his deep exhale, Mal released him from her mouth. Her jaw was already sore. She continued to work him until a bead of precum glistened at the top. Success. She bent down again and flicked her tongue out, capturing it.

Wyat groaned.

She licked her lips as she sat up to look into his red eyes. They certainly were redder in the dimness than pink. With his free hand, he reached up and cupped the side of her face. For a moment, she stopped stroking him and leaned against his touch. She couldn't believe at one time she'd been on edge with him, solely because of how large he was.

As corny as the thought was, she should have realized being so large meant he had a big heart, too. All of her men cared for her. Deeply, if how she felt was returned. But Wyat's affection felt more profound.

Mal moved up his body to kiss him, laying against the hard planes of his chest. His hand went to her, up around her waist in a one arm embrace. She tugged playfully on his ear and he smiled against her lips. No longer a hug, he now cupped her ass.

She grinned and sat up, straddling him. His phallus pressed between her heat and she rubbed herself up and down his length. "Ready?" she asked.

He smiled. "Are you?"

Mal smiled wickedly. "You know I am." She reached between them and pulled him into position. She loved handling him. It was like one of those large, heavy beer steins. And she was sure it must weigh like six pounds!

The thought made her giddy as she adjusted herself to bring her body down on him. She loved the way her body stretched to accept him. Stretched wider than she assumed it should. Then again, if she was able to push out a child, this shouldn't be a big deal. Not that she'd tried to push out a child.

She stopped thinking when the pressure turned to little lightning shots of pain. He really was a big boy. But oh, did she love having all of him. Knowing that others hadn't been able to in his past. Knowing that after the initial discomfort, he could send her spiraling into a rapture of bliss for what might be all night.

His giant hands wrapped around her waist, slowing her from putting as much of her weight down at once as she would have. Concern glowed in his red eyes. “Easy,” he murmured, voice thick with heat. “We’re not in a hurry.”

No, they weren’t. She nodded but felt her impatience to have him filling her to the brink and beyond. He didn’t let her go, easing her down bit by bit, using his thumb to distract her from the little shoots of discomfort by rubbing her clit.

He was doing such a good job at it that she forgot she was still working on getting him inside her when her first orgasm came crashing down. She threw her head back, thankful for his strong arms keeping her upright, and cried out. Her hips bucked and rocked as he continued his wonderful torment.

When she came down, she found that he was finally where she wanted him. Fully sheathed inside her. Mal grinned widely. “If I knew that was the key, I’d have suggested it long ago.”

Wyat’s answering rumble of laughter was breathless and heady. She encouraged him to take charge, to use his grip to give them both pleasure. To not treat her quite like he would split her in half.

Mal was usually pretty good about her agreement with Ryph and Eagy. They got one, maybe two good orgasms in before they went to sleep. But she wasn’t so good about maintaining her limit with Wyat. Maybe because they didn’t get their nights together as often as they should. Whatever the case was, it was a long, pleasure-filled night.

Mal Dies

CHESH

19

He swayed as he walked. Lorem's music followed them. Because Lorem had decided to follow them. Ryph was not at all pleased. Angry. His beast was glaring out more than his person.

Chesh grinned. It wasn't that he enjoyed drama. And although it would grow old pretty quickly, it was nice to see Ryph being the jealous one instead of Eagy. And Eagy humoring him instead of Ryph doing the reassuring. It made their relationship more balanced. It was good, Chesh decided.

Lorem's music announced their impending arrival at Ache's before the house came into view. Ache, Ahdem, and the wildflowers were out front waiting for them.

"All is well?" Ache asked. His attention started on Eagy when he asked, but moved to linger on Mal. She smiled tentatively at him.

Their little Mal had a thing for the Hare. Chesh glanced at Wyat. He didn't seem to care a whole lot, but Chesh knew that their resident gargoyle didn't play too well with others of his kind when kept in close proximity for too long. Hopefully, Mal wouldn't ask Ache to join them.

Then again, Chesh doubted Ache would. He had Ahdem to

think about. And Ahdem was too far gone to be joining them in this.

"Yes. The goatman has moved on," Eagy said, glancing at Chesh.

A tightness formed in his chest again. The same that had overcome him upon seeing the goatman. Here. In Laddenworn.

"Where's Rival?" Adde asked.

"Getting a message to Steele," Eagy said. "Rival and Kav will be join us at the inn later."

Perhaps they'd lose Rival to the wildflowers. He hadn't noticed that they'd taken a liking to each other but then, he usually spent this time watching Mal. It had given him nightmares to know they were back in the place they'd lost Mal before.

"Perhaps we should invite them to tea," Ahdem said in the same absent way he had yesterday.

"I'm afraid we'll have to pass this time," Eagy said. "We really ought to be on our way. We have a knave to meet." The way his eyes hooded, Chesh was sure he'd really rather lose Kav than hurry to meet up with him.

Chesh would, too. The creep set him on edge.

"Too bad," Ahdem said. "Far too choo March in glad."

Mal's brows knit together. With a sigh, Ahdem turned his slow gaze her way. His head tilted to the side and he remained staring in her direction.

Far too bad, for sure. He was perhaps one of the most ridiculously beautiful men Chesh had come across in Laddenworn. Such a shame to lose him so thoroughly before Chesh had stumbled across him. He might have been fun.

"Thank you for tea yesterday," Mal said. "And keeping our friends safe."

Ache nodded. If Chesh didn't know any better, and perhaps he didn't, he'd have guessed that Ache actually cared about Mal. He hadn't known Ache to care much about anything.

As if he was making a point, Ache handed her a canvas bag.

Chesh could smell the sweet goodness it wafted into the air. "For your journey," he said, voice low. When she took it, he handed her a soft canteen as well.

Her smile was bright and affectionate. "Thank you, Ache."

He nodded and took a step back so that he was shoulder to shoulder with Ahdem. The Hatter hadn't moved. He continued to stare at Mal (or past her or through her...) with his head tilted to the side. Chesh felt bad for him. And for the loss of one who would surely have proven to be a good time!

They turned back onto the path and walked for most of the day. Mal was filled with her usual questions, always ignited by whatever they'd recently gone through. Her voice mixed with Lorem's melody made Chesh want to dance, himself. If he thought Ryph wouldn't hate him after, he might have joined Lorem in his light-stepped frolics around them. As it were, Ryph was fit to be tied to have Lorem with them at all.

"Ache brought Ahdem back from the tea party," Mal noted.

"Ache is never far from Ahdem," Eagy said. "They're usually in the same place."

She shook her head. "He wasn't there when I came across his house during my first days in Laddenworn."

"I'm sure he was," Eagy said, smiling at her amusedly. "He isn't always up for visitors."

Her shoulders stiffened. A pretty shade of pink colored her cheeks as she contemplated what that meant. Once again, Chesh had the sudden urge to lick her cheeks to see how hot she burned. One day, he would.

"That's slightly... disturbing. And also explains a lot."

Their somewhat peaceful walk was interrupted two days later. Ryph's beast was literally just beneath the surface. Before too much longer, the gryphon would be walking alongside them, opposed to the person, if Lorem didn't stop tormenting him.

Otherwise, Lorem was a joy to have around. Chesh loved his music. It was calming and serene and it broke up the monotony of trees and mushrooms and moss. Day and night. Day from day.

But on their third day walking, they came across something incredibly bizarre. An enormous wall was built in the middle of the path. In the middle of Silence. It wasn't quite as tall as the trees, but high enough that they couldn't easily reach the top.

Looking to the left and right, it extended for the foreseeable distance.

"Is this normal?" Mal asked.

Eagy shook his head. "The door to the Cold Lands is just beyond here. You'd have seen it."

"But would I have? I must have walked in circles for days before stumbling upon Ache."

"There's only one path to Ache's house," Chesh said. "And we're on it."

She didn't look at all convinced.

Eagy raised his hood over his head. His hands came away as feathered wings, revealing a beak. A few steps further and the whole eaglet stood where the person once did. Eagy shook himself before spreading his wings and climbing through the air. He was quite the elegant, majestic bird.

They lost him from view for several minutes before he landed again on two person-feet. He was frowning as he pulled down his hood. "There's a big pool of water on the other side. Smack in the middle of Silence."

"Could you see either end?" TL asked.

Eagy shook his head.

"We're not in any kind of hurry," Wyat said. "I can't imagine it's a good thing this is here."

Eagy nodded. "You want to take Mal and head left? I'll check out the water. TL, the other side? Chesh, see what you can find around here?"

"I want to help," Onnli said.

It was probably one of the only things Chesh had heard him say since the wildflowers had taken off in the night.

"You lot can come with me," TL said as he turned to the

right and started walking. The wildflowers followed. Excited smiles danced on the girls' faces.

Chesh shook his head. Such enthusiasm for something that could very well result in death.

"Are you actually going to be useful?" Ryph asked Lorem.

Lorem's grass green eyes met the beast's through his matted hair. A moment later, Lorem had set his burden on the forest floor and stood before them gloriously naked. "I'm going to accompany the eagle."

Ryph's wings immediately burst out behind him, his claws tearing from his hands.

Eagy barely caught him around the waist. If it weren't for Wyat's stronger stone grip, Ryph would have torn free. His growls stormed around them, sending the Unnamed into quiet anticipation.

Chesh clasped his hands behind his back, a smile creeping up the sides of his face. Perhaps he shouldn't find amusement in this. But it was good to see Eagy on a different end. Not being tormented but being wanted. And Ryph not being able to handle it.

Lorem's smile was sultry and amused. He shifted his weight, bringing attention to his growing arousal. Perhaps that was his game. Ryph's anger and jealousy turned him on.

"Are you going to go in the water?" Lorem asked. "There might be something important to be discovered within the water, since it's not normally there and all."

Ryph was not in any mood for logic. The teeth he bared were more feral than person now, too.

Eagy glanced at Chesh. With something that might have been a meaningful look, he flickered his eyes towards Lorem.

He really didn't like getting in the middle of a delicious love triangle. What fun would that be?

"He's got a point," Chesh said. "None of us are good with water."

Ryph glared at Chesh hotly.

"Unless you'd like to go for a swim," Chesh suggested. *"My cat doesn't like water."* His tail flickered behind him.

Ryph's age was apparent in this moment. It took him a long time to quiet his anger and acknowledge reason. He did. Eventually. Though he was unable to put his wings away.

And then, Lorem had to enrage him again. "I'm going to need a lift over the wall, pet."

"I'll bring you over the fucking wall," Ryph said, storming over to Lorem.

"Oh, please do. I've always wanted your hands on me," Lorem purred. It wasn't an actual purr, but it sure as hell should have been.

Ryph paused before he sunk his almost-talons into Lorem. He stared. A moment later, he turned away slightly. The anger and annoyance made way for just a bit of hesitation to rear its head through. He looked at Eagy as if asking permission.

Eagy nodded. Ryph turned back. The smile he gave Lorem was not predatory in the way Lorem had intended it to be. Even so, the beast didn't seem to scare Lorem, even as Ryph sunk his talons into Lorem's biceps.

His massive golden wings spread. Three strong flaps had their feet off the ground, and they were moving higher through the air.

When they'd made the wall, Eagy sighed. "This is going to be a long day," he said, washing his hands over his face. A moment later, his eagle left the three of them.

Mal looked between Wyat and Chesh wide-eyed. "Do you think Ryph's going to actually hurt Lorem?"

"Might serve him right," Wyat said. "Lorem's instigating." He wrapped his arm around her tiny shoulders and nudged her to the left. "Come on, Bunny. Let's see what we can find."

Hours later, Chesh had found a whole lot of nothing. A little animal hole in which he enjoyed a snack. Otherwise, the surrounding trees and mushrooms were not the least bit helpful. Nothing along the path was helpful.

You'd think setting a huge wall in the middle of the path, in the middle of Silence, would leave something behind. Or conjuring a giant body of water on the other side. Either Silence itself was hiding anything that might be useful, or Chesh was not good at knowing what was useful.

The thing looked like it should have taken years to erect. It had been only several months since they'd last been in Silence. And it had not been there then.

He was staring at the wall, frowning with his hands on his hips, when Ryph joined him. His wings were away. That was nice. Or was it disappointing? Chesh was sure he was just sour since he had nothing to show for the confounding wall.

"Anything?" Ryph asked.

Chesh shook his head. "I don't get it. There has to be something I'm missing."

Ryph frowned. "A wall in the middle of nowhere that spans at least a thousand paces. It has to mean something."

"Did you drown Lorem?"

"I hope so," Ryph grumbled.

"I'll miss his music," he said, running his hand along the expanse of wall in front of him. Smooth boards with worn grain.

Chesh let out a frustrated breath. He turned and leaned back against the wall, looking out into the trees and scanning what little he could see between the thick brush and tall fauna. Again, he shook his head. Trees on one side. A body of water on the other.

Ryph's hand on Chesh's stomach brought his puzzling thoughts to a halt. Chesh looked at him, big golden eyes looking back. Golden eyes filled with avidity.

At Chesh's attempt to speak, Ryph covered Chesh's mouth with his own. Drawing his tongue into a wet dance, Chesh felt the beast's chest rumble with a suppressed growl.

His kiss was hungry, demanding, possessing. Ryph's big, hard body pressed Chesh firmly into the wall. His hands went up Chesh's flank slowly, with a heat all their own. When one of

Ryph's knees spread between his, he couldn't stop the groan from escaping.

It was a mistake since it only fueled Ryph further. Still, Chesh managed to get his bearings and push Ryph away.

"Don't fight me, pussy cat," Ryph snarled.

"I'm not sure your eaglet will approve of this," Chesh said in a quick rush before Ryph could silence him.

Ryph did pause. A torrent of emotions ran over his face. A growl, deep and menacing, thrummed on the air. With violent speed, Ryph's hand slammed into the wall to the left of Chesh's head in the same moment Ryph's mouth was on Chesh's again.

It seemed to have the opposite effect Chesh thought it should have. The beast was more aggressive now. Hungrier. Rougher as he tried to tear at Chesh's pants.

The wood beside Chesh's head splintered. He shivered as Ryph's hand found his stomach under his shirt.

So long... it had been so long, it was hard to fight against the promise of sex. And he knew Ryph knew what he was doing. All he had to do was let it happen. Yet, he tried to push Ryph away. He had to have Mal first. And Eagy simply wouldn't forgive him. Either of them.

"I think you caught the wrong animal, gryphon," Wyat's deep voice came from behind Ryph.

Ryph pulled away with effort. His eyes were almost not his own. He was close to being lost to his beast. When he tore his hand free of the wall, several pieces came with it.

Saved by the Rabbit. Saved right before he gave in.

Chesh slinked like a cat from the trap Ryph had had him in.

"Glad to have found you. Finally," Wyat said as Chesh retreated from Ryph.

Chesh nodded, grinning, falling into stride beside him as they turned back into the trees. He could feel Ryph's predatory gaze on his back. He could feel his own erection pressing uncomfortably in his pants. Chesh adjusted them to a more comfortable arrangement, though it didn't help a whole lot.

It was a long while before he felt that gaze slip away. Before he was far enough away that the tension left his shoulders.

"Thanks," Chesh said quietly.

Wyat chuckled. "You seemed to be struggling. Couldn't tell if that was welcomed or not."

Chesh huffed. "Neither could I," he deadpanned. But the further he walked, the more bothered he found himself. Bothered that he really wasn't fighting him off with any real effort. Bothered that, maybe, he wanted to fuck the stupid gryphon.

He swore under his breath. Wyat glanced at him. "It's been a really long time," he growled.

Wyat laughed and clapped him on the back.

He and Wyat arrived at the inn where they were to meet Kav sometime later. Eagy, Lorem, Mal, TL, and the wildflowers were already there. Ryph was somewhere behind them, still. Chesh found himself more uneasy. With all his anger towards Lorem, Ryph should have been up Eagy's ass. Not with his tongue down Chesh's throat.

Chesh sat with the wildflowers. Their tables were piled high with food. He absently wondered how their supply of blades were holding up. With all the traveling and their continuously expanding group, Chesh was sure they'd be running low soon.

Ryph arrived a few minutes before Kav. He didn't look at Chesh. He didn't look at anyone. The tension in his shoulders and neck was evident. Even Lorem seemed to know he needed to leave the beast alone. At least for now. Until Ryph had a chance to fuck his eaglet. And/or Mal.

Kav walked in as they were finishing dinner. He handed Eagy a paper and sat without a word.

"Did you find them?" Mal asked.

Kav nodded. Though he raised his head, he didn't meet her eyes. Wyat was far too close for that.

"Will they help?"

This time, he did look at her. "Lede assured me they would,

though Meddul was being a tool. Why should he care if Tulgey is burned to the ground?" he mocked, repeating words Meddul had doubtlessly said.

Mal's face contorted. "Maybe we need to go to Tulgey," she said.

Eagy finally looked up from the paper. He turned and handed it to Chesh before speaking to Mal. Chesh momentarily tuned the conversation out when the headline caught his attention: TWENTY-EIGHT DEAD. The article went on to say that Twenty-Eight had likely been The One since she survived so long in the dungeons, despite their heavy tactics to get her to speak. But nonetheless, the queens succeeded in destroying her, as well. Their progressive reign of bliss and purity would continue.

Get The One to speak about what, though?

There was an image of a bloody corpse that was supposed to be Mal. It even looked somewhat like Mal. Chesh glanced up at TL, who met his eyes. Chesh was glad to see he was just as disturbed by this news as Chesh was. He wondered who'd made the convincing imposter that the queens believed was still Mal in the dungeons. It couldn't have been Kav since he had been with them for the last few weeks.

Whose body was it that they'd dressed to appear to be Mal? Was the article true, or a hoax intending for them to let their guard down?

Chesh looked at the other table where Mal was arguing passionately that they needed to go to Tulgey to stop the Soldiers from destroying all the Villages and Patches and the woods. They were lives. They deserved to be saved. To be fought for.

Kav tried to assure her that Lede had it under control. She was not to be convinced.

The Gryphon

WYAT

20

He was surprised that Mal was still there when they woke up the next morning. Wyat was sure she was going to take off while they were all asleep and head for Tulgey herself. Thankfully, she either knew she wouldn't make it on her own, or trusted that Lede would take care of it.

Wyat wasn't actually sure Lede could convince his brother to look into the situation. Meddul had lost his compassion long ago. Failure after failure had tainted his will to do good. Now, he only wanted to win. The means by which he came by that win didn't matter.

A fact that set Wyat on edge. Meddul was determined to have Mal as his figurehead to rally his troops into confidence and faith once again. Where was the line he wouldn't cross to get her?

They remained at the inn for more than a few days. Eagy assured Mal it was because he was waiting on Lepa's reply. Really, Wyat thought he didn't have a game plan. If they were set on getting this seven that Mal needed, they were still short one. And that was only if you included Kav and TL.

Wyat was beginning to think the infection wasn't really the issue. Sure, there were some weird coincidences that they'd told him about but surely, one children's tale couldn't infect another. Then again, this was no children's tale they lived in. And hadn't been for far too long. He was fairly certain, in a child's book, people wore clothes and didn't rip another's still-beating heart out. Literally, not figuratively.

So, what were they waiting for? As far as inns go, this one wasn't anything special. The bed barely fit the three of them, leaving Wyat and Chesh to shrink down into animals if they wanted a place with Mal. Sure, that was the only logical way for them all to fit on the bed. Neither Eagy's eaglet nor Ryph's gryphon were small animals.

Speaking of the gryphon, he was barely contained as Lorem sat unnecessarily close to Eagy while they discussed something in the paper. Wyat was pretty sure their conversation was real and not just a ruse by Lorem to get close. He was, however, certainly antagonizing Ryph by sitting almost on top of Eagy.

Eagy, for as observant as he was, quiet and studying, was being quite obtuse in the situation. Something Adde and Saydi found amusing as they sat across the table from them and giggled behind their hands. Onnli kept rolling his eyes and shaking his head. Girls....

It was only mid-morning when the screaming started. Chesh's ear twitching caught his attention before the actual screaming. When he focused, he heard the faint cries, too. Faint, sure, but they were screaming at the top of their lungs.

Who, though? They were far within the middle of Silence. How many people could be wandering about screaming? By the sounds of it, a whole herd.

When Chesh met his gaze, Eagy finally took notice. Ryph had already stopped glaring to listen. Lorem... well, Lorem was a different kind of animal, wasn't he? A reptile. They weren't known for their hearing, considering they tasted the air for their sense of direction rather than relying on their eyes or ears.

The flowers didn't hear it. Nor did Kav or Mal.

Poor Mal. They really needed to work on her senses. She was

adept with a blade, something TL still worked her on until she nearly passed out most nights, but her senses were far too people-y. How did people even survive? Poor thing couldn't even find the path in Silence.

By the time the sounds actually filled the air, Eagy was already on his feet with a blade in hand. "Stay here," he told the flowers. Wyat was sure he meant it for Mal, as well.

"No way," Adde said. "If you're all going, so are we."

"Safer with you than we would be here alone," Saydi added, standing. The two girls gripped each other's hands tightly.

Eagy wanted to argue. Wyat could tell by his expression. But the screams were growing louder, more tortured, the longer they waited. He shook his head and headed for the door, sparing Mal a fretful glance. Yelling to the barkeep to keep their rooms booked, Eagy was out the door seconds after Ryph, with TL ahead of them.

Outside, it sounded like the screams were surrounding them. Coming from all sides. Rival met them at the front, looking at each of them expectantly. Mal spun in a slow circle, trying to pinpoint the source, while Eagy looked into the treetops.

"Something feels awful trap-y," Chesh hummed.

"The screams are fake?" Mal asked.

Chesh didn't answer. No one did. They sounded pretty real.

"Let's go," Eagy said. Whether or not he had a reason for choosing the direction he did, Wyat couldn't tell.

He enjoyed letting Eagy take lead. It left him to take the fall when something went wrong. Aside from Mal's abduction and imprisonment, he wasn't usually wrong. He had the head of a hunter and his instincts were right on. Unless he was hurt. Then, Mal got kidnapped and tortured for three months.

Their path was clear, even as the air rang with tormented cries. A particularly blood-curdling scream made Wyat's stomach flip and bile rise. He really hoped they weren't going to run into something horrible.

Eagy once again proved himself a capable leader when the

shadow beasts surged from the ground and engaged them by surprise. TL was quick enough to keep one from impaling Mal while Mal looked on, wide-eyed.

Wyat shook his head. They really needed to work on her senses next. It was a hindrance to be too much person and not enough animal, especially while in Silence. See, he could muse this whole thing while he decapitated three beasts.

They pushed through the throng of shadow things, taking no time to truly battle them. Rendering them too crippled to carry on was the goal as they pushed through.

"This means the Duchess is close?" Mal asked as she proved her blade skills. Wyat filled with pride when she sliced one through the middle and didn't stop to wipe her hands.

"Most likely," Eagy said. "These are her magic."

Wyat spared a glance at the wildflowers. Adde and Saydi were certainly afraid. Their attacks were weak and hesitant. It was a good think Onnli was with them, being a helicopter brother, with Chesh and Kav keeping close. They were going to get their petals plucked if they weren't careful. They should have stayed at the inn.

All the while, Lorem's music fluttered through the air in an odd juxtaposition to the death they were serving. With Lorem's quicker, more urgent steps, the crescendo rose and eddied while he flickered around their fighting group. Rival made up for Lorem's lack of usefulness. His teeth were sharp, his jaw was strong, and his reflexes were quick.

When they finally came upon the Duchess, having carved out a path through the shadow beasts, it was far more horrifying than Wyat could have imagined. There weren't people being tortured, sending up screams of pain and protest. It was Laddenworn itself crying for help.

The strong scent of pepper filled Wyat's nose. He somehow managed to stifle a sneeze. The wildflowers were not so well practiced.

"Like pollen," TL told them when Adde succumbed to a third sneeze. "You can resist it if you compartmentalize it."

Adde still struggled but managed to get it under control.

Wyat could only spare half of his attention for for Adde because what the Duchess was doing within her waft of pepper was far more terrible than being paralyzed with sneezes.

"What is that?" Mal asked, appalled.

The ground under the Duchess's hands was bubbling, rippling, like something had turned it into a viscous liquid. It gurgled and squelched. Silence cried out in protest.

"I think-" Eagy started.

He was cut off when the Duchess looked up. Her gaze was set, stony mad. "No!" she screamed. "You will not interrupt." With a hand thrown in their direction, shadows surged from behind her and barreled down on them like a train.

"She needs to be stopped," Eagy shouted as he engaged in defending himself from being shredded.

Wyat had no attention for what the Duchess was raising. He was too busy concentrating on getting to Mal. They would not lose her. Not now.

He carved his way through the thick shadow, which only seemed to partially solidify. Which meant the Duchess was using a lot of magic to do what she was doing.

The ground heaved under them. Saydi's cry made him turn in time to see Onnli stake a portion of shadow and pull his blade up through its spine. Adde was on her knees at Saydi's side, big crocodile tears welling in her eyes.

Wyat shook his head. You don't take flowers to a blade show.

The ground jumped again and Mal was launched off her feet. Wyat felt the panic rise through him like a storm, but then Chesh was wrapped around her in the air and they both fell to the ground together. He landed on his feet, set her on the ground, and spun in time to set the surrounding shadows on fire.

Teal flames engulfed the area. The shadows were like brush: highly flammable.

"Stop her," Eagy said, still trying to cut through the line of shadows encompassing the Duchess. "We can't let her raise it."

Dread poured down Wyat's back like ice water. Who in their right mind would try to raise Nobody?!

Kav and Eagy broke through at the same moment. Kav cannoned into the Duchess, sending her sprawling.

"NO!" she screamed. "No, you will not stop me this time!" She flung both of her hands to the ground beside her, where they sunk into the moss like it was water.

The trees themselves responded, reaching for them with branches now made of sponge and sinewy strength. The wildflowers were hurled into the air, screaming. Onnli started to cut Adde loose but stopped when he saw their fall. Rival began gnawing on the tree that held Adde within its branches, only stopping long enough to sink his teeth into any oncoming branches that tried to hinder his progress.

Every branch Chesh cut through, he apologized to while simultaneously controlling the fire so it wouldn't burn the trees but remain on the shadows. The damned demon cat was good.

Eagy and Kav were both flung away from the Duchess, spinning through the air. Kav landed with his back against a tree, where he fell to the ground in a heap. Eagy reoriented himself and caught a limb before dropping to the ground. He was just as nimble as a cat.

The Duchess scrambled back to the spot where Nobody was partially emerged. It was like a shadow itself. Solid black, smooth without defined features; just a vague people shape. Fingertips stuck out from the ground, as well as the tops of its smooth, featureless face and a hint of its chest.

"Come on," Eagy said. "We can get through some fucking trees since Chesh is doing all the damn work."

"I appreciate the acknowledgement," Chesh commented, turning with a new wave of fire.

The frustration in Eagy's voice rang through the air as loudly as the screams that took up once again. The ground bucked and caved, sending them all several feet into the air. Wyat was caught with a tree around his torso.

For a minute, he didn't get himself loose. He watched what they were up against from eight or nine feet in the air. The Duchess was struggling, but she was succeeding. Mal managed to free herself, but she stumbled and was wrapped again.

With the wildflowers safely in the trees, Wyat could spot everyone else. They were safe and beating back the forest. Except... where was Lorem? Had he not accompanied them through the shadows? Ryph would be happy if that were the case.

The trees were only trying to hinder their progress, not kill. That was evident and helpful. Chesh had the shadows under control with his heldfire - or something. It must be heldfire since it was holding the shadows back... right? Is that not how you use logic? The only one making any leeway at all was TL, who tore through the trees like a storm.

"I think we all need lessons from TL," Wyat called down to them as he pet the branch around him. "Sorry, mate," he told the tree. "But I have a girl down there I'm rather fond of and need to make sure she lives without injury." He pulled his blade through the branch and fell the distance of a house.

He put the weight of his stone behind his fall and gave the ground its own shake right back.

"Ryph," Eagy called as he landed cat-like back on his feet in a crouch.

Ryph looked up from where he was gnawing through a branch, a glint of excitement shining through his golden eyes.

"It's time," Eagy said. "I need you to stop her."

Ryph stopped teething on the tree and grinned. A big grin that spread almost as madly as Chesh's. "Are you sure?"

He sounded like he was given a dangerous gift but needed to be positive he could use it before he indulged.

"Stop her and keep it in the ground, Ryph. That's all. Can you do that?"

Ryph tilted his head, the beast shining through his eyes, swallowing the person completely. Whatever he tried to say was lost in the cry of the beast. Crossed between the bird and cat, he was all feral.

He tore free of the tree as if walking through a wall of loose sand. It shattered around him. Reaching behind him, he pulled the hood over his head and the beast freed himself from the inside. His hands lowered with talons as he came down on all four limbs, landing on them. His legs burst into the claws of his lion as his tail snapped out and his wings erupted from his shoulders.

Ryph the gryphon took a breath. With the inhale, he grew three, five, eight times his size. His bulk pushed trees sideways. They snapped with the pressure. He shook himself, his big eagle head jerking around to take in the area. His attention landing on Eagy, he let out an ear-piercing scream of the beast he now was.

Eagy grinned. "Get her," he told Ryph. "You can do it, Gryphon."

Ryph-the-gryphon turned his body, taking down trees as he did. The Duchess was too involved in what she was doing to take any notice. How she hadn't heard him, Wyat wasn't sure. But since Nobody was almost completely out of the ground, Laddenworn protesting all the more, he guessed she was working hard to finish before she was interrupted.

Too bad it took her too long.

Ryph's lethal beak sank into the Duchess, making her shriek in fear. Ryph sent her flying through the air with a snap of his head. She landed in the arms of a tree, pieces of fabric and jewelry falling in the arc she made.

Nobody was struggling to pull himself free of Silence. Ryph stepped closer and Nobody turned its missing face up to the beast. Although it held no features, Wyat was sure it was baring its teeth.

Ryph screamed at it again. With one massive talon, he stomped the thing back into the ground. It was forced down, the ground moaning in pain. But Nobody wasn't ready to be put back into the ground. Something of itself pierced through Ryph's talon like a knife, coming out the other end.

The beast roared, pulling its talon up. But he wasn't just a beast. He was a magical beast.

His golden eyes glowed. A crackling of lightning danced around his wings. He reared up on his hind legs, screaming into the forest, uprooting trees as he went, and slammed back to the ground. His talons made craters on either side of Nobody.

Another cry of anger and the beast bit into Nobody's head and chest with its sharp beak. The ground around them surged, covering Nobody like a blanket. Swallowing him as Ryph-the-gryphon released his jaws. A rumble went through the ground as if it were swallowing Nobody and digesting.

Ryph-the-gryphon looked around, studying the ground where Nobody had been. The trees stilled and snapped back up to their normal, stiff positions. The wildflowers were released and came falling to the ground. Onnli landed and rolled to catch Adde, while Chesh picked Saydi from the air, as he had Mal earlier.

The beast's head jerked in their direction, its large golden eye studying them all. Gryphons were intelligent creatures. Very curious, eager. Protective. But with so many people around, Ryph-the-gryphon was anxious for more danger.

Eagy walked up beside him and buried his fingers into the feathers of Ryph's front leg. "Nice job, Ryph," he said quietly. "You're magnificent."

Wyat was sure only those with their animal ears could hear Eagy, with as low as he cooed to Ryph. Praising him. Urging him to come back to the person.

Ryph's sharp beak jerked down and ran across Eagy's back. It looked like it should have hurt, but it was likely in affection. Eagles and gryphons took mates. Wyat was sure the two predators found a mate in each other long ago.

Slowly, Ryph shrunk down. Little by little.

"Okay," Mal said, watching Ryph with interest and awe, "I need to know about this Nobody."

"We all do," Eagy said. "There's not much that is known for sure. Just a bunch of conjecture."

"Hold up," Kav said, dragging the Duchess over from where she was heaped at the base of a tree. "We have rope or something?"

Chesh tossed one to him, and Kav tied her as she crouched, sobbing.

"What do you have to say before we sentence you to death?" Kav asked.

"It wasn't me," she cried.

Ryph-the-gryphon made a clicking, chirping sound in his throat. Yeah, he didn't believe the dumb lady either.

"It's over," Eagy told Ryph soothingly. Wyat felt his voice like a breeze on his skin. He shuddered. "Come back to be my person," he whispered so only Ryph could hear. And Wyat and Chesh with their superior animal hearing.

"We literally stopped you from raising Nobody," Kav said. "Some more than others," he added, looking at Ryph appreciatively.

"No, no. You don't understand. I *had* to," the Duchess said.

"I saw no one else but you," Chesh said.

"Years ago, I was friends with the Queen, you know," she said. "She gifted me a broach for my loyalty. I've not been myself since."

Ryph-the-gryphon made a chirp, jerking his head up.

"She lost a lot of stuff when Ryph threw her," Adde noted. She held up a piece of chain that lay at her feet.

"Let's see if we can find a broach, then," TL suggested. It was clear by his tone he was not at all convinced.

"No need to look," Lorem said as he walked around from behind a tree, his music notes filling the air. In his hand, he held a blood red pendant that was indeed a broach. One Wyat remembered the Duchess wearing at the Savage they stumbled upon months ago.

"Where were you?" Chesh asked, brow raised. He caught the broach as Lorem threw it to him.

"I did what I do best in confrontations," Lorem said.

Ryph-the-gryphon's rumble bounced off the trees.

"You're a fighter; I'm a lover," Lorem said.

"Not really a good idea to antagonize him right now," Eagy said quietly. "He's far more beast than person."

Lorem smiled and bowed his head. Wyat was positive Ryph-the-gryphon could snap Lorem in two, even with his hard, protective burden. Especially with his sheer size right then.

"So, you're saying that this broach controlled you?" Kav asked, frowning.

The Duchess nodded.

"If it's a magical object," a new voice said, "it's entirely possible. I've heard of such things."

The group turned to stare at the intruder. Ryph-the-still-quite-large-gryphon growled menacingly, lightning dancing on his wings once more.

Schoolroom

MAL

21

The man that stood in front of them was clearly something different. He wasn't human. What about him made him so, she wasn't sure. There was just... something... off.

"Fury," Chesh said, leaning back against a trunk. "What brings you around, mutt?"

"I could smell you," the man called Fury said.

"That's probably the flower," Chesh drawled, nodding his head in TL's direction. "That constant floral scent is always lingering."

TL rolled his eyes.

"Actually, I heard the screams. There have been rumors the last several weeks about Nobody rising. I came to check it out," Fury said, looking at the place in the ground where there was still clearly upturned earth. Never mind the still half-gryphon or the bound Duchess.

Eagy nodded. He continued to rub Ryph's wing soothingly as he stared at the Duchess. "It seems our friend here was being controlled," he said, gesturing to the Duchess. "She's committed some punishable crimes due to a broach."

Fury raised a brow, his fluffy black, white, and gray hair falling into his face. "A broach?"

Chesh tossed it to him. He caught it and studied it. "What is the symbol?"

Eagy shrugged. "She says she was gifted it by the Queen."

"I was," the Duchess whined, sniffling. "You must believe me. I never intended to hurt anyone."

Fury didn't look convinced. Mal didn't feel convinced.

"What of Nobody?"

"Ryph put him back," Eagy said fondly, looking at the still-shrinking part-gryphon. Ryph's head jerked sideways, big brown eagle eye blinking.

Fury relaxed, though he eyed the ground warily. "Will he stay there? Subdued?"

Eagy shrugged. "Dunno. There's not much on Nobody, is there?"

Fury didn't answer as he studied the Duchess where she sat on the ground. "What are you planning to do with her?"

"Leave her here to rot," Wyat suggested.

"Tie her to a tree and let the Unnamed take a bite of her," TL offered.

The Duchess looked at them with wide, fear-filled eyes. "Please, I swear to you, I didn't do it on purpose. I didn't have a choice. Here. Here." She pulled off her gloves frantically and offered them to the closest person, TL. "Take my magic."

TL took them without argument.

"I know a place," Fury said. "One to store her and one... other that might be of use."

Mal looked at her men and the wildflowers. If she had her choice, she'd go. It was exhausting being out in Silence all the time, watching your back for something that might try to kill you. But like they all did, she submitted to Eagy's decision. She liked that he was the leader, intentional or not.

Eagy nodded. "Let's go. I need a shower."

Fury nodded. "You do."

Eagy grinned, glancing at the Duchess. "Want to do the honors, Wyat?"

Wyat grinned and it was more gargoyle than man as he approached. Mal turned her back on them as the Duchess's whimpers filled the cool air.

Onnli helped Saydi and Adde onto Rival's back. Saydi was injured somewhere, though it wasn't clear where. Onnli walked beside Rival, his hand reassuringly on Saydi's leg.

The place for the Duchess was little more than a single wooden and metal cell within the middle of Silence. Well, maybe not the middle. Deep within silence. It was a wooden box with a door. All four sides had windows of metal pipe.

They left the Duchess whimpering and crying, looking a little bloodier than she had been before Wyat had gotten his hands on her.

Fury turned them around to head in the opposite direction.

"Where are we going?" Ryph asked in his almost-normal state. He was still partially covered in feathers with his wings and tail out.

"Uh," Fury said, glancing at him. "I'd rather not say. There are ears in Silence."

Ryph and Eagy both nodded. Mal understood this concept since it was one of the things the two had told her from the very beginning, but she was uneasy about following someone they'd just met.

Chesh seemed to know him, even if he didn't care for him.

They walked partially into the night before Fury uncovered a cave opening hidden beneath the brush of fallen trees.

The cave brought them underground. After what felt like another day of walking, it opened into a whole community. There were buildings and trees, children running around, gardens, laughter. Mal thought she might have been dreaming. She was tired enough that it seemed a legitimate possibility.

"No way," Ryph said.

Mal looked at him. His eyes were wide and excited. He was

tired, with dark circles under his eyes, but his excitement bubbled through him as he bounced on his heels.

Mal gave her surroundings another look. The largest building in front of them had a sign that read 'Derision'. To her right, another read 'Ambition'. She recognized the names.

"Schoolroom?" she asked.

Fury nodded, grinning as two rowdy children came barreling into him. He scooped them both up and nuzzled them.

"Are you immune to infertility down here?" she asked, giving the abundance of children more consideration.

Fury smiled at her. "We're not, but we have the advantage of litters."

"Litters?" she asked, blinking several times. Surely, she'd heard him wrong. Surely, she was too tired for this conversation.

But he nodded. "Once, we were Canidae shifters."

"Once?"

He met her eyes and smiled. She had thought him young before but looking at him, she realized he was likely older than all of them, save for Wyat. "We lost our shifting. Our canids are stuck inside. We kept our enhanced senses, our animal instincts and nature, and ability to carry litters."

Mal gave him a sympathetic look. She added Canidae shifters to her long list of things to right.

They enjoyed a warm meal before being shown to a room. Ryph was almost too giddy to sleep, but he passed out almost as soon as his head was down. Eagy brushed his fingers through Ryph's hair before curling up next to him. When he met Mal's watchful eyes, he smiled. "Changing doesn't hurt. But the bigger you become from something small, the more exhausting it is."

Mal glanced at Wyat as he stripped out of his forest-worn clothing. He met her eyes briefly, grinned, and disappeared behind the washroom door.

They slept most of the day away. When Mal woke the next afternoon, everyone was already up and out of the room. Mal took her time in the washroom, enjoying a long soak by herself.

As she got out and dried off, the unmistakable sounds of Eagy unpacking met her ears. They hadn't brought much so what he was unpacking, she wasn't sure. They'd left everything at the inn when they left in such a hurry. Hopefully, the innkeeper would keep their room booked as Eagy had instructed.

She smiled and dressed before making her way back into the room.

"Hey," Mal said as she rounded the corner.

Eagy turned, a soft smile tugging at his lips. "Angel," he said, his voice carrying to her as if on a breeze. She idly wondered how he pulled that off at times. It wasn't constant.

"Ryph studying?"

Eagy smiled further. "Yeah, Writhing."

"I'm surprised he's allowed you out of his sight with Lorem still with us," she teased.

He rolled his eyes. "Don't point it out. He's only barely convinced himself that he can attend a few classes without me. And I really don't want to learn Writhing today." He sat on the bed with his hands behind him where he could lean back.

He was a remarkably beautiful man. With his platinum blond hair, wind-tossed on his head, over ice blue eyes. He was lean and hard and lithe, his body covered in remarkable, intricate etchings from head to toe. There was that exotic aspect to him where he was clearly something other with his deep purple tongue. And his smile could melt steel. Soft, playful, sexy.

He was one of those people who had no idea how truly beautiful he was. Being told he was nothing all his life robbed him of that idea long ago.

Mal closed the door and crossed the room. She lowered herself onto his lap, straddling him on her knees. "Tell me why Ryph doesn't like Lorem."

Eagy's stared into her eyes. "You don't need to seduce me for answers, Angel."

She laughed. "I'm not trying to seduce you. But, you know, we never get any alone time. Just you and me."

He sighed, leaning his head against hers. She scooched in further, pressing her hips to his. She really did want alone time with Eagy. With all of them. When she managed to save the world – and she was determined to think as if she would – then she could focus on making sure her relationship with each of her men was solid individually, as well as within the whole.

"No," he murmured. "We don't."

Mal reached behind him, trailing her fingers through the short, fine hair at the base of his head.

"Years ago, decades, when we first ran into Lorem, it was while he was being restrained by the Collectors of Madness. There were more than a dozen Collectors against just one Lorem. We tend to stay away from the Collectors. They're better trained than the soldiers and their ruthlessness knows no bounds. I don't know why we stopped to help. Maybe just because he was so grossly outnumbered. We rescued him. Killed the Collectors and stayed with Lorem while he healed from a couple of wounds."

He turned his face into Mal's neck, running his lips up to her ear. As he continued to talk, she brought her lip between her teeth to try to calm her breathing. She wanted the story. First.

"He got it in his head that he ought to thank us. Ryph likes flirting, in case you haven't noticed." Mal grinned, feeling his grin against her neck, too. "He thought it was a lot of fun to have someone new to flirt with. Lorem was pretty adept at it, toeing the line between meaningless and suggestive quite regularly. I'm a bit more awkward at flirting but-" he shrugged, "- I said something right, or wrong, depending on how you look at it, and Lorem had taken it as invitation. Next thing I know, I'm pressed firmly against Ryph. We're shoved against a wall with Lorem hard on me, his mouth on mine. Seriously, he kissed me so forcefully, I didn't have a straight thought in my body."

He chuckled. Mal sat up to look at him. Eagy's face was pink, but he was in good humor. "Ryph wasn't into it?"

Eagy shrugged. "He was pissed. Sent Lorem flying across the

room. His wings tore through his shirt and his beast's roar was so loud, stars danced in front of my eyes." He chuckled. "We've only seen Lorem a few times over the years since. Lorem seems to have taken Ryph's actions as an insult. They weren't meant that way. Ryph's better at turning people away than he is with the idea that I might be interested in someone else."

Mal laughed. "I don't doubt that at all."

He sighed again. "I'm really not interested in Lorem," he said earnestly. "I think somewhere deep down, beyond the possessiveness of the beast, Ryph knows that. Lorem knows that. He intentionally antagonizes Ryph. It's a bit frustrating."

"I don't know. For a man with scales, he's rather... hot," Mal said, tracing Eagy's jawline with the tip of her finger.

He grinned at her. "He's fucking gorgeous, Mal."

"Hmm," she hummed. "But you're not interested in him at all?"

"Do you want me to be?"

She shook her head. "No, but it seems if you're attracted to someone, you must be at least a little interested in him?"

"Does that mean you're interested in him? Is this your way of asking me if he can join us?"

Mal laughed. It did sound that way, didn't it? "No. Having Ryph always so jealous is a bit... exhausting."

"It is. Lorem can't stay with us. None of us will resist succumbing to Madness if he stays."

Mal shifted on his lap, placing more of her weight down. Eagy shifted too, spreading his legs a little to give her a pocket to sit in. Her eyes locked with his, his smile growing a little in that playful way of his. "You really are gorgeous, too, you know," she told him.

A little huff of laughter met her ears as he rolled his eyes. "Perhaps you don't see me clearly."

"You don't think so?" Mal ran her hands down his chest and stomach, slipping her fingers underneath the hem of his shirt where she could pull it up. He sat forward, taking his weight off his arms for her to pull it over his head. He had a light splattering of hair on his chest and a sexy little trail between his well-defined V that disappeared into his pants. "I think *you* don't see you clearly," she said, using her finger to trace a line of his etchings along his ribs.

She looked up to see open vulnerability shining brightly in his eyes. "Mal," he whispered.

It sounded almost like a plea. Mal wrapped her arms around his waist, leaning against him to press her lips to his. His kiss was reverent, as were his hands at her back, behind her shoulders. Holding her to him gently. She rocked her hips to his, gaining herself a groan from him.

He pressed her firmer against him, kissing her more ardently. She had meant to make this slow, to show him that she really did think he was as beautiful as Ryph. But his hands on her excited her blood far too much.

She broke from his lips and kissed down his neck. Eagy pulled at her shirt, taking handfuls and lifting it over her head. She pulled away long enough to allow him to pull it off her before she continued to kiss down his chest, running her fingers through the soft hair there. It was feather fine, something she was not at all surprised about.

Mal slipped from his lap to her knees onto the floor in front of him. "Someday," she said against his abdomen as her fingers undid his pants, "you're going to have to let me watch you and Ryph do this."

Eagy's sudden snort of laughter made her look up. He lifted his hips at her tugging, and she slipped his pants down. Exposing his already hard shaft, ready and weeping for her. "Not happening," he said, brushing her hair back from her face.

"Why?" she pouted, wrapping her hand around it. His eyelids fell to half closed as soon as she had him in her hands. "You let me watch you have sex."

His huff of a laugh was cut off by her hand tightening around him. His lips parted.

"You really are beautiful," she said quietly.

His eyes opened as he looked at her smiling. He leaned down and captured her mouth again. It was not just hunger this time, but affection and weakness. She swore it felt like he was opening his soul to her.

Eagy pulled her back into his lap. She pulled her lips from his but before she could speak, his mouth trailed down her neck, leaving a wet path that the cool air kissed and sent chills rising on her skin. He undid the wrap around her breasts, dropping it onto the floor before starting to untie her pants.

"Eagy," she breathed. "I really wanted to-"

"Later," he said against her skin.

"But I want to learn how. That's why I want to watch you and Ryph," she said as she dug her fingers into his hair.

"Later," he said again, pulling at her pants. She hadn't tied them that tightly.

"You'll let me watch you two later?"

A quiet, breathless laugh and he shook his head. "No. I mean you can take me in your mouth later if you still want to."

"Eagy," she whined.

Frustrated, he ripped at her pants, causing the seams to give. "Knots are not necessary," he said, hooded eyes meeting hers.

Mal laughed. "I didn't tie a knot and seriously, I want to see. How else will I learn?"

He took her mouth in his again, cutting off her argument from expanding. She pulled him to her, their chests together, hearts beating frantically against each other. Her heart felt so full with the way he touched her and held her against him.

When he had her pants bunched around her ass, she pulled away long enough to let her ruined pants fall. But with her breath regained, she grinned. "Please?"

Eagy grinned, shaking his head. He reached for her and she was only too happy to climb back on his lap.

"Please?" she whispered again.

He took a breath, his cheeks hot as his hands ran smoothly

across her back. "Maybe," he said. "I still dream you'll change your mind about us. That it won't be okay, and you'll leave."

Mal shook her head. "No, Eagy. I'm really okay with it. In fact, it's fucking hot."

His cheeks heated further as he buried his face in her neck. "How did we ever get so lucky to find you?"

"I think I found you," Mal said, scooting in further.

Eagy nodded, reaching between them to position himself. He pushed his head in before wrapping his arms around her again, bringing her chest flush to his. It was almost an odd angle with their lips against each other's too, but she pushed her hips down on his, taking him inside her. Any awkwardness there might have been was lost in the sensual connection between them.

They moved slowly, feeling their heartbeats as much as their sex. There was something almost more carnal about this as they stared in the other's eyes with their lips parted just an inch apart. Their heaving breathing and shared air increased the sensual feel of their slick bodies as the friction built between them.

Mal rocked her hips, his arms tightening around her. She rolled into him over and over, Eagy allowing her complete control.

"Come for me," he whispered. "Can we? Without Ryph to help?"

Mal's mind was so thick with desire and warmth that it took her several minutes for her to understand his question. "We don't need Ryph to help with that," she said at last.

"Are you sure?"

His voice was filled with trepidation. She knew he didn't get that insecurity from anything Ryph had done. She'd seen them together.

"More than sure," she assured him. "Look at me."

He opened his eyes again, those piercing blue shards penetrating her soul.

"You're all I need, Eagy. We don't need anyone's help for this."

The breath he took was shaky, even as he nodded with small, jerky motions. When he started to look away again, she asked him to keep looking at her. She wanted to see his emotion. She wanted to make his insecurities go away. She wanted to take them away.

One by one, she wanted to give Eagy back the confidence he shouldn't have had stripped from him by the cruelty in the world. All because he was born something he didn't have control over.

Mal kept his gaze with hers as she worked them both into a long, sweet orgasm. He somehow still managed to keep himself still and allow her to control the rhythm in which they finished. When they finished. How they finished.

His eyes remained on hers, steady, even as she couldn't keep hers open when the peak of her pleasure rolled through her. The enormity of emotion mixed with pleasure on his face was almost heart-wrenching. She could only begin to imagine what he was thinking.

She rested her forehead on his and closed her eyes. It shouldn't have been possible, but he pulled her closer, tighter, squeezing her to him like she might vanish. "Mal," he whispered.

"I told you we didn't need any help," she said.

He chuckled.

She wondered if it was too soon to tell him she loved him. She was sure she did. There was no one who made her feel so loved, so valued and treasured, yet respected her strength and need to be heard.

Eagy took a breath. "Join me in the tub?"

Mal nodded. "I did just take a soak," she said.

"I know," he murmured. "I want to wash you myself."

She grinned. He picked her up and headed for the washroom. She watched him run the water and light the fire from where he sat her on the counter. After several considerations, Eagy placed three bottles of cleansers by the tub, along with two towels.

When he was satisfied, he picked her up and brought her

into the water. For a moment, he continued to hold her. Then, he made sensual work of washing her. He gently bathed every nook and crevice before moving on to her hair. When he was satisfied and they got out, he dried her just as attentively before rubbing her body down with lotion. He even dressed her in clean, not-torn clothing, though she had to maneuver the wrap herself.

He watched her carefully as she did, scrutinizing every hand movement. "I'm not as good at this as Chesh," she admitted.

He met her eyes with that heart-skipping, playful smile. "I'll need him to teach me. It's all a bit... confusing."

Mal laughed, agreeing wholeheartedly.

Finally clean and dressed, they returned to the room. Eagy crossed back to where he was unpacking their meager belongings.

"I'm going to get some answers," Mal told him. He looked up as she placed a kiss to his lips. With a smile and an assurance that she had her blade on her and that she'd keep safe, Mal left in search of Lorem.

He didn't need the music that came along with his burden to announce where he was. She could hear his deep baritone as he sang. She followed his music until she found him dancing around a copse of trees.

Mal was sure the man didn't own any clothing. He never wore anything but the thing he carried on his back. Otherwise, he was bare to the world and happy for it. Always very happy.

She watched him dance around, singing in a language she didn't understand. And then he must have saw her, for his words changed to English and the song clearly changed, as well.

"In the winter, when the fields are white,
I sing this song for your delight-"

He spun around a tree, his feet coming off the ground.

"In spring, when woods are getting green,
I'll work all day to make you scream."

A spin and a dip before he executed an elegant backwards cartwheel. One of those where their hips don't move in space and they don't use their hands.

"In the summer, when the days are long,
Perhaps you'll let me lick your thong."

With his hands over his head, he made some very suggestive moves with his hips, where his fully erect cock swayed invitingly.

"In autumn, when the leaves are brown
Let's talk our kinks and we'll go down."'

His hands washed down his face, his chest, his stomach, his hips as he turned his face to profile. His long, white hair fanned with the turn.

"I put a message in the dish
I tell you, this is what I wish."

He spun, his hair once again fanning out. As he slid across the ground, bringing his heels together and his hands above his head once more, he looked like he was suspended at a forty-five-degree angle, defying gravity.

"Tie you up so you can't see
Then you do it back to me."

He righted himself, bringing a hand across his eyes. When it finished its course, his grass green eyes were locked with hers.

"Bury myself in so deep

Making your hips buck and leap."

Her heart leapt as he took several steps to her. She found it hard to keep her eyes on his when the entirety of his body was on display for her. And right now, for her alone.

"'Just like that' you start to say,
No, my love, time to obey."

His hand thrust out to his side between lines. When his fist closed, he brought it back in over his heart.

"You beg and cry; my giddy grin
When I thrust back in again."

He rolled his back, thrusting his hips out.

"I drive, and plunge, once then twice
Ram and lunge, that feels so nice."

He turned on his side and repeated the moves. She hadn't realized he had such a nice ass until then. Tight and perfectly shaped. Her hand tingled to slap it, so she clutched her fist tightly at her thigh.

"Let us now try something new
Fit for the deed I crave to do."

And he turned another ninety degrees, bringing his back to her. The muscles in his back were just as impressive. When he rolled his back this time, the scales shimmered like a wave.

"My heart went hop, my heart went thump;
Your hips buck up, I pump and pump."

His hand over his head, gyrating like he was spinning a lasso, he turned back to face her in two steps.

"I'm coming, I'm coming," you said.
I drove you hard into the bed."

In a move that seemed a little too modern for Laddenworn, he brought his lasso-wielding hand down in front of him, palm to the ground, and made a thrusting motion with his hips.

"I say to you, I say it plain,
"Are you ready to get it again?"

Part of her thought she should be completely annoyed by him. Was he trying to seduce her? She couldn't quite tell. He was always dancing and singing.

"Breathing heavy, loud and clear
I bend to whisper in your ear."

A cat-like grin curled his lips as he languidly blinked at her, turning his head to profile.

"I'm mighty stiff and oh so proud
You must like it; you were quite loud."

Before she could stop him, he grabbed her by the waist and brought her flush to him. Her heart pounded loud in her ears as she met his bright, grass green eyes.

"Not just stiff, I'm long and strong
Time to get our fucking on."

He moved their hips together in a tight circle, making sure she felt exactly what he pressed between them.

"I took the oil from the shelf
Then I stroked it on myself."

Mal swallowed loudly, pressing her hands against his shoulders. His scales were smooth, sleek, and riveted like a small, spiral-bound notebook. She was mortified when her hands brushed down to his biceps, exploring if the rest of his scales felt that way.

"Looky what you've done, I'm cocked
Not to brag, your world will rock."

She was beginning to think this wasn't part of the song. He moved them through the little clearing and into the shade between two large trunks.

"Come here, babe, I'm about to nut.
But first, let's try it in your butt-"

He pushed her roughly against the trunk of a tree, the bark biting into her back through her loose shirt. His smile was nothing but sensual. His hold was pure heat and seduction, as his hands moved from her hips to her waist.

"Well, hello, my pretty little thing," he said in a sound that was absolutely a purr. Who knew reptiles could purr? "What brings you my way? Care to join the dance?"

Mal shook her head, trying desperately to think of the reason she'd sought him out. Oh. Oh, right. "Why are you here? Why are you constantly antagonizing Ryph? What's wrong with you?!"

His smile displayed wonderfully white teeth. She was distracted by his mouth getting closer to hers. Her feet left the ground as he pushed her up the tree, bringing her eye-level to him. He didn't answer her, ghosting his lips along her jaw.

Her breaths were labored as she fought to keep her hold.

At the crook between her jaw and her ear, he whispered, "Ryph's a mess. Surely, you can see that."

Anger rushed through her, clearing her mind of much of the fog he was creating. But before she could retort, he continued.

With a sigh that tickled her skin, he said, "The rarer they are, the fiercer the Madness grasps. Deeper its talons go. Ryph is almost lost completely."

"That's not true," Mal insisted. "You're purposefully making him-"

"Oh, come now," he purred. "I know you can see the beast at the surface all the time. Madness cannot touch animals, but the person it's attached to is not immune. We all have our coping mechanisms. Our own strategies for warding off the madness for as long as we can. Sometimes, we're only awarded with windows of clarity. Others find better ways to keep it down."

"What's yours?" Mal asked. "I'm pretty sure you're really deep in madness."

"Oh, I am," he said, his lips moving against her ear. "I dance. I sing. For me, it keeps the dreadful fog away."

"Then why are you pushing him? What are you trying to gain?"

He chuckled, feathering his nose up her hairline. She shivered. "He's letting his person out more and more. If the beast sleeps, the Madness will take hold and Ryph will be lost. He's far too young to be able to hold the Madness back without his beast." A hand on her waist moved up to her ribs. "No worries, sweet little thing. His beast is the only thing awake since I've been here."

Mal thought about Ahdem. Not everyone had an animal to keep the madness at bay. "You're trying to tell me you're doing this for his own good?"

"Yes, though coming upon you was happenstance. I meant what I said bout the reason why I left Tulgey. Sad, really. That's my home."

Mal refused to allow herself to be sympathetic just yet. "Why are you with us? Just to torment him?"

"No," he breathed and nipped her neck. She swallowed and tried to push him away. She really shouldn't have tried. He pressed his weight harder to her, grinding his hips to hers. She felt his smile against her neck. "I am with you because I'm not sure where else to go. Silence is a lonely place."

That, she knew only too well.

She was suddenly free of his grip. Mal fell to her feet and stumbled, trying to gain her balance. She lost her footing completely when she was whisked up, bridal style. Her world spun until she saw Eagy's irritated gaze looking beyond her.

Lorem was sprawled across the ground, his hair tangled over his face. His chest shook with laughter. His phallus was standing up straight, swaying as if waving at them. Mal blushed and turned away.

"You crossed a line, Lorem," Eagy said.

"Just now?" Lorem sat up, brushing his hair back. "Was that all it took?"

Eagy's gaze hardened. "Don't touch her. Play your damned games, but don't touch Mal."

"That means... I can touch you...?"

Eagy sighed and turned away. "You're draining."

Lorem's laughter followed them out of the trees and into the area that made up the grounds of Underground Schoolroom. When Lorem's laughter could no longer be heard, Eagy said, "When you said you were going to get some answers, I didn't realize you meant from Lorem."

She smiled sheepishly.

"Mal-"

"I only went to ask him why he's such an ass and can't he just leave Ryph alone," she said quickly, before he could get upset with her.

He paused and met her eyes. "Did you?"

She nodded. “I thought, on his own, he might be more forthcoming.”

“Was he?” He continued walking, bringing them back to the room they all shared with the big, comfortable bed.

“If what he says is true, Ryph uses his beast to stave off madness, which settles in deeply to rare animals. But Ryph has been bringing his person to the surface more and more and if his animal goes to sleep, Ryph will be lost for good.”

Eagy stopped walking. She studied his face for some time as many thoughts sped through his expression. He frowned and looked at her. “We’ll talk to Ryph.”

She nodded, wrapping her arms around his neck and burying her face in his shoulder. He hugged her tighter.

“You okay?” he asked.

Mal nodded. “What is he?”

“Lorem?”

She nodded again.

“Mock Turtle.”

“Ohhhh,” she said, laughing. That explained the burden on his back and scales.

Messenger

MAL

22

Mal didn't leave Eagy for the rest of the day. She spent a lot of time in her memorandum book, looking at all the things she'd learned from Eagy and Lorem about Lorem and madness and why he was being such a pain in the ass.

Ryph returned from class stoked. He talked excitedly about what he'd learned and what they'd be teaching the next day. Mal studied him through a smile. Ryph was always in a good mood, always laughing and happy and ready to embrace anything. But this Ryph was damn near ready to explode with giddiness.

She tried to see if what Lorem claimed was true. But she was so used to seeing those big, golden eyes. Happy and full of mirth.

Oh! There... Mal sat forward to look. His eyes weren't so round, so big today. Not so much... animal. And yes, there, was a hint of absence. Not Absence but absence – as in he wasn't all there. The madness. His gaze would shift, go far away, for a split second.

Was she seeing it because it was there or because Lorem had suggested it was?

"We need to talk," Eagy said, taking his hands and sitting him on the bed.

Ryph's expression changed immediately. Rage leaped forward and the beast was back at the surface, for sure. "Did he fucking touch you? I swear, I'll-"

"No," Eagy said, smiling. "He didn't touch me." He glanced to Mal for a split second. She got the message. Best not say that Lorem touched *her*, either.

Ryph took a breath and settled back. "Then...?"

"First, you know we need to leave soon, right? We can't stay here."

Ryph sighed. "Yeah. I know." His tone was so sad, Mal was sure she felt her heart crack a little.

Eagy smiled softly and set a hand on the side of his face. "I'm worried about you."

Ryph titled his head, just a bit. Not enough to pull away, but enough that they knew he was curious. "Why?"

"When your beast is too far inside, there's Madness in your eyes," Eagy said gently.

Fear made Ryph tense. He glanced at Mal before staring at Eagy. "I..."

Eagy kissed him, pulling him to his chest. "Until we figure out how to get rid of the Madness, keep your beast close, okay?"

"Eagy," Ryph whispered. "I'm scared."

Eagy's arms tightened around Ryph. "I got you. Just stay with me. Keep your ferocious animal near the surface for a bit."

Ryph tensed further. "He's... a bit unstable," he confided. "He wants things."

"We'll work it out. Whatever it is, we'll work through it, but I can't lose you."

"No," Ryph said, his fingers digging into Eagy's back. "No, I won't let it take me."

Ryph sunk his teeth into Eagy's shoulder. Eagy flinched, his fist tightening the hold in Ryph's hair.

They remained like that for a good, long time while Mal looked on, tears in her eyes. It was one thing to hear someone talking about madness. About someone else having it. Having it affect someone she cared deeply about was a little too much.

She added that to her list of things to fix. But if it was anything like mental illness back in the Outside, she doubted any amount of magic could fix it.

Their door swung open and Chesh popped in. "Grab your new gloves, Kitten. You're about to go to your first lesson."

Ryph jumped from the bed with a huge smile, grabbing Eagy's hand and pulling him to his feet with him. "Let's go, too."

Eagy nodded and handed Mal her gloves that had been sitting next to him on the bed. She was surprised they hadn't been lost in the blankets from their earlier romp. Then again, they hadn't gotten too involved with blankets.

Chesh led them to an empty building without a name.

"This is newly built," Ryph told them. "They're preparing for more subjects."

Mal smiled to herself.

"Put them on," Chesh said, leading them to the other side of the room. He had a table set up with various objects. A bowl. A towel. A book. A small rock. He picked up the rock. "We're going to start small. Turn the rock into sand."

She held it in her palm and stared at him. "What, no instruction?"

Chesh shrugged. "Magic works different for everyone. You have to find how you touch it."

"How it touches me, you mean," she said.

"No, I mean what I said as I meant it."

Mal glanced at him. "Then give me some advice on how I touch it."

"It started with stolen tarts, they say. I tend to believe it was the Frabjous day," Chesh offered with his too-wide smile.

She frowned as Ryph snorted a laugh.

Mal was thankful when Eagy came up behind her. His hands rubbed down her arms, enclosing hers with his. His lips at her ear, he said in a soft, windy voice, "Just feel for it. Close your eyes and pull the brightest thing to you. Feel for it and ask it to do as you wish."

He was rather distracting this close. So sweet and kind and beautiful. Thoughtful. Caring. He was the brightness in her. With amusement, she thought she'd just see if his brightness would help her find the brightness of the magic.

She imagined herself wrapping Eagy around her. Feathers, wings, etchings. The bright light coming out of the wrap that was Eagy, breaking through each twist. The warmth it caused as it ran down her arms, into her palms, through her fingers.

"See, I knew you could do it," Eagy whispered.

Mal opened her eyes, shocked to see there was sand sifting between her glove covered fingers instead of a rock. "Oh!" she exclaimed. "But I don't think that was my magic. I was using yours."

Eagy's head shifted in confusion. "Mine?"

She nodded as heat rushed to her cheeks, now suddenly embarrassed. "You're the bright spot. So, I pretended to wrap your bright light around me. And..." She shrugged, letting the rest of the sand fall to the floor.

Eagy was grinning widely when he stepped away, pink high on his cheeks, too.

"Try again," Chesh said, highly amused. "Turn the bowl into a tea tray."

Mal closed her eyes and imagined the same thing. Eagy around her. The light coursing through her. Down her arms. To her hands. Filling her hands so full they no longer cupped the bowl between them, but lay flat, opened. She only opened her eyes when Ryph cheered loudly for her. The bowl was gone, and a beautiful tea tray lay in her hands.

"Either this is really easy, or these things are already magic," she said skeptically.

"Book into bread," Chesh prompted. "This time, keep your eyes open."

Mal nodded. Holding the book in her hands, she still

pictured Eagy around her. Felt his light, his warmth, travel down her arms into her hands. Before her very eyes, the book changed into a loaf of focaccia.

"Oooo," Ryph said, holding his hand out eagerly, "What kind of bread have you made?"

"The kind vaguely shaped like a book?" she offered, handing it over. She was momentarily mortified to see him stick a large hunk in his mouth. That was a book! You don't eat books. Not even ones without pictures in them.

But Ryph hummed his enjoyment, his eyes closing as he savored the bite. He shared with the other two, offering Mal some, too. She refused, not able to get behind the idea that the book was now in their stomachs.

"Let me choose something this time," Mal said, picking up the last item. A towel. "Just to prove you didn't already hand me objects that turned into what you suggested."

Chesh shrugged and stepped back.

Mal repeated her Eagy-wrap-light-warmth exercise with her eyes opened. She was ecstatic to find that it turned into a mirror. When she looked up at the three men, they stared at her in surprise.

"You're not supposed to be able to do that," Chesh said. "Part of the Queens' destruction of all looking glasses was their eradication of the magic in creating new ones."

"Are you sure they managed that or just convinced everyone they had and so no one would try?" Mal countered, holding it up to look at her reflection.

The three didn't answer for a time.

"Power of suggestion," Mal said, turning with her new mirror. A gift for Adde.

SHE TAPPED her pen absently on the memorandum book, staring at the wall. She had a whole lot of theories and almost no facts at all. Nothing to be of any help in locating the original, prophesizing looking-glass – whether it was Snow White's or not was another question. Where the Vorpal blade might be - or if it was even necessary. Did she need these items to defeat the queens? Better yet, were they items the queens could use against her? Whether a different fairy tale had actually poisoned this one or whether it was all mad coincidence.

And then, what of the prince, the king? The poisonous apple? The poisonous apple might have been the cursed red mark vaguely in the shape of an apple that she'd escaped from the dungeons with. Did that mean the poisonous apple was now accounted for?

Hell, maybe none of that mattered in the least. Maybe the only thing that really mattered was getting rid of the Bloody Queens.

The door to their room swung open suddenly. Startled, Mal jerked out of her chair to her feet.

TL paused, looking at her. "Sorry," he murmured. His eyes scanned the room. When he quickly noted she was alone, his lips pressed together into a hard line. "Where is everyone?"

"Scared of me, Flower?" she asked as she took her seat again.

His gaze landed on her and he frowned. When he shut the door behind him, she raised her brow. He'd spent the last month keeping himself far out of reach when she was alone, unless it was strictly necessary for him to be with her. Then again, he did seat himself as far away as he could in that moment.

Mal rolled her eyes. "Wyat is getting food. Chesh is doing whatever a demon cat does. The other two are in the tub." She gestured to the washroom door as a splash met their ears. "No idea where the wildflowers or Lorem are. And Kav is your responsibility."

"And you're alone in here?"

She looked up. "No one is looking for me. Why should they?

According to the papers, I died in the dungeons. Everyone is waiting on number twenty-nine."

He didn't answer or argue.

It was the better part of a long, silent hour later that Chesh came back as Eagy and Ryph came out of the washroom. They had all gathered on the floor when Wyat stepped in, bearing a giant tray of food.

Conversation was pleasant throughout the meal. Mal enjoyed sitting back and watching them interact. They liked each other. Genuinely. She wondered if all harems got along as well as hers. Even TL seemed to fit in with their joking and stories, as if he were meant to be there.

As they plowed their way through the food, Chesh asked, "What brings you to our meal, TL?"

TL finished eating his meat pie before leaning back on his hands. "Kav," he said.

All five sets of eyes looked at him. Satisfied everyone was paying sufficient attention, he continued. "I've seen him meet messengers at every stop. I brushed it off initially, but his behavior is very peculiar when he interacts with them. He is careful to make sure no one is around that could overhear. He whispers his reply low enough that I can't get even a hint of it on the air."

Wyat growled. "Are we finished?" he asked as he got to his feet.

Mal was pretty sure they weren't, but the platter was removed from their little picnic area as Wyat stormed out of the room to retrieve the knave once again. And like last time, he threw Kav to the ground like a rag doll.

"I haven't touched Mal," Kav said angrily. His dark eyes looked at her intently.

Mal shook her head. "I didn't say you had."

"Then what-"

"What's with the secret messengers?" Wyat asked, arms

crossed. The man looked like a bouncer when he stood like that. Big, muscular, and mean.

Kav sighed. "I'm the Knave of Hart. I have a job to do. Remember? I'm out on the pretense of making sure I get my hands on Twenty-Nine before anyone else does."

"Why is that a secret?" Eagy demanded.

"It's not a secret. That is the official reason I'm not at the palace."

"You're not telling us something," Wyat said. "You're looking pretty suspicious whispering to all your messengers, sneaking around to meet them."

Yeah, he'd added that last part on conjecture.

"Look. If I thought I could have managed, I'd have killed the queens myself. They murdered my family: my mother, my wife, three sisters, and my daughter. I literally watched two of my sisters' still-beating hearts removed from their chests." Grief filled his eyes. "I went to the palace after they were taken - once I managed to get out of the barn the soldiers locked me in. I went posing as a soldier. I worked my way up, into their good graces, so I could have free access to the palaces. Hart took more of a liking to me than Redd, so I kept on her side as much as possible. Even so, they don't trust me enough to move beyond Knave.

"I had to change my plans. Now, I wait until they capture One after One. They don't last long in the dungeons. Even when I bring them sustenance. They're usually dead within a few days. Mal survived for more than seven weeks. I knew before then that she was the Right One, but I couldn't find a way to get her out without blowing my cover. We'd both lose our hearts. When I finally managed to get her out of the dungeon, I couldn't get her conscious for more than a few minutes. Dressing her in armor to escape the palace was impossible until she was at least fully lucid. It took me three weeks to get her to keep enough down for the medicinal teas to work.

"Do you really think I'd risk my life helping her if I planned to turn around and get her killed?"

The room let that settle for a few minutes.

Not satisfied, Wyat pushed on. "Yet you've still managed to avoid my question."

He nodded warily. "There's a troop of soldiers I'm tracking. Hunting soldiers is treason. If I let anyone hear what I'm doing, someone with a stupid idea of advancing their position in life could march right to the palace and turn me in."

"We hunt Bloody Soldiers constantly," Ryph said, crossing his arms.

"Yes, you hunt them and terminate every last one. You dispose of their bodies pretty well and leave nothing of yourself behind. I'm not trying to kill them but keep eyes on their movements. Being out of the palace means I am not privy to what's going on there. And right now, between the two queens, there are nine troops moving through Laddenworn, which seems high to me. Thus far, whatever is going on has been kept quiet since no one I trust has any answers as to why they're out in droves."

They contemplated his words for several minutes before TL looked at Mal. "You have a map, don't you?"

Mal titled her head. Had he read her mind? She'd never taken her map out around him.

The corner of his mouth quirked ever so slightly. "In your ramblings of yelling at me your first few days in my Marden, you mentioned a map you once had."

She narrowed her eyes on him but got to her feet and retrieved the rolled-up parchment from her messenger bag, handing it to him as she sat back down next to Eagy.

TL thanked her and unrolled it. After studying it and deeming it slightly outdated (why? Because Silence had spread further into Redd as it skirted around Garden to reach Tulgey), he decided it would do. He placed it on the floor in front of Kav.

Kav didn't wait for him to say what TL wanted him to do. He

pointed to nine different places on the map. The places where the nine troops of soldiers were located at last report. Three alone were within Tulgey. Another larger one was in Childhood, preventing rebuilding. One close to both palaces, Redd and Hart. The remaining three were apparently on the move. One in Silence, south of Childhood, one by the Pool of Tears and another passing the river at And Curiouser.

"What does it mean?" Mal asked.

Kav shook his head. "They're trying to burn Tulgey to the ground, last I heard. A messenger two days ago suggested that they were newly running into some opposition. I don't think Steele could have made it there yet. Perhaps the Raptors?" He shrugged.

"Which way are the moving troops headed?" Eagy asked.

Kav pointed. The one within Silence was moving west, in a direction south of their current location. The one crossing the river was moving toward Memory, out of And Curiouser. And the one by the Pool of Tears was heading toward the Palace of Dymund.

"Are there any towns or settlements or anything around the moving groups?" Mal asked.

Kav shook his head. "Not that I know of."

They discussed the troops for quite some time, throwing out one unlikely idea after another. They ended their discussion on the idea that the queens were looking for something. It couldn't possibly be a someone, but maybe it could...

At the door, Kav turned. His eyes met Mal's. He hesitated, as if contemplating something, undecided on whether he wanted to say it.

"Spit it out," Ryph said.

Kav inclined his head slightly, his eyes not leaving Mal's. "I petition to join your harem, Mal."

Her eyes widened in surprise. She'd spent almost no time with him since Wabe, since her harem had almost beaten him for their earlier relationship. He gave her a small, flirty smile and hurried out the door before anyone could say anything.

And they had a lot to say. Well into the night, they had many things to say. Mal didn't even argue with them. She wasn't sure if she trusted him, either. TL still insisted he was leaving something out. There was no way troop movement would be such a quiet conversation. He was the Knave. Part of his job was to know what the troops were up to.

Well past the time Mal was usually deep asleep, TL finally got up to leave. He opened the door to their very own messenger who asked for Chesh.

With a sigh, Chesh walked over like a proud, annoyed cat, tail standing up and the tip flicking with irritation. "Do you know what time it is?" he asked the messenger.

"Yes, sorry," he said, offering Chesh the piece of paper and leaving.

TL shut the door and turned.

A smile crept up Chesh's face. "Finally. We have a destination."

"Wally?" Wyat asked as Eagy asked, "Where?"

"Dark Water," he said, nodding at Wyat's question.

"We leave after breakfast," Eagy said. "Especially since we need to head back to the inn for the rest of our travel gear first."

The Cats

CHESH

23

For wanting to get to Wally after waiting months to hear from him, no one was in a hurry that morning. Probably because they'd been up too late last night. Kav, then conversation after Kav, then the messenger. Then the beast couldn't go a night without spilling his seed in Mal.

He was exhausting.

As Wyat went to fetch them breakfast and Mal passed through the tub again (Eagy and Ryph on her heels), Chesh volunteered to find the wildflowers and Lorem to let them know they were leaving. Ryph had suggested Chesh might forget to mention it to Lorem. But that was just rude. He would, however, propose Lorem stay behind.

Lorem seemed the more draining of the two stops, so he sought him out first. He was already up and dancing around by the time Chesh was close enough to hear him. In a grove of small trees, light-footed, despite the burden on his back.

Chesh paused a minute to listen. Lorem really did have a nice, soothing voice. He leaned against one of the saplings and waited until Lorem noticed him or found a natural break in his song.

It was a while. Longer than Chesh thought was polite to

ignore someone openly watching you and presumably waiting to have a few words.

Tired of the delay, Chesh walked further into Lorem's little grove and stopped in the path Lorem was taking. Lorem came to a sudden halt, lyrics cut off mid word.

"Well, that was rude," Lorem said, frowning.

"Tell me about it," Chesh said, crossing his arms. "I've been waiting for you to break for half an hour and I'm hungry."

Lorem lifted his head. "What is it, already? I have a headache."

Ah, he was dancing to fight back the Madness this morning. "We're leaving," Chesh informed him. "We found our prey and will be taking off within the hour. I thought you might like to know."

Lorem nodded. "I think I will not burden you with my slow presence," he said, taking a step back.

"I'm glad we agree on that, though our ideas of why differ."

He grinned widely. "No worries. We shall cross paths again, demon."

Chesh nodded. He held no doubts about that. He waved vaguely and turned to head toward the wildflowers' room. It was quite a walk from their own. They'd been housed with the families because Mal's harem was large enough to warrant a bigger bed. And, you know... there was the giant that was Wyat. The wildflowers, unhusbanded and unwifed, were housed with those just there for education. Rooms with multiple beds.

It was a nice place. He was surprised he hadn't heard about it until Fury.

Damned mutt.

If he remembered correctly, they were on the third level of the small, inn-like dormitory. He paused at the first door on that floor. Then the second. At the fourth, he heard Adde's giggle. Well, then. He not only found the wildflowers, but they were awake.

He probably should have knocked. For when he opened the

door, the two girls were in bed, wrapped around each other, very much without clothing. Chesh tilted his head, his ears perking up. *That*, he hadn't expected.

Adde sat up, startled at his sudden appearance. Saydi gave a little yelp and pulled the covers up to her neck. At their distress, Onnli came out of the washroom, strangely enough, fully clothed.

Not so strange, really. Chesh had spent a lot of time in the washroom before Wyat came along. Now, he was happy enough to leave the younglings with Mal since Wyat didn't go far.

"Beg my pardon," Chesh said. He turned away to give them some semblance of privacy, choosing instead to address Onnli. "We're leaving shortly."

"We'll be there in a few minutes," Onnli said. "Once I manage to get the girls out of bed." He frowned at them, though it was clear he was not at all unfamiliar with this scene.

How awkward. There was no way Onnli and Adde weren't siblings.

Chesh nodded and shut the door as he backed out of the room, apologizing once more. He meandered back and found that there was still food left.

Mal looked up at him from the floor with a wide smile. "I saved some for you, Cheshy Cat."

It might as well have been a purr. One that went straight to his heart. Or was it his cock? Both, perhaps. He took up a seat beside her and dug right into the food.

"You'll be pleased to know that Lorem will not be accompanying us," he told the room at large.

Ryph smiled broadly, the beast almost bursting from him with joy.

Eagy just looked relieved.

"The wildflowers?" TL asked, sitting in the far corner at the table.

Chesh finished a breakfast pie while nodding. "Onnli will get them out of bed and meet us here any minute."

"They were still in bed?" Ryph asked, perplexed. "There's so much to do."

Chesh nodded, though he didn't expand. It wasn't his tale to tell. If they wanted to keep it a secret, he would keep their secret, too.

They were up and packed with the few parcels they'd acquired by the time the three wildflowers arrived. Adde was looking a little sheepish, while Saydi all but hid behind Adde and Onnli. Once again, Onnli rolled his eyes.

"Ready?" Eagy asked, curiously watching their odd behavior.

"Actually, we'd like to stay here. If that's okay?" Adde asked.

Chesh wasn't convinced Onnli wanted that at all. His expression said he surely didn't want to stay behind, but that he wouldn't leave his sister. Chesh understood that. There was a very big part of Ryph that wanted to stay, too. But he wouldn't stay without Eagy and Mal, even if he would leave Chesh, Wyat, and TL behind.

Eagy nodded. "You'll be safe enough here."

"Did you leave anything at the inn?" TL asked.

The three shook their heads.

Adde's eyes constantly darting to Chesh, a bright pink blush on her cheeks, was only calling more attention to a situation he hadn't addressed. He smiled at her, hoping to convey that her secret was her own.

Onnli sighed. "Look," he said, ushering the two girls further into the room. He shut the door and turned to face the room of men and Mal. "Saydi is my wife. She's also Adde's wife. So, what you walked in on this morning," he said, looking at Chesh, "was quite regular and pretty obnoxious." He glared at the two.

All the men looked at the girls with interest, fascination, before turning to land curious eyes on Chesh.

"For the record," Chesh told the girls, "I hadn't said anything. What you do is your business, not mine. And," he turned to look at the others, "I probably should have knocked. I heard Adde laugh and assumed they were up for the day." He shrugged.

"You share a wife?" Ryph asked, fascinated.

Onnli nodded, a small smile playing at the corner of his lips. "It's even weirder than it sounds." He pulled Saydi out from behind him, resting his hands gently on her arms.

"If men can share wives, why can't a man and a woman share a wife?" Adde asked, her voice small and hesitant. Like she was doing something wrong. "Why can't I have a wife?"

"You can," Mal said, giving everyone in the room a very pointed look. "Whatever makes you happy."

"You're not bothered by it?" Adde asked.

"Only if this relationship is at all fake," Mal said.

All three wildflowers looked at her with confusion. "Fake?" Onnli asked.

"I mean, you're not pretending to be Saydi's husband so Adde and Saydi can be together, right?"

Saydi's face turned a bright shade of red. She shook her head furiously as Onnli laughed.

"No," Onnli said. "Saydi was my wife first, actually. If I recall, she and Adde didn't care for each other much." The grin on his face was the biggest Chesh had seen. "It was more disturbing when they actually started getting along than it was when they were constantly at each other's throats."

Adde shrugged, having regained some of her composure. "Don't fight. Don't kiss. If you'd have just made up your mind what you wanted..."

Onnli rolled his eyes again, but this time he was smiling.

"You'll be okay here?" Mal asked. "Truly?"

Onnli and the girls nodded. "I'll keep them safe," Onnli promised. "There's a few classes for just that purpose, actually. I doubt it'll be as good as TL, but I'll take it."

TL smirked but remained quiet.

The wildflowers walked them to the passage that took them from Underground Schoolroom. Mal hugged Adde and Saydi, telling them to make sure they kept their mirror hidden. Who knew what kind of attention they'd bring if someone saw it?

She was surprised when Adde and Saydi wrapped their arms tightly around Rival's neck. He bowed his head, resting it on the girls' backs.

Kav watched them, perplexed. When Rival raised his eyes, meeting Kav's, there was some silent exchange between the two of them. "Why don't you take care of Rival?" Kav suggested after the moment lingered on. "Give Onnli some comfort when he's in class."

Adde turned with a wide grin. "Really? You won't mind?"

Kav shook his head, an amused smile. "As long as Rival doesn't."

Rival nudged his muzzle into Adde, encouraging Adde to wrap her arms around his head. "Goodbye, Knave," was his only reply.

The walk back to the surface took a little over an hour. It was still late morning by the time they left the tunnel entrance, hidden back under the dead and decaying trees.

Chesh immediately smelled something he hoped he wouldn't come across. Something that he dreaded and, given the direction it seemed to be wafting from, he knew they'd be coming across them soon. He inwardly grumbled, but hopefully kept his expression neutral.

"I'm going to miss them," Mal said.

"We didn't spend a lot of time with them, really," Ryph said, rubbing his big, bronze hand down her back.

"No, I know. But it was some time. And it was nice to have another girl around," she mused.

"Too many men?" Eagy asked, warily.

Mal must have caught his hesitancy because she turned to him with a beaming smile. "No. Enough men, sure. But I'm happy with you all."

His smile in return was still uncertain, but he nodded. Mal was getting good about reading Eagy's insecurity. She twined her fingers with his and wrapped her other hand around his arm, too, cuddling into his side as they walked.

This time when he smiled at her, he knew she was trying to comfort him. Assure him. He kissed the top of her head. "Alright," he said. "I'm good."

She nodded but didn't release her hold on him. He was just as happy to walk with her like that.

"Is that...?" Wyat started to ask, raising his twitching nose into the air. He glanced at Chesh.

Chesh tried very hard not to scowl or grumble. Instead, he nodded.

"What?" Mal asked. She looked at Wyat and then at Chesh. Both Eagy and Ryph lifted their noses to the air, then, too.

"Cats," TL said.

As if he'd cued them, the cats' yowls and hisses filled the air.

"Really?" Mal asked, looking back at Chesh. "I didn't realize there were others like you. More demon cats!"

Chesh shook his head. "Just cats, dear. Normal, lame cats."

She grinned.

They listened to the antics of the cats get louder the closer they got. When the finally arrived, it was obvious the colony had picked itself up and was moving around. There were boxes here and there, set up haphazardly. Strings hanging from branches as kittens played. And down the center of the long clearing was a table piled high with dead rodents and cooked food alike.

A couple of cats in the corner were fighting, clawing at each other and hissing. Their ears were flat on their heads as they prowled towards each other, swatting with quick, claw-extended paws.

Another few were playing. Laying on their backs, batting at the strings.

There was a rather large group of kittens and grown cats singing around a small fire. Too small to warrant the singing.

But the vast majority of the group was around the table eating.

"Huh," Mal murmured.

Chesh glanced at her. She was studying them curiously.

Surprised. He turned back to look at them, trying to see them through her eyes.

They were tall and sinewy, lithe in build. Their cat ears and tails were much like Chesh's, but that's where the similarities stopped. Their skin was covered in a fine coat of fur, velvety feeling. Their coloring was just as varied as a domestic, ***normal*** cat's. Their faces were slightly scrunched with cat-like features and cat eyes. Their hands were more on the paw-side than people hands.

Yes, he supposed they were strange.

Before Chesh could suggest they just move on, two kittens rolling around, wrestling, stopped their mad tumble at their feet, where they splayed out. One was pure white, while the other was abyss black.

"Oh," the white one said. She was female. Her voice gave it away.

The other, her brother, hollered for their mother.

Chesh sighed.

"You're a cat, too!" the little male kitten said. He sat up, grinning excitedly at Chesh.

"Something like that," Chesh replied.

The boy licked his paw and ran it across his ear.

"I'm Kitty. This is my sister, Snowdrop," Kitty said. "We're traveling to the mountains."

"Why?" Ryph asked. "I didn't think the cat colonies liked to travel long range."

Kitty shrugged, pulling his sister to sit beside him. "They don't actually tell us anything, but we smelled it."

"Fire," Snowdrop whispered, shuddering.

"You're from Tulgey?" Mal asked anxiously.

Both kittens shook their heads. The last time Chesh ran into the colonies, they were at the outer edge of the Creeping Silence. Close to Tulgey, yes, but within Silence.

"The fires weren't close, though," Kitty told Snowdrop. "But they burned our noses and hurt our lungs. So, we decided to get away."

"Momma doesn't think Silence can burn. We just hafta watch out for the Unnamed," Snowdrop told Mal.

Something Snowdrop said must have put Kitty's whiskers in a titter. He turned and pounced the girl. She mewled loudly, trying to bat him away.

"There are kids," Mal remarked happily.

"Like the Canidae, they have litters. Unlike the Canidae, they're stuck in mid-transition between cat and person," Chesh offered. There was a time he'd tried to fit in with the cats, since it seemed the most obvious place for him.

"Fascinating," Mal said. "Adorable."

Chesh snorted as a striped tabby pulled the two kittens from the ground. "Hello," she said with a smile. "Traveling? Would you care to join us for some food?" She waved her paw at the table filled with equal amounts of unappealing and edible food.

"We really ought to be traveling through," Eagy said. "In a bit of a rush."

She nodded. "Understandable. Then we wish you-"

Her words were cut off by a whizzing through the air.

"What now?" Eagy asked exasperatedly. "I swear, if the fucking Duchess escaped-"

His words were met with the one thing they all wished they'd never see again. Sheep.

Mal took several steps back as chaos erupted around them. The cats were a fight or flight species, heavy on the flight. They scattered abruptly, leaving Chesh and the others to fend for themselves. It was actually quite remarkable and impressive how quickly they vanished.

"Please tell me we have a better plan than last time," Mal said, her voice shaking.

Eagy wrapped her in his arms. "Don't worry, Angel. We'll get you out of here."

Chesh pulled his scythe from his back. Spinning it, the mirrored blade on the opposite end extended.

"Something's wrong with them," TL said, closing in to block their way to Mal.

Chesh paused to look at them. They looked like... corpses. Sallow. Mindless. Well, they were sheep. Mindless followers. As all flocking animals were.

But no, TL was right. Something was certainly off about them. They stumbled, reached out blindly. Slow.

Yet, when they engaged, they were strong enough to be a challenge. Their damn wool prevented Chesh from getting a good swing and clear shot with the scythe.

They had Mal surrounded before the Sheep could get close.

"What's wrong with them?" Mal asked. "Why do they look so.... Like *that?*"

"I think they lost their shepherd," Kav said. "Flocks fall apart when they have no leader. Run around frantically trying to carry out their last orders because they don't know what to do."

"They can't think on their own," Chesh added.

"Did you kill the shepherd, Wyat?" Ryph asked as he swung a sick looking blade at one of them.

Their heads were thicker. As if whatever had happened to them had dulled their senses. Took away their ability to reason. They followed a mindless doctrine now.

"They all look the same," Wyat said. "How was I to know?"

"That's not a bad thing," TL said. "Their days are numbered now."

"Not saying it was bad," Ryph amended as his blade finally broke through their thick wool. "Just funny. They're like..."

"Zombies!" Mal exclaimed.

What's a zombie? Chesh wondered as TL voiced the exact question.

"Uh... mindless, basically dead things. Like reanimated corpses. They eat people."

"Why are they so hard to kill?" Eagy asked exasperatedly.

"Zombies are hard to kill because they're already dead," Mal told him. "How do you kill something already dead?"

"Tearing it a part?" Kav offered.

"Fire?" Chesh suggested.

"Both," Mal said. "Duck!"

The men dropped around her and her hands flew out at her sides like wings. A stream of fire soared from each glove-covered hand and the Sheep burst into flames. Wool was flammable, after all.

They stumbled and bleated, running into each other and setting the cats' camp on fire. Mal stomped a foot and the ground bucked. The Sheep went down like dominoes. And they stayed down, as if they were a turtles caught on their backs, where they screamed until they burned to death.

The air was filled with an acrid scent that made even Chesh want to gag.

"Well," Mal said, a nervous smile on her lips as she took off her gloves. "I'm glad that actually worked."

Eagy laughed, wrapping her in his arms and squeezing her. "Wonderful, Angel. We knew you touched the magic all along."

"Hmm," she hummed, burying her face in his chest when he set her feet back on the ground. "I hope that's the last of the Sheep."

"I do believe you finished what I started," Wyat said.

"Now," Chesh said, getting to his feet and brushing moss off his trousers. "Let's get out of here before the cats return. They smell just as bad as burnt Sheep."

The Betrothal

EAGY

24

They arrived back at the inn the next afternoon. The inn was a chilling place. The walls were dark with peeling paint. Stuffed heads were custom in inns, but these were grotesque. Their eyes bulging, their fur tufted and skinned, mottled all over their bodies. It was as if they took long-dead corpses and then hung their heads.

This was never his first choice of places to stop. He wasn't even sure why they were spending the night again or why they'd been lounging before they had been interrupted before. Oh, right; finding rooms big enough for more than three was near impossible. They were at five now. And Wyat alone counted for three.

Eagy glanced at Chesh sitting with Mal and Ryph. For the life of him, he couldn't figure out why he wished Chesh would go away. He liked Chesh, really. Had he not, he wouldn't have suggested the demon cat in the first place.

Then again, never had he had to be around others for so long. Maybe that was the problem. Sharing Ryph's attention.

Ryph's boisterous laugh made Eagy look over once more. Mal's back was to Eagy so he couldn't see her face, but she looked like she was laughing, too. At Chesh, presumably, since he had a mischievous grin that spread up the sides of his face in a very demonic way.

No, it wasn't having him around. It was Ryph's attention on the stupid cat that bothered Eagy.

Wyat, Kav, and TL came back into the room then and Eagy was glad for it. Their arrival meant they could go upstairs. Wyat made for the small group Eagy had been trying to ignore, which stood the moment the others had come in. He wrapped a big arm around Mal's shoulders and followed as Chesh and Ryph led the way to the stairs.

Eagy scowled. He only barely noticed when Kav left the inn. Annoyed as he was, it might have escaped his attention, except that TL was frowning at the door Kav disappeared through. Their eyes met. TL joined him.

"You know, I don't trust him to take Mal tomorrow," TL said.

"You'll be with them," Eagy said, trying to dismiss it. He turned and headed for the stairs.

TL's hand on his arm made him pause. The look on the flower's face made Eagy frown. "Eagy, *he* is her coter."

The tone in which he said it gave Eagy chills. He looked at the ceiling, knowing the rest of their retinue was already upstairs.

Eagy took TL's wrist and dragged him behind as he made quick time to their room. Pushing TL inside, he shut the door, sending the old bolt home with a rusty grind.

He ignored Chesh and Ryph where they sat on the hearth, tending the fire. He equally ignored where Wyat was perched on their bed, Mal in his lap, his lips on her neck. Why did his life have to be so aggravating? Why couldn't he just have Ryph and Mal and everyone else go the fuck away?!

The knowing smirk on TL's face told Eagy he wasn't hiding any of his emotions well at all. Rolling his eyes, he turned back to the room at large and made some snarky comment that gained everyone's attention.

Silence followed as all eyes looked at him. He sank into one of the ratty chairs, trying like hell to keep his scowl from his face. "Kav just snuck out when he thought we were all going to bed."

Wyat made a face that betrayed everyone else's energy: distrust.

Ryph's eyes were on Eagy. He could feel them. But he didn't want to look at Ryph when he was so irritated. Jealous.

"Kav is lying about his family," he said at last.

"What do you mean?" Wyat asked.

"Ryph and I have traversed Silence for decades, trailing each One as they enter Laddenworn. We've seen the last eight come." He looked at Mal. "That's why we were in Silence. That's also why the Bloody Soldiers were. We were late because we were busy disbanding their hunting party."

Mal nodded. She shifted in Wyat's lap to face him more fully. Once, before their little party expanded, she'd be in his lap right then.

Eagy turned back to looking at no one in particular. "Five Ones ago, Kav stepped out from the Cold Land. Obviously, a family did not accompany him."

"Why would he lie?" Mal asked. "He looked genuinely upset when he was telling us about them."

"To gain our trust?" TL asked.

"I still don't understand why he would go through so much trouble to rescue me from the palace if he only plans to kill me later," Mal insisted.

She liked Kav. Still.

Eagy couldn't stop himself from looking at Ryph. Both he and Chesh were frowning at Mal. At least he wasn't the only one who didn't approve that Mal liked the stupid knave.

"Mal," TL said, stepping away from the door, "*why* doesn't matter. The point is that he's keeping a whole lot of secrets. If he was fully committed to this - to *you* - he'd be completely honest. Don't you think?"

She sighed. "Yes. You're right. I know you are. But I still don't-"

"Neither do we, but until he decides he trusts us enough to tell us why he's still sneaking around, we cannot trust him. That includes you, Mal," TL said in a hard voice. A voice that made her flush and lower her eyes.

"There's another problem," Eagy said. They looked at him. His shoulders tensed, but he forced himself to speak to the room. "Mal goes with TL and Kav tomorrow. Since we don't really know what Kav is up to, that puts Mal at risk."

Mal frowned. "But you trust TL, don't you?"

Wyat nodded behind her. As did Chesh. Ryph looked to Eagy for his answer. Did he? Well... more than he did Kav.

"Trust isn't really the issue," Chesh said when Eagy didn't answer right away. "Not the whole issue."

Mal groaned and leaned back into Wyat. "What haven't you told me this time?"

Chesh smiled a little. "It hasn't come up and I didn't think it would. It doesn't change anything, Kitten."

"Out with it, demon cat," she said. Her lips quirked, making it clear that she wasn't upset.

Yet.

"A wife has the final say in the safety of her husbands. She can make decisions on her own welfare when she is able. She also trusts them that what they say is for her wellbeing. With her best interest. And vice versa," Chesh waved a hand in the air, indicating it went both ways. "You don't have husbands, but you do have coters and a betrothed. There's a bit of a hierarchy because, presumably, you only accept one as a betrothed when you absolutely trust them, and later to a husband when you're sure you want to spend your life with him."

"So far, that sounds reasonable," Mal said warily.

"The hierarchy is pretty obvious, too. Husband has most authority in these matters, then the betrothed, followed by the coters. There's another level before coter where you're getting to know each other to determine if you'd like to court. You don't have any intrins. Lastly, there are those who are friends." Chesh looked at TL. "Or whatever our blossom here is."

TL's eyes were hooded. "I'm here as a friend who'd like to see the Queens' reign end."

Chesh shrugged.

"Okay, good. Thank you," Mal said. "Still-"

"It means that tomorrow when you're out with Kav and TL, we trust TL more, but it's Kav who's opinion and decisions will be honored, should the need arise," Eagy said.

"Wouldn't Kav be on the same level as TL?" Mal asked, brows knitted in confusion.

She was so beautiful, Eagy couldn't stop from smiling at her.

"He's a coter. I'm not," TL said.

Mal shook her head. "But I didn't accept him when he asked."

"Here's the part that we should have pointed out sooner," Chesh said gently. "You have three days to deny a statement whereas a question needs an answer. We asked if you'd accept us and you did. He stated that he was petitioning to join your harem. You didn't tell him no. It's been three days, so he is now a coter."

"Giving him more influence in your safety and wellbeing than TL," Wyat said. "Not acceptable."

"We can change our plans," Ryph offered. "Technically, I outrank him. TL can go to the smithy."

Chesh's head cocked to the side. "Even if we do that, this does not change the situation. It puts the majority of us, who are all about Mal, on an equal chess board as Kav. I don't know about you, but I'm a little uncomfortable with that."

Wyat smiled and dipped Mal back so he was cradling her. She laughed and relaxed into his hold. Eagy wanted to be annoyed and snap that now wasn't the time, but his words caught in his throat when she reached a hand up to place on Wyat's cheek.

"Can I ask you, my little Bunny, if you plan to wed us one day?"

"Are my words binding if I answer?"

He grinned. "Not if you give me a yes or no."

"Yes. I-" She broke off and frowned. "I'd like to say more, but I don't know what that will do."

"I'd like to make a suggestion."

She nodded.

"Make us your betrothed now. A betrothal can last a forever so there is no pressure on you. It will give us the higher card."

"Even better," Chesh said, his wide smile curling up his cheeks, "we don't tell him anything has changed. He keeps on with his keeping on and we are there to interfere with whatever he might do to our Mal."

"I love that you all act as if *your Mal* is a helpless, fragile doll," Mal said, frowning at Chesh.

"You are more fragile than us," Ryph said. "No one thinks you're helpless, though."

She let out a breath of frustration.

"What do you think?" Eagy asked. "Of Wyat's suggestion."

Mal nodded. "Yes, fine then. I agree to this." She sat up and hopped off the bed. "What do I need to do?"

"Do you want to ask us as a group or individually?"

Mal looked around at each man. Examining. When she stopped on Ryph, she said, "I made a mistake before and I intend to make it right when we feel it is right. You know that, right?"

Ryph smiled his mega golden smile. "Yes, I know."

"I consider this the same thing. Not the mistake part, but it's a move out of necessity. I need your help and protection. When it's right, I will make it right. Understand?"

As one, Chesh, Eagy, and Wyat agreed.

"Then as a group. Tell me what I need to say."

"You've already said it once," Ryph suggested.

Mal looked down to her arm. She pulled up her sleeve to

examine the ribbon. Absently, she nodded, as if agreeing. "One day in the future, I wish to make you my husband if you will accept me as your wife."

Once more, as one, all three agreed.

Eagy flinched as his skin seared with magic. He pulled up his sleeve in time to see the same purple ribbon Mal and Ryph had embedded into his arm. And the same words 'Promised to Mal on this day and that day forevermore' scrolled across it.

He knew that this wasn't the real thing. He knew that it was done because it would keep their Mal safest. Still, his chest felt full. His heart pumped loudly in his ears. Right now, he wanted nothing more than to bury himself deep inside her and know that she was his.

The other three were smiling as broadly as Eagy. And on Mal's arm, three more silhouettes joined that of the gryphon: an eagle, a rabbit, and a cat.

"One more problem," Chesh said.

Mal looked at him with a sigh. "We solved one tonight. Haven't we met our quota?"

"We didn't fully solve the problem. This is in tandem." Chesh looked at TL. All eyes moved to him, as well. Eagy could almost feel TL's wariness from where he sat, several feet away. "You are still outranked by Kav."

"I'm not-" he said, hands in the air in front of him in defense.

"It can be canceled later," Chesh insisted. "If you will truly help us, then it needs to be done."

"That means you also need to carry on with the ruse. You move in here," Wyat said.

The distress on TL's face would have been comical if it wasn't so real.

"It's only pretend," Mal said, her voice quiet and tight.

His chest was heaving with his rapid breaths. The room was suddenly filled with his anxiety, as if it were the scent of a flower wafting through the air.

"You don't have to," Mal said.

Eagy wasn't sure if that was hurt or irritation in her voice. Her expression seemed a bit clouded, too, so he couldn't read that either.

When TL finally moved, it was quick enough that the other four men in the room jerked. He stood in front of Mal, his hand on the back of her neck. His stare was dark, tormented, intense. "Please understand that you don't understand me. I don't want a wife. I don't want a lover. I don't want a partner of any kind. It has absolutely nothing to do with *you*, in particular."

Mal's wide eyes stared at him. Eagy thought she made an effort, albeit a small effort, to move away from him. TL held their position for long, quiet moments.

"I want you to be the Right One, Mal. I want the Bloody Queens' rule to end and Laddenworn to be righted again. That's why I'm helping you. As long as you understand that, and if you promise to break the contract when I ask you to, I'll agree to join your harem in name. I'll keep up appearances and whatever else so it's convincing."

Mal nodded. "I promise."

"Then ask me, Sunshine. Ask me to accept you as my someday wife." TL's voice was strained. Like his anxiety through the air, the fear deep in his voice reached every corner of the room.

For a moment, Mal didn't say anything. She felt it, too.

"Ask me," he insisted.

"I would make you my husband after the world is fixed if you accept my promise," she whispered.

"I accept." This time, his tone was normal. Firm and confident. It almost sounded like he truly did accept.

The flower silhouette on Mal's ribbon formed before their eyes.

TL did not release her. Not her head nor her eyes for several silent minutes. When he did, he did so slowly, backing towards the door. "I'll get my bag," he said, disappearing into the hall.

Mal looked around the room. Her shiver seemed to reach them all.

Eagy couldn't help but wonder if TL realized that the promise Mal had made him was outdone the moment he accepted her betrothal. If he really wanted her words to bind into her promise, he should have asked for the promise after.

Mal climbed back up into Wyat's lap and snuggled into his big embrace that enveloped her body until she was almost entirely out of sight. Before Eagy could turn away, Ryph had climbed into the chair Eagy was in, nuzzling into his neck. He could feel Ryph's lips brush his skin, moving with words he didn't speak.

Eagy smiled and closed his eyes, wrapping his arms tightly around his beast. *I love you, too*, he thought.

It took TL almost no time to return to their room. He dropped his bag with the others and took up the chair opposite Eagy and Ryph.

Wariness didn't seem to cover his expression. Dread was likely a far better word.

"Let's go downstairs," Ryph said. "I'm still hungry. Maybe they have some tarts."

Eagy nodded, allowing Ryph to pull him to his feet and toward the door. TL and Chesh followed. Glancing back, he realized it was probably because Wyat intended to have their girl. Jealousy spiked through Eagy and he turned away.

Part of being in a remcule was sharing their wife. As long as he didn't have to share Ryph, he might be able to get through it. Get to a place where it didn't bother him quite so much to see others with their hands on her. Inside her. Giving her pleasure and receiving her affection.

He shook his head to rid himself of the thoughts. As they hit the bottom of the stairs, a messenger was heading up. He looked at Eagy, decided that's who he was looking for, and handed over a small square of paper.

He recognized the handwriting, if you could call the little

image handwriting. There were four rectangles, each with a different suit inside. Heart. Diamond. Club. Spade.

Lepa was suggesting they use cards to get into the palaces? Curious. Curiouser that he hadn't thought of the damn illusionists to begin with. Probably because it had been so long since he'd seen any cards. They weren't exactly uncommon, but they were never what they appeared.

"What is it?" Ryph asked, setting his hand on Eagy's waist, pressing his chest to Eagy's back so he could peer over Eagy's shoulder.

Eagy showed him the little paper as he pulled Ryph behind him toward the tavern. Ryph frowned. "I don't-"

The room was abuzz with activity. Fear. Eagy stopped at the bar where Kav was sitting, a paper in his hands.

"What's going on?" TL asked, looking over the knave's shoulder.

"I'm not sure you really want to know," Kav said, handing over the paper. As TL read, his face draining of color, Kav looked at Eagy, Ryph, and Chesh. "The queens have completely annihilated a Patch. They've declared the Final Purging of Laddenworn."

Books by Crea Reitan

THE IMMORTAL CODEX

Immortal Stream: Children of the Gods

Mortal Souls

The God of Perfect Radiance

The Hidden God

The God Who Controls Death

Gods of the Dead

Gods of Blood

Gods of Idols

Gods of Fire

Gods of Enoch

Gods of Stone

INFECTED FAIRY TALES

Wonderland: Chronicles of Blood

Toxic Wonderland

Magical Wonderland

Dying Wonderland

Bloody Wonderland

Wonderland: Chronicles of Madness

The Search for Nonsense

The Queen Trials

Veins of Shade

Finding Time

Neverland: Chronicles of Red

Neverwith

Nevershade

Neverblood

Nevermore

OTHER/STANDALONES

Hellish Ones Novels

Blood of the Devil

House of the Devil

Harem Project Novels

House of Daemon

House of Aves

House of Wyn

House of Igarashi, 1

House of Igarashi, 2

House of Agni

House of Malak

House of Darkyn

House of Savage (2024)

Brothers of Eschat

Unsolicited

Equipoise

Paranormal Holiday Novel

12 Days

Satan's Touch Academy

A Lick of Magic

A Touch of Seduction

A Taste of Darkness

Fae Lords

Karou

Sweet Omegaverse

Alpha Hunted

Knot Interested

Omegas of Chaingate

Get Pucking Knotty

The Princess and Her Alphaholes Anthology (excerpt of *Wrecked)*

Wrecked

Hell View Manor

Stroking Pride (A Sons of Satan Novel)

A Tale of Steam & Cinders

Terror

Haidee (A Ladies of MC Novel)

Silent Night (Femme Fatale Freakshow - 2024)

MM NOVELS/SERIES

For Puck's Sake

Shiver

Starting Line

Lucky Shot

The Crease

Wingman Score

Coach Stare Down

Stick Lessons

The Defending Goal(2024)

For Your Love

For Your Time

For Your Heart

For Your Mind

For Your Forever

Van Doren

Loren

Rainbow Dorset University

Collide

Longwood U

Rumor Has It

Author's Note And Acknowledgements

One of my favorite things about writing is creating the world. My worlds are constantly evolving as I write and as such, I have a hard time keeping up. My desk is scattered with scraps of paper, reminding me of what I had written in the last book.

Thus the reason there are three weeks between releases and why the series is near complete before I release book 1. I do not envy those authors who wait a year between releases (nor can I fathom taking that long to write a single book). To remember what happens from one day to the next is exhausting sometimes.

But, here we are. I hope you enjoyed the second book of Mal's journey. I am so psyched for you to see what happens in the next! No, really... I can't wait.

Throughout writing this, I had the immeasurable support of some very important people. My sister, who once again, was always full of sarcasm and corrections, marking up my manuscripts enough that it looked like I had a fun border on every page. My husband, who doesn't like to read, but was constantly lending me support and encouragement. (Yes, I said he doesn't read. Don't ask!) And all my family and friends who liked, shared, and spread the word of my new writing career. Thank you, from the bottom of my heart!

About the Author

Crea lives in upstate New York with her dog and husband. She has been writing since grade school, when her second grade teacher had her class keep writing journals. She has a habit of creating secondary, and often time tertiary, characters that take over her stories. When she can't fall asleep at night, she thinks up new scenes for her characters to act out. This, of course, is how most of her meant-to-be-thrown-away characters tend to end up front and center - and utterly swoon-worthy! Don't ask her how many book boyfriends she has...

When not writing, Crea is an avid reader. Her TBR pile is several hundred books high (don't even look at her kindle wish list or the unread books on her tablet). Sometimes, she enjoys crafting; sometimes, exploring nature; sometimes, traveling. Mostly, she enjoys putting her characters on paper and breathing life into them. Oh, and sleeping. Crea *loves* to sleep!

Thank You

Thank you for reading *Magical Wonderland* and sticking with Mal as she navigates her way through a fairy tale she thought she was prepared for. She was not expecting to find men she cared about so quickly, nor to see such cruelty. To that end, would you be so kind as to take a moment and leave a review? Reviews play a big role in a book's success and you can help with just a few sentences.

Thank you!!

Crea Reitan

PS - If you find any errors, spelling or the like, please do not use your ereader to mark them. The algorithms pull the book! Instead, please reach out to me on Facebook or via email. Thank you!!

Printed in Dunstable, United Kingdom

78948008R10174